FRACTURED SOULS

Fallen Messengers # 1

AVA MARIE SALINGER

silver
orb
publishing

COPYRIGHT

Fractured Souls (Fallen Messengers #1)
Copyright © 2021 by Ava Marie Salinger
All rights reserved.
Registered with the US Copyright Office.
Paperback edition: 2021

www.AMSalinger.com

Edited by Right Ink On The Wall
Cover Design by 17 Studio Book Design

Want to know about Ava's upcoming releases? Sign up to her newsletter for exclusive stories, new release alerts, sneak peeks, giveaways, and more.

WANT A FREE PREQUEL STORY?

Sign up to Ava's newsletter to get Unbound now, as well as new release alerts, sneak peeks, giveaways, and more.

FALLEN MESSENGERS GLOSSARY

Aerial: An angel or demon who can control wind.

Alchemist: A human who can create new matter or manipulate existing matter into new forms. Emits a scent of powdered iron.

Aqueous: An angel or demon who can control water.

Argent Lake: Home of the Naiads.

Argonaut Agency: Organization responsible for law and order in the supernatural and magical communities. Headquarters in New York. Agents include angels, demons, and magic users.

Astrea Sea: Home of the Nereids.

Bloodsand: A black tree with red veins that grows in the

Nine Hells. Created by warlocks who made pacts with the Underworld after the Fall. Can be used to summon war demons from the Nine Hells.

Blossom Silver: A silver derivative that can heal injuries caused by demonic weapons or black magic. Made by the Naiads.

Cabalista: Demonic organization. Agents include demons only. Headquarters in London.

Dark Blight: A powder black-magic users use in their rituals and which is poisonous to angels and other magic users. Made by Shadow Empire alchemists from the heart of a Dryad.

Demi: The offspring of a God of Heaven/God of the Underworld and a human.

Electrum: Naturally occurring alloy of gold and silver, as well as copper and other trace elements. Used extensively by Argonaut in their weapons. Combined with steel, titanium, and Rain Silver to make their bullets.

Empyreal: The highest order of angels or demons, with powers equal to those of a Demigod.

Enchanter/Enchantress: A human who uses illusion magic. Emits a scent of cedar.

Fiery: An angel or a demon who can wield Heaven or Hell's Fire.

Fractured Soul: A human's damaged soul core, extracted from the body – a powerful source of magic.

Ghoul: An evil spirit who consumes the flesh of humans. Emits a scent of rotting meat.

Glitterfang: A pale powder white-magic users employ in their rituals and which is poisonous to demons and black-magic users. Made by Nereids.

Hexa: Guild of magic users. Agents include magic users only. Headquarters in Seattle.

Incubus: A male demon who gains power from sleeping with humans and divine entities.

Ivory Peaks: Home of the Dryads.

Lucifugous: A heliophobic demon who abhors light and who can control darkness.

Mage: A human who uses an arcane staff to focus their magic powers. Emits a scent of Juniper.

Magic Levels: Classification of magic users based on their abilities, with Level Six being the weakest and Level One the strongest.

Messengers: Those belonging to the Third Sphere of Heaven and Third Hierarchy of Demons.

Order of Rosen: Religious order affiliated with the

Catholic Church. Agents include angels only. Headquarters in Rome.

Rain Silver: A liquid-silver derivative that can injure and kill demons. Made by the Nymphs.

Rain Vale: Home of the Nymphs.

Reaper: A soul collector and guide of the dead. Emits a scent of camphor.

Reaper Seed: A drug that can intoxicate most beings and which is fatal in high doses. Mined by Lucifugous demons in the Shadow Empire. Potent hallucinogen for Lucifugous demons.

Shadow Empire: Home of Ghouls, Lucifugous demons, and Dark Alchemists.

Sorcerer/Sorceress: A human born with powerful soul core magic. Uses the energies around them to manipulate magic. Emits the scent of Valerian.

Soul Core: A living being's life force. Red for demons, white for angels, and dirty gray for humans.

Spirit Realm: Home of Pan, the Gods of the Underworld, and lesser spirits.

Stark Steel: Strongest and most magic-resistant metal on Earth. Found exclusively in the weapons and armor of the Fallen.

Succubus: A female demon who gains power from sleeping with humans and divine entities.

Terrene: An angel or demon who can control earth and its derivative metals.

The Fall: An unexplained event five hundred years ago that resulted in an army of angels and demons falling to Earth.

The Fallen: Angels or demons who fell to Earth.

The Nether: The space between Heaven, Earth, and the Nine Hells.

The Abyss: A forgotten realm beyond the Nether from where there is no escape.

War Demon: Demon soldiers created for battle. Remnants of an ancient war between Heaven and Hell. Banished to the deepest parts of the Hells.

Warlock: A human who draws power from demons and the Hells and converts it to magic. Emits a scent of sulfur.

Wizard/Witch: A human who learns to use magic through spell books, and who utilizes potions and rituals to access their soul-core magic. Emits a scent of Frankincense.

1

SHIT.

Cassius Black frowned at the dark waters soaking the hemline of his brand-new jeans.

If I'd known I'd be going down the sewers today, I would have worn something different.

The faint smell of rotten eggs wafted toward him as he gazed along the tunnel he'd entered. He stepped out of the beam of moonlight that had followed him down the manhole and the fifty-foot ladder he'd just descended and headed north, the sound of the night-time traffic on 3rd Street fading in the distance above him.

I should have charged more for this gig.

The face of his latest client rose before his eyes at that churlish thought, bringing with it a pang of guilt. He hadn't had the courage to tell Joyce Almeda that the cat she'd hired him to find was, in fact, a demonic spirit. Cassius had detected the sulfurous taint that characterized its kind the second he'd entered the old lady's house on a run-down street in Mission District two hours ago.

That Joyce Almeda was still alive and well and had yet

to realize that the stray she'd picked up outside her home six weeks ago was a supernatural entity told Cassius the demon cat was injured in some way. It was the only plausible reason as to why the creature's presence hadn't drained the old lady's life force and made her ill. A wound would also explain why the cat was leaking demonic scent.

Whatever state Cassius found it in, he couldn't return it to his client. Demonic animals and humans were never a great match even at the best of times, not least because the creatures didn't possess the ability to stop their powers from using up the vitality of their masters. Unless there was an animal shelter in San Francisco that took in demonic pets, and depending how badly the creature was injured, he would have to either put the cat down himself or release it into the wild and hope it stayed away from the city.

The sewer gradually widened and dropped, the floor sloping gently downward. Cassius reached an intersection and paused. He took a shallow breath and filtered out the stench of human waste, stagnant water, and hydrogen sulfide filling the labyrinthine spaces stretching out around him. The trace of the demon spirit came from his right, a trail of intangible red energy dancing in the air.

Cassius turned, his footsteps raising faint splashes in the darkness. He didn't need a flashlight to see what lay in his path. His unearthly eyes were more than enough to pierce the shadows around him.

The cat's scent grew stronger.

Cassius slowed.

There was something else. Something that had just teased his nostrils and stirred his supernatural senses. His hand rose to the Colt strapped to his waist.

There was another demon in the sewers up ahead. One

who was giving off a distinctive whiff of human flesh and blood.

Fuck.

Cassius frowned. Part of him wanted to turn around and retrace his steps. He could tell Joyce Almeda her cat was dead and he'd disposed of the body to spare her feelings; something told him the creature had left her for a good reason and was unlikely to return. The other part of him, the part that always landed him in trouble, urged him to forge on ahead.

Cassius hesitated.

He'd only been in San Francisco for a couple of weeks. He couldn't afford to get in the crosshairs of the agencies that oversaw the supernatural beings in the city so soon. Unfortunately, as he'd found out to his detriment over the years, life had a way of screwing up his best-laid plans.

Cassius sighed and removed his gun from its holster.

Besides, I've always been a bad liar. The old lady would see through me in a heartbeat.

The coppery smell of blood grew stronger as he navigated the tunnel, the odor made more pungent by the warm, August weather. So did the scent of the demon he could sense up ahead.

Cassius's pulse quickened.

Please don't let it be what I think it is.

The darkness started to abate. Pale light framed the end of the sewer pipe in the distance. Cassius carefully approached the tunnel exit and paused on the threshold of a cavernous space.

Moonlight streamed through a narrow grating high above him. The pale beams swirled with dust motes as they arrowed down to the center of the confluence chamber framed by a narrow, circular, concrete walkway and three weir gates.

Cassius's stomach twisted.

Damn it! It's a Lucifugous!

The monstrous shape crouched in the middle of the shallow basin before him seemed oblivious to his presence as it feasted on the lower half of a man's naked body, its stone club lying at its feet.

Movement to the right drew Cassius's gaze.

A small, slender, black form slinked toward him, vertical pupils glowing a vivid yellow in the gloom and tail swinging lazily as it approached.

Cassius grimaced.

Of course you're here, you stupid cat.

If the feline read his mind, it gave no indication of it. It stopped a short distance from Cassius, sat on its haunches, and observed him with an expression that seemed to say, *So, what are you going to do about this shitty situation we currently find ourselves in, pal?*

Cassius noticed it was favoring its left foreleg. He clenched his jaw when he detected the thin bolt of magic that had pierced the demon cat's limb. Invisible to human eyes, it was the weapon of choice when it came to incapacitating supernatural creatures.

From the rumors he'd heard before he left London, hunting demonic animals was a hobby wealthy humans on the West Coast liked to indulge in. Not that they would ever dare go after a supernatural creature without some backup. Cassius scowled.

Damn elitist magic users.

Despite their supercilious attitude toward demons, some humans born with magic soul cores liked nothing more than making money from their non-magic-wielding counterparts – people they loved to hate, looking down on them as an inferior race. Killing a few weak demonic spirits in the process only added to their sick thrill.

A grunt echoed around the concrete chamber.

The Lucifugous had finally noticed him.

Cassius slowly re-holstered his gun, his pulse racing as he held the creature's boorish gaze. Though he could easily injure or kill the demon with the Rain Silver bullets in his Colt, he saw no need to shed blood tonight.

"Look here, big guy. I don't want any trouble." His gaze flitted to the dead man behind the Lucifugous. "I can tell it wasn't you who murdered that human. Why don't you step away and—"

Darkness swirled around Cassius. He cursed, the cat's startled hiss reaching him dimly through the wall of inky blackness closing in around him before all sound faded. Cassius's breaths sounded loud in his ears as he cast out a weak pulse of his energy.

There!

2

Cassius snatched his dagger from the sheath strapped to his back. It swiftly transformed into a sword and blocked the demon's weapon inches from his head. The stone club smashed soundlessly against the double-edged, Stark Steel blade, the impact rattling Cassius's bones.

It would have broken his arm had he been human.

A shift in the air told him the demon had retreated. It wouldn't be for long.

Cassius gritted his teeth and called forth his divine powers. He had to end this fight and soon, before anyone with magical or otherworldly abilities detected their energies. A pale glow lit the gloom as his pupils radiated seraphic light, the brightness piercing the blanket of solid darkness surrounding him.

Lucifugous demons specialized in shadow manipulation, confusing their would-be victims' senses by wrapping them in a soundproof bubble of pitch blackness while they attacked.

Unfortunately, that sort of trick didn't work on someone like Cassius.

Sight and sound returned in a violent rush. The creature appeared above Cassius, its grotesque shape arcing through the fading gloom as it descended toward him with a savage roar. It blinked and froze a couple of seconds later, its shriek ending on a shocked grunt.

Cassius's heart slammed against his ribs as he stared into the demon's eyes. Dark blood flowed down his sword and dripped onto his hand, hot and sticky.

The blade had pierced the creature's chest and impaled it straight through its back.

A hint of redness flashed in the demon's pupils as it sagged on the weapon, its body growing limp in death. For a second, Cassius imagined he saw relief in the creature's dying gaze.

A soft meow rose in the gloom beside him.

Sadness oozed from the cat as Cassius withdrew his blade and carefully lowered the Lucifugous to the ground. However much they were feared and reviled, demons still mourned every loss of life of their kind. It was a bond that had existed between them since they fell to Earth five hundred years ago, just as it did for the angels who had followed them that fateful day the Nether tore open.

Cassius grimaced. *Well, except for me.*

He knew no angel would grieve his death when he passed from this wretched world. He clamped down on the age-old bitterness that the thought prompted and closed the demon's eyes with a gentle hand.

"Rest in peace."

Of all the creatures Cassius had slain in his long and cursed life, Lucifugous demons earned the most pity in his heart. Most had been unable to adapt to their new lives on

Earth after they fell and lived like animals, skulking in hidden spaces under cities and the few untouched pieces of wilderness left on the planet. They were another favorite prey of human magic users and often died at the hands of those who liked to practice their high-end spells on them during magic hunts.

Cassius clenched his jaw, rose, and drove his blade back into the demon's body and through the red core he could sense deep within it. The demon's soul shattered with a sound only he heard.

With it came pain.

Cassius sucked in air as the familiar agony squeezed his chest and robbed him momentarily of breath. It wasn't until the creature's body had crumbled into a pile of fiery ash that the throbbing abated. He stared blindly at the darkening cinders, wondering if this affliction would forever burden him.

As far as he knew, he was the only one on Earth who could see and destroy another living being's soul core. And he always experienced crippling suffering when he did so. It was as if the Heavens had damned him when he fell, punishing him for a sin he could not recall committing.

Whereas Reapers claimed the souls of humans and returned them to the cycle of rebirth and death the race of man was destined to go through until their final redemption, the only way for an otherwordly to go through the same process was if their soul core was completely destroyed and their physical remains returned to ash. Despite the pain the rite brought him, Cassius still chose to perform it. He knew, deep in the marrow of his bones, that it was his solemn duty, even if he could not recall why.

The sword shifted back into a dagger as he withdrew

his power from the weapon. He wiped it clean, put it back in its sheath, and jumped down into the basin.

The man whose remains the Lucifugous demon had been feasting on had died a terrible death. Cassius could tell from the runes that had been burned into his skin and the aura of corruption tainting his flesh.

The cat growled beside him. Cassius looked down at the creature and followed its unblinking gaze to a sewer pipe on his left.

The scent of evil was coming from that direction.

The cat kept pace with him as they headed that way, its body rubbing against his leg from time to time, as if to mark him. They found the other half of the man's remains in a second confluence chamber a quarter of a mile to the north. A cold foreboding swept over Cassius as he stared at the mangled torso lying on a stone dais in the center of the basin.

The altar did not belong there.

"Well, *this* situation just went from bad to hell in a handbasket," he muttered to the cat.

The creature glanced at him before crouching on the edge of the walkway and springing clear across the basin. It landed on the altar and turned around a couple of times before sitting and looking proudly at him.

"You little—!" Cassius scowled. "Exactly what part of hell in a handbasket did you not understand?!"

The demon cat lowered its head and sniffed the corpse curiously.

Cassius blew out an exasperated sigh, eyed the stagnant pool filling up a third of the basin, and stepped carefully into it. He scanned the shadowy tunnels radiating off the gloomy space as he made his way to the altar, the dark brown waters sloshing around his shins.

The cat moved out of his way as he climbed onto the dais. Cassius took care not to touch any of the black lines and symbols on the stone; he could smell Dark Blight and human blood on the complex pattern of runes that had been etched into it. He squatted, pulled back the corpse's left eyelid, and stared into the fixed, dark pupil.

Whatever remained of the dead man's soul was long gone. Which was strange, considering the condition of the corpse.

Cassius studied the signs on the floor with a frown, his unease deepening. It was clear someone had performed a black-magic ritual down here. But to what intent? The runes were unfamiliar to him and the victim had been abandoned and left exposed to the elements and scavengers, the usual as well as otherworldly ones.

An eerie awareness tickled the back of his mind. Before he could make sense of it, a shout echoed from a sewer pipe behind him, startling him.

"Hey, you there! Don't move!"

Cassius looked over his shoulder and cursed at the sight of a man running toward him with a flashlight in hand. It was an Argonaut agent.

And when there's one of these bastards, there's bound to be more!

As if to prove him right, more shouts came from the other tunnels. The beams of a dozen flashlights washed over Cassius where he crouched on the altar. He scowled.

I really don't have time for this shit.

He tucked the demon cat under his arm, spread his wings, and rose. Angry yells followed him as he smashed through a metal grating and disappeared into the balmy night.

THE NOISE STARTED AGAIN AT EXACTLY 5 A.M.

Cassius stirred, lifted his face off the pillow, and blinked sleepily at the dark bedroom.

"Oh!" a voice shouted faintly through the wall opposite his bed. "Oh *yes!* Right there! That feels *so* good!"

Cassius groaned, jammed the pillow over his head, and pressed his face into the mattress. Alas, nothing he did could drown out the racket coming from the adjoining apartment. The man's cries of pleasure intensified and were soon accompanied by a steady thumping.

Cassius swore and sat up, the bedsheets falling around his bare waist. He glared at the wall separating his apartment from his neighbor's.

It's a miracle that asshole hasn't broken his bed yet!

The demon cat was sitting on his dresser and staring avidly at the spot the sounds were coming from, its swinging tail matching the tempo of the lovemaking happening in the next apartment.

Had he known when he'd moved into the building two

weeks ago that he would be living next to a sex addict who liked to fornicate with a different person every night, Cassius would never have signed the lease on the penthouse. As it was, he'd hardly gotten any sleep since he'd come to San Francisco, bar the couple of nights he'd relented and slept on the living-room couch.

"Oh God! *Harder!* Fuck me harder, Morgan!"

Another man's low grunts reached Cassius, the creaks from the rocking bed escalating as he pounded his partner and gave him exactly what he was begging for. Heat flooded Cassius's cheeks as he felt a stirring in his own groin.

His neighbor only got loud right near the end, before he climaxed. And, for some insane reason, the sounds he made always quickened Cassius's pulse and made lust pool in his belly. Cassius told himself it was because he hadn't had sex in months. Deep inside, he knew that lie was starting to wear thin.

The first man cried out in ecstasy when he came.

A feral noise left the other man a moment later as he orgasmed.

Blood pounded in Cassius's ears in the silence that followed. He could almost picture the two men on the other side of the wall in his mind's eye, their faces flushed with pleasure and their bodies damp with sweat as they lay in each other's arms. The ache in his groin intensified.

Cassius dropped his head on his knees and closed his eyes, his erection throbbing between his legs. He was about to touch himself when he became conscious of an intense stare.

The demon cat's gaze was locked on him.

He'd had no option but to bring the creature to his

place when he'd fled the sewers last night. Luckily, there hadn't been any angels or demons among the Argonaut agents who'd surprised him in the underground chamber, or else they would have followed him when he'd escaped into the darkness. Not that they would have been able to match his speed in the air.

It had taken but a moment for Cassius to remove the magic bolt from the demon cat's leg once they'd reached the safety of his apartment. The wound was already healing, the creature's otherworldly energy hastening the process.

The demon cat meowed, its stare all knowing.

"Look, it's because I haven't gotten any in a while, alright," Cassius told the creature defensively.

The cat blinked, its expression indicating it wasn't buying that bullshit.

Cassius blew out a heavy sigh, threw the sheets off his body, and walked naked into his bathroom, his erection at full mast. He gritted his teeth and stood under an ice-cold shower for a good ten minutes until his body calmed down, all the while cursing his neighbor.

"Fucking Morgan and his fucking stamina."

The demon cat ignored his mutterings while he got dressed and followed him when he headed into the open-plan living area overlooking a private, rooftop terrace and a dark San Francisco Bay. Cassius made a fresh pot of coffee, rooted around in a cupboard, and unearthed a can of tuna.

"It's a good thing I did some shopping yesterday or else you'd be having cereal," he muttered to the cat as he opened the tin and upended the contents onto a plate.

The creature perked up, leapt onto the table, and sniffed carefully at the processed fish before biting down on a mouthful. Both angels and demons had had to adapt to consuming human food when they'd first come to Earth. From the way the demon cat was chomping down hungrily, this was its first meal in days.

"I should call Joyce." Cassius frowned faintly as he watched the creature eat. "You can't go back there."

The cat licked its chops, raised its head, and bumped Cassius's chest affectionately, a low rumble leaving its belly.

Cassius narrowed his eyes. "You are *not* staying here."

The cat yawned, exposing small white fangs, and went back to eating. Cassius swallowed a sigh and headed out onto the terrace with his coffee.

The sky was lightening on the horizon when he heard a noise next door. A man walked out of the neighboring penthouse and crossed the adjoining terrace to the railing overlooking the bay. Orange light flared as he leaned on it and drew on his cigarette, the glow briefly illuminating his features. He removed the stick from between his full lips and lazily blew out a trail of smoke.

Cassius swallowed hard.

The guy was a good six foot three, stark naked, and had the kind of face and body that would make most modeling agencies and Hollywood casting studios weep for joy. Cassius cursed his preternatural sight and hastily looked away, his neighbor's arresting features and toned, muscular frame burned into his retina.

"Hey there."

Cassius stiffened before carefully peering around.

It seemed the man had noticed him despite Cassius doing his best not to draw attention to himself.

Wait a minute. Cassius frowned. *I dampened my aura. He shouldn't have been able to pick me out at all.*

The guy smiled, his turquoise-blue eyes twinkling in the breaking dawn. "You must be the new neighbor."

He came over to the balustrade separating their terraces, heedless of his nakedness.

Cassius's gaze skittered down the faint scar that cut across the man's chest from his left clavicle to his right flank, before dropping briefly to his groin. His mouth went dry. An ache ignited in his lower body.

Fuck.

His neighbor's dick was long and thick, just the way Cassius liked it. Cassius gripped his cup of coffee and did his best to subdue his stirring libido.

"I'm Morgan. Morgan King."

Morgan offered his hand over the railing.

Cassius stayed put where he sat on a deckchair and glared at his neighbor. A lazy smile curved Morgan's mouth. Cassius blinked at the luscious, pink curves.

Why does this guy have such ridiculously full lips?!

"I get the feeling you're upset with me," Morgan drawled.

Morgan's voice danced across Cassius's skin and raised goosebumps on his flesh.

Shit.

That was not the only thing his neighbor's voice was raising.

Cassius shifted on the deckchair, hoping the gloom masked his growing erection. "You realize you're naked, right?"

Morgan's smile widened at his cold tone. "Is my nakedness bothering you?"

Cassius flushed. "I'm not a fan of exhibitionism. Also, do you make it a habit of having loud sex with a different person every night?"

Morgan blinked at Cassius's scathing words. He burst out laughing the next instant, his teeth gleaming in the shadows.

"I'm sorry," he chortled. "Did we wake you?"

Cassius frowned, more than a little incensed. "Our bedrooms are next to one another, so yeah, Mr. I-can't-keep-my-dick-in-my-pants!"

Morgan grinned and took another suck of his cigarette. "Well, it's hardly my fault my partners are so noisy in the bedroom."

Cassius tried desperately not to imagine that sinful mouth wrapped around his cock. The way Morgan's pupils flared slightly told him he was just as aware of Cassius as Cassius was of him.

"From the way you were doing that incubus tonight, I'm prepared to lay the blame completely at your feet," Cassius said frostily. "And FYI, the women are even louder, especially that super model and the sorceress."

Morgan chuckled. "Damn. You're making me blush with all the compliments. So, do I get a ten?"

Cassius stared. "What?"

Morgan arched an eyebrow, his tone teasing. "Am I a ten on your sexual prowess scale?"

Cassius scowled. *Arrogant fucker!*

"If you're asking if you deserve a medal for your stamina in the bedroom, you're not gonna get an answer from me," he growled, rising to his feet. "Self-important pricks who think they are the center of the world are the lowest of the low."

Morgan winced. "Ouch." His gaze dropped. A wicked smile stretched his mouth. "Somehow, I think you're lying, Mr. Neighbor. That's a pretty impressive hard-on you're sporting there."

Cassius cursed his own body and stormed back inside his apartment, Morgan's low laughter following him until he slammed the sliding doors closed.

4

"Asshole!" Cassius snarled at the empty living room, his dick throbbing.

He marched into the kitchen, made himself another coffee, and stared at it mutinously before walking over to the liquor cabinet and pouring a generous shot of whiskey into it.

It took a while for his lower half to quieten down again. Cursing his neighbor helped. He'd just finished his drink and was pondering his grim findings last night in the sewers when the demon cat ran out of the bedroom and came over to where he paced the floor by the couch. It leapt onto his shoulder, its claws sinking into his T-shirt, and stared unblinkingly at the front door of the apartment. Cassius stiffened as a warning growl rumbled from the creature's belly.

"What is it?"

The cat's growl intensified.

Cassius's gaze darted to the bedroom door. *Damn it!*

He'd left his gun and dagger on the nightstand. He

frowned, took a shallow breath, and sent out a faint pulse of energy.

It took but a moment for him to detect the heavily armed group gathered outside his apartment. There was another group on the rooftop. They smashed through the front door and the terrace doors and stormed inside seconds later, the trigger-mounted laser beams on their guns lighting up his body in a macabre dance of red dots.

"Cassius Black? This is the Argonaut Agency! Get down on the ground and put your hands behind your head!" someone yelled.

The demon cat hissed, its eyes flashing red and an aura of crimson energy flaring from its body as it arched its back threateningly.

One of the agents in the hallway fired.

Cassius swore, snatched the cat from his shoulder with lightning speed, and twisted around, his wings sprouting defensively from his back. Heat flared on one of his right pinions as the bullet punctured it and passed right through.

Shock reverberated through Cassius. He stared at the crumpled projectile where it had lodged itself in the wall of his living room, his heart thundering where he held the trembling demon cat to his chest. Hot blood dripped onto the floor from his wound.

An ordinary bullet would never have pierced his flesh.

Anger surged through Cassius when he realized what was in the slug. He lowered his wings and glared at the agents surrounding him.

"Stark Steel and electrum?! Are you fucking kidding me? That shit is illegal!"

An agent standing by the door pushed her tactical goggles up on her head. She was a tall blonde with hazel eyes, a hard expression, and the faintest whiff of magic about her.

"I'm sorry about what just happened." Her cold gaze shifted to the man who'd discharged his weapon. "I'm sure Agent Driscoll didn't mean to *accidentally* fire on a suspect."

Driscoll hunched his shoulders at her tone. Somehow, Cassius had the feeling he was in for a serious ass-whooping later.

"But you'll understand when I say we can't exactly use standard ammo on someone like you," the woman added, her gaze flitting to Cassius's feathers.

Cassius gritted his teeth and retracted his wings, conscious of the distrustful stares the other agents were directing at him.

Of all the angels and demons who had fallen to Earth when the Nether tore open five hundred years ago, he was the only one who had wings as black as night and as red as blood. That fact had contributed to him becoming the most feared and ostracized supernatural being to walk the planet since that fateful day, the grim colors a dark portent that both humans and otherwordly associated with back luck. Cassius scowled.

Still, it doesn't give these assholes the right to barge into my home and shoot at me and my *cat!*

The demon cat had gone still in his arms, its instincts evidently telling it it needed to lie low for the time being.

"Are you the person in charge?" he asked the blonde icily. "On whose authority are you trying to arrest me?"

The woman narrowed her eyes. "You know very well who we are. You are a suspect in the murder of a man whose body was discovered in the sewers under Bayview

Park eight hours ago. You were seen fleeing the scene of the crime."

Cassius drew himself to his full height.

"So, you decided to come in here and gun me down?" he snarled. "Is that the modus operandi of the San Francisco branch of the Argonaut Agency? Kill first and ask fucking questions later?!"

The blonde frowned. "Like I said, that was an unfortunate accident. Now, how about you—?"

"What's going on here?" someone said behind Cassius.

He whirled around.

Glass crunched under Morgan's bare feet as he stepped inside the apartment from the terrace. He was wearing jeans, an almighty scowl, and little else.

Cassius stilled. The glass was not cutting Morgan's skin.

Alarm had Cassius's pulse spiking. He hadn't sensed anything unusual about his neighbor when they'd just spoken out on the terrace. His stomach dropped.

Except for the fact that he knew I was there when I'd deliberately masked my aura.

"Morgan?" The blonde gaped. "What the hell are you doing here?!"

Cassius's heart stuttered. *Wait? They know each other?!*

"I live next door," Morgan replied irritably.

Cassius registered the expressions on the other Argonaut agents' faces with a sinking feeling. It was clear they knew Morgan too. Not just knew him, but regarded him as their superior.

Shit. He's an Argonaut agent.

Cassius fisted his hands. The demon cat protested with a soft meow when his fingers sank into its hide.

"Since when?" the blonde asked Morgan, still shocked.

"Since a month ago," Morgan snapped. "Now, how about you tell me what the hell you're doing in this guy's apartment, Adrianne?"

"I should renegotiate my salary," the blonde muttered, looking around the luxurious penthouse. Her gaze focused on Morgan and Cassius once more. "Your neighbor is a suspect in a murder," she told Morgan. "FYI, your neighbor is Cassius Black."

Morgan visibly stiffened. He observed Cassius with an inscrutable expression before turning to Adrianne. "That still doesn't justify you guys coming in here in full tactical gear and shooting at him, Adrianne."

Cassius blinked. *That's a first.*

It wasn't every day an Argonaut agent came to his defense.

He clenched his jaw. "I happened to be looking for this cat. That's why I was in those sewers. My client is a woman called Joyce Almeda. Her phone number is on my cell phone." Cassius studied Morgan and Adrianne coldly. "Seeing as your agency appears to be as biased against me as every other one on this planet, you'll excuse me for not having stuck around long enough for you assholes to pin the blame on me for something I had nothing to do with."

Adrianne frowned at Cassius.

"We found another victim," she told Morgan, a muscle jumping in her cheek.

Morgan froze. "What?"

"We found another human sacrifice. It was a man this time. Your neighbor was at the scene of the crime when our agents got there." Suspicion glittered in Adrianne's eyes as she glanced at Cassius. "And yes, before you ask, it was a magic circle made from Dark Blight and human—"

Wind exploded inside Cassius's apartment. It wrapped

tightly around his body in overlapping bands, locking his limbs in place and robbing him of his breath. Cassius gasped as he was lifted bodily into the air, his wings straining uselessly against his back where he sought to spread them and escape.

Morgan's pupils glowed with blinding-white light as he wielded his powers, imprisoning Cassius in a painful tempest of seraphic energy. The demon cat leapt onto the floor and hissed angrily at the angel who was glaring at Cassius as if he'd committed a grave sin.

Black spots burst across Cassius's vision as the constraints squeezed his ribs to near breaking point.

He thought he heard Adrianne shout Morgan's name.

Darkness encroached upon his world as his consciousness faded.

"*Jesus*, Morgan! You nearly killed him!" Adrianne snarled.

Morgan clenched his jaw and kept silent, his gaze on the unconscious man lying opposite where he and the sorceress sat in the back of the van taking them downtown.

The other Argonaut agents had chosen to ride in the second vehicle, even though they'd had to cram inside. If Adrianne and Morgan's expressions hadn't been enough to deter them, then Cassius Black's presence had.

The demon cat they'd found in Cassius's apartment was currently perched protectively on the motionless angel's chest, its yellow eyes radiating pure loathing as it glowered at Morgan and Adrianne.

Morgan could hardly blame it. Just as he couldn't explain why he'd done what he'd done in Cassius's apartment to Adrianne and their subordinates.

Cassius Black was infamous not just among the other-worldly, but among humans too. The Cursed Angel with the Black Wings. The Devil Who Walks Amongst Us. The Possessed Fallen. He was known by many names, some more unpleasant than others. Although the angel had never committed a crime that justified the degree of hostility and distrust directed at him, he had been involved in enough troubling incidents over the centuries to be labeled a dangerous liability by most people.

Remorse stabbed through Morgan as he gazed upon Cassius's pale face. He'd chosen to let Adrianne and the other Argonaut agents believe that it was news of the human sacrifice they'd discovered last night that had made him fly into a fit of rage. And it was, partly.

Two months had passed since he and his team had been assigned the case of the mysterious human deaths that had been taking place over San Francisco. All were attributed to black-magic rituals. They were still nowhere near finding the who and the why behind the sacrifices.

But that wasn't the sole reason Morgan had been overcome by the strength of his feelings when he'd heard Cassius's name. It had been a gut instinct borne from the very depths of his soul. One underscored by bitter resentment. He couldn't tell Adrianne that, in that moment, he'd just wanted to lash out at Cassius. To tear into the angel for a reason he still couldn't explain. A reason he was beginning to suspect might have something to do with why he barely slept most nights.

Morgan had multiple bed partners not because he was addicted to sex, but because the slumber he fell into after making love was often dreamless. Unfortunately, his stamina far outdid that of the men and women he bedded, hence why he rarely had the same partner on consecutive nights.

"Hey, you okay?" Adrianne asked.

The sorceress was frowning at his fisted hands.

Morgan grimaced. He'd clenched them so hard he was close to drawing blood.

"Yeah." He sighed and raked his hair with his fingers. "I'm sorry about what happened back there."

"Well, this case has all of us jumpy as hell," his second-in-command murmured, her eyes darting to Cassius. "Still, I've never seen you lose your shit like that before."

Morgan studied the unconscious man. *She's right. And now, it looks like we have another headache on our hands.*

Despite meeting Cassius for the first time, Morgan couldn't help but sense that they were connected in some way. He'd felt it the moment his powers had touched the angel. Though it had lasted but seconds, Morgan had experienced an oddly familiar resonance when their soul cores had come into contact. The animosity he'd initially felt toward the other angel had faded, only to be replaced by intense curiosity.

I wonder what that's about.

Morgan stiffened.

Cassius was finally stirring.

Color returned to the angel's striking face as he blinked his eyes open. He stared at the ceiling of the van for a moment before shifting his body on the bench. Metal jangled as he moved. He froze and looked at his hands.

Stark Steel handcuffs were locked around his wrists, securing him to a metal bolt in the floor of the van via a chain. Stark Steel was the strongest and most magic-resistant element in existence. It was found exclusively in the weapons and armor of the angels and demons who'd fallen to Earth five hundred years ago. It was also the only element that could inflict mortal wounds on angels beside Dark Blight, a poison that could incapacitate angels and which was used exclusively by black-magic users in their rituals and spells. Rain Silver, a liquid-silver derivative, was similarly toxic to demons.

Anger turned Cassius's gaze a stormy gray as he glared at Morgan and Adrianne. He sat up slowly, mindful of the cat that landed in his arms. Morgan observed the feline where it huddled against Cassius's chest and fought the insane urge to rip it from the angel's hold and take its place.

I am losing my fucking mind.

The stirring in Morgan's groin told him it wasn't his mind doing the thinking right now. Cassius Black was drop-dead gorgeous and everything Morgan liked in a man. He'd felt the instant spark of attraction between them when they'd met a short while ago, on their respective penthouse terraces.

Despite Cassius's bad-tempered attitude, it was clear he'd sensed it too. It had not just been his dick that had betrayed him. The way his eyes had darkened to molten slate and the hint of color that had stained his cheekbones had been a dead giveaway too.

"Where the hell am I?" Cassius growled.

"In a van," Morgan said blithely.

Adrianne glanced at Morgan with a frown.

"We're on our way to the local Argonaut Agency bureau," she told Cassius gruffly. Her gaze flickered to the cat. "So, does demon kitty have a name?"

A muscle danced in Cassius's jawline. He hugged the creature close to his chest and stayed mutinously silent.

Morgan swallowed a sigh. *Lucky cat.*

They pulled into an underground garage beneath the agency's San Francisco branch office a short while later. Adrianne unlocked Cassius's cuffs from the chain and was about to fasten the spare bracelet to her left wrist when Morgan stopped her.

"Let me."

Surprise flashed briefly in the sorceress's eyes. She passed him the handcuff wordlessly. The look Cassius gave Morgan as he shackled them together would have turned a lesser man into a bloodied stain on the ground. Morgan bit back a smile, not quite sure why the current situation amused him so.

Brightness flared briefly in Cassius's pupils. "What's so funny, asshole?!"

Morgan kept a straight face by a sheer act of will. "Nothing."

Cassius glowered at him. He glanced around warily as they stepped down from the van. Four Argonaut agents fell into step around them as they headed for a bank of elevators. Ten seconds later, Morgan started to heavily regret their presence. The tension inside the cabin they rode was so thick he could have cut the air with his dagger. Bar Adrianne and him, the Argonaut agents did nothing to mask their obvious hostility toward Cassius. The way their fingers occasionally twitched told Morgan they would happily shoot the angel if he so much as breathed the wrong way.

Relief flooded Morgan as they came out into the agency's main office space, on the tenth floor of the high rise. It was short-lived.

A deadly hush descended in the bullpen when the men and women gathered there registered the unwelcome stranger in their midst.

"Hey, isn't that—?" a female agent hissed sideways to a colleague.

Zakir Singh – an Asian man with a scar running across his left eye and down his face – spat on the floor and earned himself half a dozen scowls.

"Cassius Black," he said in a voice dripping with contempt.

"Hey, I hope you're gonna clean that up, dickwad," Bailey Green told him. The wizard spun a rune-covered dagger on his knuckles as he narrowed his eyes at the other agent.

"Wow," Cassius murmured sardonically. "I can literally feel the love in the air."

Morgan sighed. He couldn't exactly come up with a riposte against the angel's sarcasm in the face of the Argonaut agents' open resentment.

"It might be a good idea not to antagonize them," he said instead.

He might as well have asked Cassius to perform a sexual act in public from the incredulous look the angel gave him.

Bailey's gaze shifted curiously to Cassius before moving to Morgan and Adrianne. "You guys are here awfully early. I thought our meeting was at nine."

Adrianne frowned. "Something came up. Get your ass out of that chair and come with us."

Even though his abilities as a wizard more than matched Adrianne's powers as a sorceress, Bailey lifted his feet off his desk and meekly obeyed her command.

"I think he's still hoping to get back in your pants," Morgan told Adrianne as they headed down a corridor lined with offices and conference rooms, a stony Cassius and the curious demon cat between them.

"The only way that's ever gonna happen is over my cold, dead body," the sorceress retorted.

"I'm *right* here, you guys," Bailey protested behind them.

6

CASSIUS'S PALMS GREW SWEATY UPON ENTERING THE office of the director of the San Francisco branch of the Argonaut Agency. He prayed the man beside him didn't notice his sudden nervousness.

Despite his bravado, Cassius knew he needed to be careful. Not only was it evident that the Argonaut agents in San Francisco were prepared to use illegal ammunition on him, they had an incredibly skilled Aerial angel working for them in the shape of Morgan King.

A tall, charismatic black man with receding, gray hair and a goatee turned from where he was standing at a bay of windows overlooking the Embarcadero. His dark eyes gleamed shrewdly when they landed on Cassius, the sunlight reflecting off the water framing him with a halo.

Cassius wasn't fooled by his benign appearance.

Francis Strickland was a Level One mage and one of the most powerful magic users in the country. He knew more about Cassius than most people did, including his best-kept secrets, which was another reason for Cassius's edginess.

He's aged pretty gracefully.

Strickland no longer gave off a strong whiff of Juniper, unlike the first time they'd met. Only the most seasoned magic users could mask their abilities as effectively as he was doing. Cassius was aware the man and woman standing next to Morgan and him were likely one level below Strickland, judging from their almost undetectable scents. The Valerian smell emanating from Adrianne's soul core marked her as a sorceress, whereas the blue-eyed blond redolent of Frankincense seemed to be an equally powerful wizard.

Following the Fall, the magic that had always existed deep inside the souls of humans had flourished, a side effect of being exposed to the seraphic and demonic cores of angels and demons. It had taken many forms, from sorcerers who could use the energies around them to create and manipulate magic, to wizards who had to rely on potions and spells to access theirs. There were also enchanters who manifested illusion magic and mages whose staffs acted as a medium for them to focus their powers.

Of all magic users, warlocks were the rarest and most feared, their ability to draw power from demons and the Hells an art that was once forbidden.

All magic users were required to make themselves known to Hexa, the guild of registered magic users. They were subsequently assessed and classified based on their abilities, with Level Six being a novice and Level One being the most powerful magic user.

There were probably a dozen people in the world who could discern the power in the souls of magic users of the caliber of Strickland and the other two. The fact that

Cassius was one of those people had made him a target of Hexa for as long as it had existed.

"Mr. Black," Strickland said. "I would like to say it's good to see you again, but current circumstances prevent me from doing so." The director walked over to his desk and indicated the chairs on the other side. "Please, sit."

Cassius followed Morgan as the angel headed for the seats. It was that or be forcibly dragged across the floor.

To Cassius's surprise, the demon cat jumped on Strickland's desk and padded over to the director. It sniffed the air in front of Strickland's face, froze, and darted back to Cassius, hackles raised and an angry hiss leaving its throat. The feline leapt down onto the floor and hid under Cassius's chair, still spitting.

"Damn," Cassius murmured. "That cat is the smartest thing I've met since I've come to San Francisco."

"Is that a dig at me?" Morgan said, his blue eyes twinkling with amusement.

Cassius masked a frown. *What's with this guy? He nearly killed me back at the apartment and now he wants to be friends?*

"I don't know," Cassius said coolly. "From what I've seen so far, the IQ levels of the Argonaut agents in this city leave a lot to be desired."

A palpable wave of displeasure washed over him from the two agents framing them.

Cassius flashed a bitter smile their way. "Don't take it personally. I think most Argonaut agents are dumb as fuck."

Adrianne and the blue-eyed magic user scowled at him.

Strickland sighed. "Really, Cassius? Insults?"

Cassius narrowed his eyes at the man across the desk. "Since it seems we're going to get personal, yes, *Francis*. One of your agents shot at me barely an hour ago and *this* asshole—" he jerked a thumb at Morgan, "—tried to kill me in my own goddamn apartment. So your people can piss off if they think I'm gonna play nice!"

Strickland's gaze shifted to Morgan. "You tried to kill him?"

Morgan's expression sobered. He didn't reply.

Strickland steepled his hands on the desk and dropped his forehead on his knuckles. He murmured something under his breath.

"What's he doing?" Cassius asked Morgan.

"Praying for patience," Morgan replied morosely.

Strickland finally looked up, his eyes dark with irritation. "Uncuff him."

"What?!" Adrianne said, shocked.

Strickland's tone turned arctic. "I said uncuff him, Agent Hogan."

"But, sir, Black is a suspect—" Adrianne protested.

"Whatever you believe this man has done, he hasn't. Trust me on this." Strickland arched an eyebrow when the agent opened her mouth to voice another objection. "I am well aware of Cassius's abilities, Adrianne. In all the time I've known him—and known *of* him—he has never attacked someone without being heavily provoked first."

Adrianne faltered before stiffly unlocking the handcuffs shackling Cassius to Morgan, a muscle jumping in her jawline.

Cassius rubbed the red marks on his wrist. "Thanks."

"How do you guys know each other?" Morgan asked Strickland curiously.

A dry smile curved Strickland's mouth as he studied Cassius. "Cassius saved my life when I was a starry-eyed Level Three mage working in London, thirty years ago."

From the way Adrianne and the wizard sucked in air,

Cassius guessed it was unusual for their director to be so frank in their presence.

"To be fair, you were starry-eyed because you were under the spell of that woman's enchanter," Cassius muttered.

The cat jumped onto his lap and curled up in a ball. He petted its head and was rewarded by a low, demonic rumble.

"That guy was good," Strickland admitted with a grunt. "There are only a handful of people who can match his skills these days."

"Wait." Morgan frowned. "Thirty years ago in London? Are you talking about—?"

"Tania Lancaster?!" Adrianne gasped, some of the color draining from her face.

"Who's Tania Lancaster?" the wizard asked blankly. This earned him a battery of stares. He grimaced and shrugged. "What?"

"Tania Lancaster was a Level One sorceress whose sect terrorized Europe over a period of twenty-five years," Adrianne explained. "She was a black-magic user who excelled in necromancy and she had incredibly powerful acolytes working beneath her, including one of the best enchanters this world has ever known. A lot of people died at their hands, regular humans and magic users alike. They even killed a few demons and angels. All the agencies worked together to bring them down when they went underground in London." She cast a troubled frown at Cassius. "I never heard anything about Black's involvement in that incident. It was Victor Sloan who killed her."

"Victor was there," Strickland said mildly. "But it was Cassius who landed the killing blow on Tania and saved everyone's life that day, including Victor's. Cassius insisted

Victor take credit for his accomplishment." His sharp gaze moved to Cassius. "How is Victor, by the way?"

Cassius kept his expression neutral at the mention of his friend and former lover. "He's okay. He's enjoying being the new head of Cabalista."

Morgan frowned faintly. Argonaut agents had as much love for the demonic organization as they did for Cassius.

"Why was this kept a secret?" Anger underscored Adrianne's words. She tilted her chin challengingly at Strickland. "If Black was responsible for Tania's death, then why wasn't this fact made public?" Her irate gaze shifted briefly to Cassius. "It would have helped change people's opinion of him."

Silence fell in the wake of her question.

Strickland leaned back in his chair, his eyes on Cassius's carefully blank face. "Because none of the organizations who govern the supernatural beings of this world wants anyone to know that the most feared and shunned Fallen on this planet does their dirtiest work for them."

7

Surprise jolted Morgan at Strickland's words. Adrianne and Bailey startled.

Cassius sighed and pinched the bridge of his nose. "Should you really be telling them this, Francis? You know the other agencies will be pissed if you blab about their classified information to unauthorized agents."

"Morgan and his team know how to keep a secret," Strickland said dismissively. "Besides, that's not what's important right now."

Morgan stiffened slightly at the calculating light in Strickland's eyes.

If Cassius noticed, he gave no indication of it. He picked up the demon cat and studied it solemnly face to face. "What'd I tell you? Argonaut agents are idiots."

The feline yawned before giving the angel's nose a tentative lick with its pink tongue. A bolt of jealousy stabbed through Morgan.

Stupid cat.

The demon spirit turned its yellow gaze on him.

Morgan wouldn't have been surprised if the creature had suddenly smirked.

A knock came at the door.

"Come in," Strickland called out calmly, seemingly immune to the strained atmosphere in his office.

Agent Driscoll opened the door and walked in. He slowed when he clocked everyone's expressions, cast an uneasy look at Cassius, and came over to murmur something in Adrianne's ear.

The sorceress frowned. "Thanks." She waited until Driscoll had left before turning a chagrined gaze on Strickland and Morgan. "Black's story checks out. He was hired to find that cat yesterday."

Something that felt a lot like relief darted through Morgan. Though his instincts had told him Cassius didn't have anything to do with the mutilated body the agency had discovered in the sewers last night, it was still reassuring to hear proof of his innocence.

"Great." Cassius rose to his feet, the cat in question under one arm. "Now that that's sorted, I'll take my leave. I hope the agency will foot the bill of repairing and cleaning my apartment." He turned and headed for the door with a casual wave of a hand. "It was nice to see you again, Francis."

"Wait," Strickland ordered in a hard voice.

Cassius stopped. He looked over his shoulder, his expression turning frosty. "No."

Strickland narrowed his eyes. "You haven't even heard my offer yet."

A muscle jumped in Cassius's cheek. "The answer will be no, whatever it is."

"We still need to take your statement about what you saw in the sewers last night," Adrianne told Cassius stiffly.

"You can do that at my place." Cassius's tone turned mocking. "I'm afraid being in a building full of people who hate my guts will make me...uncooperative."

"Why did you apply for a license to operate as an independent operator?" Strickland asked Cassius. "Last I heard, you were still working for Victor and Cabalista."

Cassius twisted on his heels to face them, his eyes darkening with displeasure.

Morgan masked a frown. Few Fallens chose to work independently of the organizations that governed supernatural entities and magic users. Independents were not as well respected as those who worked for the Argonaut Agency, The Order of Rosen, Cabalista, and Hexa, the four main agencies that came about in the centuries after the angels and demons fell to Earth and magic became all too powerful once more. Nor did they enjoy the money, protection, and benefits that came from belonging to an influential institution.

As an angel, Cassius had the right to ally himself with Argonaut, the agency responsible for maintaining law and order among the Fallen and magic users, or The Order of Rosen, the organization of angels affiliated with the Catholic Church.

Morgan grew thoughtful. *Of course, him being an outcast means those are probably not viable options.*

He'd heard rumors of Cassius working for Cabalista in an advisory capacity about a decade ago. It seemed the demonic organization wasn't as fearful of a backlash from its members as the other agencies were. Somehow, Morgan suspected Victor Sloan had something to do with that. He'd met the demon a handful of times in the past, when their paths had crossed on business for their agencies. He hadn't been able to get a read on the man, which only convinced him of one thing: Victor was a suave politician through and through and good at getting what he wanted.

Though Cassius had done his best to hide it, Morgan had noted his reaction when Strickland had mentioned the demon's name just now. He couldn't help but feel that there was more than just a business relationship between Cassius and Victor.

Strickland glanced at Morgan, as if he'd detected his deepening irritation.

"Have you and Victor parted ways?" the director continued, plainly ignoring Cassius's scowl.

"The answer to that question is no one's business but mine," Cassius grated out. "Now, if you'll excuse me."

He had his hand on the door handle when Strickland spoke again.

"I can revoke your license, Cassius."

Morgan straightened in his chair.

No one could have missed the threatening wave of seraphic energy that had just washed through the office from the man standing frozen at the door.

Cassius's back trembled as he fought to stop his wings from sprouting from his body, his knuckles white where he grasped the metal knob.

"Do not test me, Francis," he said between gritted teeth. "I'm having a shitty day."

The hairs rose on Morgan's nape at what he sensed from Cassius then. He saw Adrianne and Bailey reach for their guns and shook his head jerkily. They stopped at his command, their faces wary.

"You would never intentionally harm me, Cassius, and we both know it," Strickland said sedately.

Morgan couldn't help but glance at his old friend in admiration. Though he'd surprised Cassius back at the apartment with his powers, he doubted he could do so easily right now. He'd heard rumors of the black-winged angel's abilities over the centuries but had never believed them. It seemed Strickland had witnessed what Cassius could do during Tania Lancaster's execution in London.

And it appears he deliberately didn't unleash his full powers when I attacked him this morning.

"The secrecy spell that Victor had his mage cast on us in London prevents me from telling the agents in this room the full extent of your...talents," Strickland continued, confirming Morgan's suspicions. "Look, I know you just want to be left alone." The director sighed. "Believe me, as your friend, I want to respect your choice. But I can't. Morgan and his team are working on something big. And I think you can help them."

Morgan narrowed his eyes at Strickland. "Wait. What the hell are you trying to pull? You want to offer him some kind of position on the team?!"

Cassius's expression when he twisted on his heels would have turned Strickland to stone had he been a lesser man.

"Are you saying you'll have the city revoke my license if I don't help that—" he glared at Morgan, "—that douchebag and his friends? Because that sounds a lot like blackmail to me!"

Morgan grimaced. "Ouch."

"You deserved that," Adrianne muttered.

Cassius pointedly ignored them.

"You only need to go down to the bullpen to see how your agents feel about even having me in the same building," he told Strickland heatedly. "I have no wish to work with people who would stab me in the back with their next breath!"

Morgan saw Adrianne twitch out the corner of his eye. He knew the sorceress had taken that dig personally. Still, none of them could blame Cassius for his wariness.

"I don't trust any of you," Cassius continued, his angry gaze landing on each and every one of them. "Argonaut. Rosen. Cabalista. Hexa. You're all the same. Your self-righteousness has bitten you in the ass over and over again in the past few centuries, yet you keep making the same mistake. You keep assuming that the only reason I haven't fought back is because I'm scared of you."

Morgan's skin prickled at the light that flared in Cassius's eyes. The windows trembled and the room shook. Adrianne and Bailey straightened, their apprehension palpable.

Only Strickland remained indifferent to the overwhelming power emanating from the angel.

"Someone is stealing human souls again, Cassius," the director said quietly.

8

Cassius landed on the terrace of his penthouse, entered his apartment through the smashed glass doors, and scowled when he saw the mess inside.

Damn Aerial!

Morgan's smug face rose before his eyes. A mixture of anger, frustration, and wariness swirled through Cassius. Anger because his next-door neighbor had turned out to be an Argonaut agent. Frustration because of the undeniable spark of sexual attraction that had ignited between them from the moment they'd laid eyes on one another. And wariness because of what he'd felt when Morgan had touched him with his powers. Could still feel.

A connection he could not explain.

One that gave off a dark, twisted scent full of pain and longing.

The demon cat leapt from Cassius's arms, landed lightly on the floor, and padded across the apartment.

"Don't get too comfortable," he muttered. "This is just a temporary arrangement."

The cat flicked its tail, happy rumbles rising from its chest. It could evidently sense the lie in Cassius's gruff words.

Cassius sighed and grabbed a dustpan and brush from a cupboard. Strickland's words echoed through his mind as he started cleaning up.

"Stealing human souls?" Cassius had repeated, growing deathly still.

"Yes." Strickland had dipped his chin. "The rituals aren't quite the same as those Tania was performing in England, but they're pretty damn close."

The grim foreboding Cassius had experienced in the sewers had rushed through him once more.

"That doesn't concern me," he'd muttered, turning to open the door.

"You know what our suspicions were regarding what Tania was planning," Strickland had argued. "If the same is true of what's happening in San Francisco right now, then this concerns all of us."

Cassius's fingers had clenched on the doorknob. "Be that as it may, you can't force me to work for you. I can be very unhelpful when I want to be." His gaze had flitted to Morgan. "That guy would regret having me on his team."

Cassius frowned as he put the broken glass in a trash bag. Despite what he'd told Strickland, he couldn't help but brood over what he'd stumbled upon in the sewers. He now understood why he hadn't detected any trace of the dead man's soul when he'd looked inside him. Considering the fresh state of the body, there should have been a lingering vestige of the victim's essence.

There were only a dozen or so people in the world who could attempt the kind of black-magic ritual required to fracture and remove a soul core from a living human's body. Tania Lancaster had been one of them.

Looks like someone else might be attempting a similar move. But that isn't my problem to solve.

Cassius clamped down on the guilt that surged through him at that last thought. He was well within his rights to refuse to assist Strickland and Argonaut.

"Need a hand?" someone said behind him.

Cassius looked over his shoulder, his gut clenching at the familiar, smoky voice.

Morgan was leaning against the smashed-up front door where it hung off its hinges. He'd changed into a black T-shirt, tactical Defender jeans, and a leather jacket with the badge of the Argonaut Agency on the left breast pocket.

Irritation shot through Cassius.

He had a feeling Morgan would look good even if he were wearing a trash bag.

"Unless you can undo what you and your agents did to my place this morning, then no," Cassius said coldly, doing his best to shrug off the sexual awareness rippling across his skin.

Morgan ignored him and walked inside the apartment. "Let me help. I feel bad enough as it is about what happened."

Cassius was about to snap at the angel to get the hell out when an idea came to him. "If you're truly sorry, then do me a favor. Stop having loud sex every night."

Morgan blinked, pupils flaring in surprise. "Excuse me?"

Heat flooded Cassius's face. *Shit. I can't believe I just said that.*

"I can't sleep with all that racket you make," he said defensively.

An alluring smile split Morgan's mouth when he noticed the color staining Cassius's cheeks. "I'm afraid I might struggle with that request. I have a pretty high sex drive."

Cassius's dick responded to Morgan's words and smile. He cursed his lower body.

"Besides, it helps with the nightmares," Morgan added lightly.

"Nightmares?" Cassius said curiously.

He silently berated himself in the next instant. He and Morgan weren't close enough for him to be asking the man about such an intimate topic.

Morgan didn't seem in the least bit upset by his interest. "Yes."

He came closer.

Cassius found himself taking an involuntary step in the opposite direction. The backs of his knees struck the couch. Morgan stopped, the look on his face shifting into that of a hunter stalking its prey. Cassius licked his lips nervously.

Somehow, he really didn't mind being the prey right now.

"What kind of nightmares?" he murmured, hoping to distract the man observing him as if he were the most tempting morsel of food he'd seen in a long time.

Something dark flitted in Morgan's blue gaze. "The kind that haunts you even when you're awake."

He moved again.

This time, Cassius stood his ground. He had to tilt his chin up slightly when Morgan stopped toe to toe with him. His heart pounded as Morgan's heat surrounded him, cocooning him in sensual warmth.

The scent of arousal emanating from the Aerial grew stronger as his gaze roamed Cassius's face and body. Cassius shivered, the feeling of Morgan's searing stare so potent it felt like a caress. Morgan took the trash bag from Cassius's unresisting hand and dropped it on the floor.

Cassius swallowed, too mesmerized by the fire in Morgan's eyes to even dare breathe. "I thought you were gonna help."

Morgan smiled. "I *am* helping."

Cassius's dick throbbed at the sexy smirk. "No, you're not."

Morgan chuckled. "Busted." His expression slowly sobered. "You're right."

He lifted a hand and traced a thumb across Cassius's mouth.

Electricity sparked on Cassius's flesh. His entire body focused on where Morgan was touching him.

"What are you doing?" he whispered.

Morgan's pupils dilated as Cassius's breath washed across his skin. "What I've yearned to do since the moment I laid eyes on you. Kiss you."

Blood thrummed heavily in Cassius's veins, lust a tight ball growing in his belly.

Morgan's gaze dropped to Cassius's mouth. "Tell me if you don't want this."

Cassius hesitated. He couldn't deny that he craved Morgan's kiss just as badly. He parted his lips slightly.

Desire darkened Morgan's eyes at the silent invitation. He clasped Cassius's cheeks in his hands, angled his face, and took his mouth fiercely.

Oh God.

Heat exploded inside Cassius. He shuddered, body

instantly melting and mind growing blank at Morgan's demanding touch and scalding lips. The front of his jeans grew uncomfortably tight as Morgan explored the contours of his mouth with masterful skill.

This kiss was out of this world and he wanted more of it.

Cassius gasped as Morgan slipped his tongue inside and frenched him. His hands rose to clutch at Morgan's strong shoulders, the feeling of their mating tongues lashing against one another so wickedly good he almost came there and then.

His instincts screamed at him to push the angel away. To stop this madness before it consumed them both. But his desire for Morgan had him brushing his body closer to the man.

Morgan made an approving noise at the back of his throat. He lowered a hand to Cassius's ass, pushed his thigh between Cassius's legs, and pressed their groins together. Cassius moaned, a wave of dizziness washing over him at the feel of Morgan's rock-hard cock digging into his belly.

It had been ages since he'd experienced the frenzy of feelings coursing through him.

The next thing he knew, he was flat on his back on the couch with Morgan kneeling above him. The angel's touch was rough and just a little desperate as he yanked Cassius's T-shirt up, his eyes a brilliant sky-blue and his cheeks flushed with passion. He sneaked his hands under the material and touched Cassius's quivering abs and chest, his lips still hot and heavy on Cassius's mouth as he held his gaze.

Cassius trembled, eyelids fluttering closed and a sweet ache building inside him as Morgan's fingers danced across his flesh in sweeping strokes. Morgan circled Cassius's hardening nipples with his thumbs, let go of his mouth, and leaned down to nip at the left nub with his teeth through Cassius's T-shirt.

"Fuck!" Cassius hissed, eyes slamming open and body arching instinctively closer to the man above him.

Morgan smiled sultrily. He grazed a knuckle up and down Cassius's stiff dick through the material of his jeans, igniting a trail of fire along Cassius's aching length.

Someone knocked on the front door of the penthouse, startling them both.

"Hey, Black, are you in there?" Adrianne called out warily.

"Shit," Morgan mouthed where he crouched above Cassius, an irritated frown wrinkling his brow.

Debris crunched under Adrianne's feet as she entered the apartment. "Black?"

Neither Morgan nor Cassius were visible from the doorway.

Cassius bit down hard on his lower lip, the sudden urge to laugh sweeping over him like a tide.

Morgan narrowed his eyes.

"You're not helping," he berated Cassius in a whisper only the two of them should have heard.

"They're on the couch," a woman said blithely.

"'They?'" a man said warily.

Cassius recognized the blue-eyed wizard's voice.

"Are they fornicating?" another man asked drily. "Oh. Hello, Kitty."

"Seeing as how the room reeks of sexual arousal, I'd say possibly," the unknown woman replied.

"What?!" the wizard gasped, aghast.

Footsteps approached Cassius and Morgan. Adrianne's scowling face appeared over the back rest.

"I can't believe you!" she snarled at Morgan.

Morgan sighed.

"Excuse me," he told Cassius in an exasperated tone. He straightened, moved off the couch, and glowered at Adrianne and the people Cassius couldn't see, heedless of his raging erection. "What the hell are you guys doing here?"

Cassius carefully raised his head and peered at the group standing inside the hallway of his apartment.

The tall, Oriental woman who'd detected their presence gave off the almost imperceptible, electric scent of an angel. She was flanked by a man emitting the muted, sulfurous taint of a demon. He was holding the cat in his arms.

The blue-eyed wizard and a young man who smelled of cedar stood next to them, mouths gaping and expressions horrified.

Adrianne ignored Morgan and directed a tense stare at Cassius.

"Did this asshole jump you?"

"Hey," Morgan protested. "I'll have you know I don't sexually attack people. They attack me."

Cassius frowned at that. "Really?" He climbed off the couch, straightened his clothes, and gave Morgan a withering look. "So, you're saying I assaulted you, tripped, fell on my back, and somehow ended up with your tongue down my throat and your hand on my dick?"

The Oriental woman and the demon turned away slightly, faces crunched up and shoulders trembling as they fought to suppress their snorts. The wizard and the enchanter made choking noises. Adrianne blinked, her expression a mixture of shock and reluctant admiration.

Morgan grimaced and rubbed the back of his neck. "Okay, I admit I'm the one who tried to seduce you." He paused, his eyes growing heated as he held Cassius's irate gaze. "By the way, you talking dirty is a real turn-on."

Adrianne slapped Morgan on the back of the head.

9

S<small>UNLIGHT SPARKLED ON THE GREEN WATERS OF THE PIER</small>, casting dazzling reflections across the outdoor seating area and the table they sat at. Considering how busy the restaurant had been when they'd entered it, Cassius was surprised their order had reached them in such record time.

He only had to observe the way the waiters and waitresses were exchanging heated whispers and the admiring glances their group was drawing from the other customers to realize Morgan and his team likely had this effect on people wherever they went. Cassius frowned faintly.

I can't say I blame them. Angels and demons have always been rather striking in their appearance.

Julia Chen, a Terrene angel with sculptured cheekbones, long, shiny, black hair piled in an elegant topknot, and dark eyes full of wisdom, was stunning enough to be a super model. Seated to her right with the demon cat asleep on his lap was Zach Mooney, a broodingly attractive Aqueous demon with brown hair and blue eyes.

Compared to them, Charlie Lloyd, the Level Three

enchanter with dark hair and gray eyes, and Bailey Green, the blond wizard from Strickland's office, looked positively mundane despite their above-average looks.

Cassius turned to the most arresting figure of them all. "What am I doing here again?"

He frowned at Morgan and waved a vague hand at their surroundings.

"Adrianne and I wanted to apologize for what happened this morning," the Aerial replied.

Cassius cursed his treacherous heart when it skipped a beat at Morgan's faint smile. Adrianne dipped her chin at Cassius, oblivious to his mixed feelings.

"Lunch is on me," the sorceress said. "I've ordered the agency's admin pool to organize the repairs to your apartment. And you'll be pleased to know Driscoll is on my watchlist."

"Why do I get the feeling I never want to be on your watchlist?" Cassius said warily.

A cool smile stretched Adrianne's mouth. "You would be right."

"We call it the Watchlist of Death," Zach told Cassius helpfully as he poured ketchup on his French fries.

"As in, the agents who end up on it barely make it out alive after she's through with them," Bailey added before biting into his burger.

Adrianne cut her eyes to the demon and the wizard.

"How about I give you some details about the murders we've been investigating?" Morgan asked Cassius.

Cassius paused, his hand on a slice of extra-hot pepperoni pizza. "I haven't agreed to help you guys, so you'd be breaking the law if you did. Besides," he looked around, "this place isn't exactly a secure location."

"Strickland gave me permission to discuss the case

with you." Morgan looked across the table. "Charlie, do your thing."

Charlie sighed. "I wish you wouldn't call it that."

The enchanter murmured a spell. An invisible privacy shield formed around them, enclosing them in a sound-proof bubble only a magic user or supernatural being could detect. All anyone outside it would hear was what would pass for a normal conversation if they were to spy on them.

"It started two months ago," Morgan said, ignoring Cassius's frown. "The first body was discovered in the Mission Dolores Cemetery, in front of the sculpture of Junipero Serra."

"The Saint of California?" Cassius asked curiously. He bristled slightly when he saw the amused light in Morgan's eyes. "This doesn't mean I'm taking on your case."

"Sure, sure," Morgan drawled.

"Serra was hardly a saint," Julia observed as she cut into her lasagna. "He forced many Native Americans to convert to Catholicism."

"I thought you angels were all for Catholicism," Adrianne said drily, popping a French fry in her mouth.

Julia shrugged. "Only if people sign up to it of their own free will."

Zach stabbed a lettuce leaf with his fork and chewed on it thoughtfully. "Serra also worked for the Spanish Inquisition, during which time he accused many magic users and demon practitioners of witchcraft and sorcery. That guy was definitely *not* a saint."

"Oh." Julia raised an eyebrow. "Wasn't that the time he accused Melchora of devil worship?"

The demon cat woke up, stretched, and studied Zach's plate with avid interest.

"Yup," Zach said. "She was pissed. She said the only way she'd idolize Satan was if that bastard licked her feet and worshiped her back."

"How is Melchora?" Julia said curiously. "I haven't seen her in decades."

"She's good. She runs a chain of hair salons in Mexico City." Zach grimaced. "That demon is filthy rich."

Bailey sighed. "Sometimes, I forget how old you guys are."

Charlie nodded.

"Who was the first victim?" Cassius said.

"It was a college student," Adrianne replied. "Her name was Anita Hernandez. She was a sophomore in the Liberal and Creative Arts Department at SFSU."

"She had no links to the magical or supernatural world that we could find," Julia said. "The girl was a high-school Valedictorian and pure as the driven snow as far as we can tell."

"No one is that innocent," Cassius said skeptically. "Not in this day and age."

"You're not wrong," Julia said. "You're sitting next to a very depraved soul."

Morgan narrowed his eyes at the angel. "You know I'm your superior, right?"

A cool smile stretched Julia's mouth. "I'm willing to take you on anytime, anywhere, Aerial."

"You guys did that once," Zach said drily. "Remember?"

"What are you talking about?" Cassius asked Zach.

"Julia and Morgan were in opposite factions during the Napoleonic Wars," Zach explained. "They tore a pretty big chunk out of the Spanish coastline during their one and only battle."

Morgan frowned. "I still can't believe you supported that little French twerp."

"His arguments were pretty convincing at the time," Julia muttered without a trace of remorse.

Charlie's eyed rounded.

"Are they talking about Napoleon?" he asked Bailey.

"Yeah. They're like a walking history book," the wizard replied, indicating the angels and the demon with a vague wave. He studied Julia shrewdly. "By the way, did you and Bonaparte ever—you know?"

He waggled his eyebrows suggestively.

Adrianne grimaced. "Eww."

Julia rolled her eyes. "No. Unlike our esteemed leader over there, my brain is not located in my gonads. Besides, there's no way Bonaparte could have satisfied me."

Zach leaned back in his chair.

"Is that a challenge?" he asked Adrianne behind Julia's back. "I can't help but feel it's a challenge."

"Stop it," Adrianne berated him. "The last time you flirted with her, she buried you at the bottom of San Francisco Bay and we had to save your sorry ass."

Morgan's frown deepened. "Are you clowns quite finished?"

There were general mutters around the table. Cassius swallowed a smile. Despite their grumblings, he could tell Morgan and his crew were close.

"What about the other victims?" he asked Morgan, no longer bothering to hide his interest.

10

THE SUN WAS SINKING ON THE HORIZON WHEN CASSIUS parked his Vincent Black Shadow outside Joyce Almeda's cream-colored, Stick-style, three-story home. The house was located at the end of a cul-de-sac, with a metal fence separating it from the abandoned rail tracks that cut through the neighborhood.

Despite the area being one of the roughest in San Francisco, Cassius could tell the locals took pride in their properties from the pretty, painted clapboard exteriors and the neat front yards. He crossed the sidewalk and strolled past the brightly colored flowerbeds framing the path leading to Joyce's porch steps, his mind full of what Morgan and his team had revealed to him earlier that day.

There had been nine human sacrifices to date, including the man who had been discovered in the sewers last night. This meant whoever was behind the black-magic rituals in San Francisco was killing an average of one person a week. Considering the time required to gather the necessary ingredients for such high-powered sorcery and for the person performing it to recover their strength after the considerable energy they would have had to expend for the ceremony, that kind of made sense.

The victims had nothing in common as far as the Argonaut Agency had discovered to date. They were of both sexes, with ages varying from twenty to fifty-four, and came from different backgrounds and socio-economic classes. They had never been in contact with one another and all of them had been discovered in the same state as the man Cassius had stumbled upon in the sewers, their flesh covered in runes and their bodies torn asunder.

The only trait they shared was that they were all ordinary humans. With only a tenth of the world population able to access the magic that lived in their soul cores, that put them in the majority of the city's residents.

Cassius reached the porch and knocked on Joyce's front door, a thoughtful frown on his face.

It could also mean having a normal soul is an important element of the ritual.

Something wriggled inside his jacket. The demon cat poked its head out the top.

Joyce had wanted to say a final goodbye to the creature, hence their visit. She had sounded more sad than shocked when Cassius had told her about its true identity over the phone that afternoon. He suspected the old lady wouldn't have minded keeping the creature even if it meant making her ill.

"We won't stay long," Cassius told the demon cat. "And we should really come up with a name for you."

The demon cat blinked at him before staring at the front door.

Cassius was about to knock again when the creature stiffened, ears rotating forward in sudden alertness. They both heard the weak cry that came from inside the house.

Alarm shot through Cassius. "Joyce!" He banged on the glass panel, rattling it. "Joyce, are you alright?!"

A door creaked open to Cassius's right.

Joyce's neighbor, a woman in her sixties, came out onto her front porch, her expression hesitant. Her face cleared when she saw Cassius.

"Oh. You're that charming young man who visited Joyce yesterday." She paused, her rheumy eyes growing troubled. "Is everything okay?"

"I don't know." Cassius swallowed, knowing the words were a lie the moment he uttered them. Something was very wrong. He couldn't say why or how he sensed this, but he could feel it in his bones. A darkness that scratched at the very marrow of who he was. "She's not answering the—"

A crash sounded at the side of the property. Cassius bolted to the railing and peered down the narrow alley separating the house from the fence and the rail tracks.

A man jumped out of a second-story window and landed on the grass, fragments of glass crunching beneath his boots.

"Hey!" Cassius shouted. "You there! *Stop!*"

The man frowned at Cassius over his shoulder before taking off in the direction of the rear yard. Cassius's pulse spiked when he caught the whiff of black magic in the air.

It was the same scent he'd picked up in the sewers last night.

He retraced his steps, kicked down the front door, and barged inside the house, Joyce's neighbor's shocked shout following him. The demon cat leapt from his hold and rushed on ahead.

They found Joyce in the dining room. Blood pooling rapidly beneath the old lady's frail body where she lay on the floor, her chest shuddering with her rasping breaths. There was a deep depression in the middle of her breastbone.

"Joyce!"

Cassius dropped to his knees beside her and pressed down on her wound, his heart thundering with fear. The man who'd attacked Joyce had blasted her with a shot of black magic that had caved her flesh and bones, destroying most of the lung tissue beneath.

"Hang in there," Cassius said grimly, his gaze on Joyce's ashen face.

She clasped his arm with trembling fingers and nodded, her eyes opening briefly. A weak smile curved her lips. "You brought the cat."

The demon cat crouched down next to Joyce's head, its tail flicking agitatedly.

Cassius yanked his cell from the rear pocket of his jeans with a bloodied hand, dialed 911, and put it on speaker. He placed the phone on the ground and continued applying pressure to Joyce's wound, the ringtone echoing with a macabre timbre around the room while hot blood seeped between his fingers and stained his skin.

"Joyce?!" someone mumbled behind him.

Cassius looked over his shoulder. Joyce's neighbor had followed him inside the house.

"What's your name?" he asked in a gentle voice despite the urgency coursing through him.

"Ines," the woman whispered, her dark eyes locked unblinkingly on her bleeding neighbor.

"Ines, I need your help," Cassius said firmly.

The woman nodded and came over, tears streaming down her face. The operator came online just as she knelt shakily beside him.

"911, what's your emergency?"

"I am at the home of a woman called Joyce Almeda!" Cassius barked. "The address is 265 Libertine Street, in Mission District. She's in her fifties and has been attacked by a black-magic user. She has an injury to her chest and is bleeding out fast. I'm gonna put you on to Joyce's neighbor. Contact Morgan King at the Argonaut Agency and inform him of this call. Tell him Cassius Black wants him at this address ASAP!"

Cassius removed his jacket, folded it, and pressed it on Joyce's wound.

"Take over," he told Ines, placing her hands on top of the jacket. "Help is on the way." He frowned at the cat. "Stay with them."

The cat meowed.

Cassius rose and headed for the hallway, anger pulsing through him in thick waves. He paused on the threshold of the dining room and cast a final glance at Joyce before storming toward the back door.

He took to the sky the moment he cleared the rear porch, his gaze searching for Joyce's attacker in the falling twilight even as he sent out a wave of his energy to pick up any magic in the area.

He can't have gotten far!

A bitter scent teased his nostrils when he turned north. *There!*

Cassius tucked his wings and dove.

11

A FIGURE JUMPED DOWN FROM A FENCE COVERED IN climbing plants, landed on the hood of the car parked some thirty feet below, and headed for the road fronting the row of houses behind Joyce's home at a dead run.

Cassius caught up with the man on the edge of the park.

The sorcerer turned a fraction of a second before Cassius swooped down and brought him to the ground. They tumbled along an embankment in a tangle of limbs and wings, Cassius hanging on grimly to Joyce's assailant.

A grunt left the sorcerer as they smashed into the low concrete wall surrounding a playground. He whipped a knife out from under his sleeve and stabbed at Cassius.

Heat flared on Cassius's left arm. He swore.

The sorcerer's weapon was made of Stark Steel.

The man scrambled to his feet and murmured an incantation, his dark eyes gleaming with evil in the growing dusk. The air grew heavy with magic.

Cassius rose, unsheathed his dagger, and brought out

the sword within. His gun would be of no use in this situation.

"What did you want with Joyce?"

The sorcerer's gaze flicked nervously to the blade. Darkness pooled around his hands as the spell took shape. A savage snarl left his lips as he hurled a sphere of destructive magic at Cassius.

Cassius batted the attack away with his sword.

The black ball crashed into the playground and exploded with a force that shook the branches of the nearby trees and rattled the windows of the closest houses. A ten-foot-wide crater appeared in its wake, melted lumps of rock and rubber mulch tumbling down into the depression.

Cassius narrowed his eyes. "That's not nice."

He closed the distance to his attacker in the blink of eye and smashed shoulder-first into his chest. The sorcerer grunted and sailed backward over the wall.

Cassius grabbed his leg before he landed, climbed fifty feet into the air, and released the screaming man above a bridge spanning the playground. A burst of dark magic cushioned the man's fall at the last second.

"Now, tell me why the hell you tried to kill Joyce Almeda!" Cassius roared as he dropped toward his attacker.

The sorcerer cursed and twisted sharply out of the way of his descending blade.

The sword vibrated in Cassius's hands as it sliced the ground inches from the man's head. He tugged the weapon free and turned to face the sorcerer. The magic user had leapt to his feet and was already firing off another incantation, his voice low and urgent.

Cassius scowled. "Your attacks won't work against me.

Now, why don't you tell me—?" He stopped, his skin prickling at the intense, dark energy he sensed gathering around them. "What the hell are you doing?!"

The sorcerer laughed at Cassius's low growl. Darkness pooled in the air next to him. He reached inside the wavering wall and extracted an ebony cane with red veins embedded in the wood.

Cassius's eyes widened.

It was a summoning staff, a magical weapon banned by all agencies. Just having one in your possession meant an automatic death sentence.

Cassius clenched his jaw. All known summoning staffs in existence today were currently held in a secure vault deep under the headquarters of Cabalista, in London.

"How the hell did you get your hands on that?!"

"That's for me to know and for you to die without ever finding out!" the sorcerer hissed.

He cut his finger on a sharp edge on the staff, smeared his blood on the wood, and slammed it onto the ground at his feet.

"*I call thee, my dark brethren*," he shouted, his eyes full of madness. "*Come forth and lay my enemy to waste!*"

Cassius leapt out of the way of the expanding circle of blackness that exploded where the staff touched the ground.

Shit!

The pool thickened, the darkness sloshing around and spilling over onto the bridge. Violent ripples tore across the surface, as if something were moving beneath it. Cassius knew all too well what would come out of it in a moment. He shot up into the air and drew on his seraphic powers, his fingers tightening on the handle of his blade.

Macabre figures emerged from the living darkness

beneath him. The creatures were some eight feet tall and gaunt, with narrow, bat-like faces, forked tongues, and claws as long as their hands and feet. Leathery, spiked wings sprouted from their deformed backs, the membranes so thin they were almost see-through.

Cassius gritted his teeth. Though the monsters looked like they would fall over at the mere suggestion of a breeze, he knew better. These were war demons from the Nine Hells.

Goddammit!

The summoning staffs created by the warlocks who made pacts with the Underworld in the century following the Fall were made out of Bloodsand, a black tree with red veins that only grew in the Hells. When the governments of the world finally realized the destructive powers the weapons could unleash on their own citizens, they had them confiscated and banned their use. Cabalista was put in charge of sealing the demonic artifacts; once created, a summoning staff could not be destroyed by any power on Earth.

Dozens of crimson eyes locked on Cassius where he hovered above the playground. These demons were vastly different from the ones who had tumbled to the Earth with the angels five hundred years ago. They were the remnants of an old war between Heaven and Hell, soldiers created solely for battle, dark beings without soul cores who thirsted for one thing and one thing only. To kill everyone in their path. Once the forces of Hell had realized what they'd inadvertently created, they'd banished the monsters to the deepest parts of their dimensions.

The air trembled as the war demons rose, their wings swinging with powerful thumps that washed across Cassius in waves. The monsters faltered and screeched as white light poured out of Cassius's eyes and flared across his skin. Having lived in the shadows of the Hells, light was poison to them.

Cassius took advantage of their hesitation and bolted straight into their midst, his blade humming as he slashed and stabbed at them with lightning-fast moves. The best way to dispose of war demons was to take them by surprise.

The monsters retaliated swiftly. Claws sliced into him from every direction and fangs snapped uncomfortably close to his flesh. His wounds closed almost as fast as they formed, his seraphic energy hastening his healing abilities.

Movement below caught his gaze.

The sorcerer was using the battle to make his escape, his figure fading in the gloom as he sprinted north across the park.

Cassius scowled. *That asshole!*

He blocked the claws headed for his face, kicked a war demon in the gut, and sliced the two coming at him from the left in half. Since war demons didn't possess soul cores, he didn't experience the pain he would normally have suffered had they been ordinary otherworldly beings.

The pool of blackness was shrinking rapidly on the ground, the portal closing in the absence of the weapon that had opened it.

Where the hell is Morgan?!

Cassius glanced from the remaining six war demons blocking his path to the fleeing man.

Damnit! I can't let that bastard get away. I have to end this fight myself!

He hesitated for scant seconds. It was dark enough that any witnesses would struggle to make out what he intended to do next. The sound of approaching sirens took the decision right out of his hands.

It was now or never.

Cassius let the war demons surround him, took a deep breath, and called upon his true powers.

12

MORGAN WAS OUT OF THE SUV BEFORE ADRIANNE pulled to a stop at the curb. An ambulance was parked sideways in front of a vintage, black and silver cafe racer motorbike opposite the cream-colored house Cassius had called emergency services from. The front door of the property was wide open.

People huddled on the porches of the nearby homes, their faces full of worry. Most of them were elderly. Sirens rose in the distance as patrol cars converged on the neighborhood.

Morgan and his team had been re-examining the scene of the latest human sacrifice at Bayview Park when they'd received the dispatch about a black-magic attack in Mission District. Fear had twisted Morgan's stomach when he'd heard the identity of the caller who'd phoned for an ambulance.

He stiffened when he picked up the acrid taint of magic lingering in the air. It was coming from the house and somewhere beyond it. Adrianne and Zach followed him as he strode briskly toward the property.

Julia climbed out of the second SUV with Bailey and Charlie.

"There's a disturbance at a park north of here!" she shouted. "That's where most of the cops are going."

"You guys head over there. And watch your six." Morgan clenched his jaw. "This smells like the same black magic we've been investigating. Whoever this sorcerer is, we need him alive."

The EMTs were tending to an elderly woman in the dining room when Morgan and the others entered the house. One glance at her injuries and Morgan knew she would not survive the next hour.

Another woman sat holding the victim's hand, her face full of grief while she mumbled reassuring words to her. Morgan was somehow not surprised to see Cassius's cat sitting by the head of the injured woman. The demon spirit looked at him before staring at the ashen-faced figure on the floor, its agitation plain to see.

"That's Joyce Almeda, the client Cassius was working for," Adrianne said grimly.

Zach headed over to the EMTs. "Let me help."

Though the demon couldn't stop the woman from dying, his powers as an Aqueous meant he could at least stem the flow of blood pouring out of her wound.

The technicians hesitated before nodding. Morgan and the others' badges identified them as Argonaut agents. As such, they had authority over all cases involving magic in the city.

"The guy who called for help," Morgan indicated the bloodied cell phone on the floor, "where did he go?!"

"He went out back," the woman holding Joyce Almeda's hand said in a quavering voice before the EMTs could open their mouths. "He was chasing the person who did this to Joyce. Please, help him!"

Morgan's gut twisted with a fresh wave of dread.

"Stay with Zach, in case there are any more of these bastards around!" he told Adrianne.

Morgan turned and made for the rear yard of the property without waiting for a reply from his second-in-command. A warm breeze ruffled his hair as he spread his wings and rose into the balmy night. He followed the scent of magic toward a large, open space less than a quarter of a mile to the north.

Flashing lights punctured the darkness as patrol cars screeched to a stop around the park. Morgan cut across a road. He had just entered the south perimeter when dazzling light flared in the gloom ahead. His heart stuttered.

The brightness broke through a giant, writhing ball of blackness hovering in mid-air, the slivers of intense brilliance seeping through the cracks in the sphere emanating a strong electric scent. Alarm prickled Morgan's skin when he recognized the grotesque shapes making up the living globe.

Shit! War demons!

He unsheathed the dagger strapped to his thigh and released the Stark Steel blade within. A figure rose from the ground and headed for the ghastly manifestation, gray wings beating the air with strong thumps as it ascended. It was Julia.

The angel had also unleashed her sword, the scent emanating from her full of the same blood lust coursing through Morgan.

Though the Fallen had lost the memories of their

pasts, the history of their kind had remained embedded in their very consciousness.

War demons were their enemies of old.

They converged rapidly on the creatures. A massive wave of power blasted into them when they were twenty feet from the globe.

What the—?!

The world went supernova a heartbeat later.

Morgan braced his wings as he was swept violently backward. He raised a hand to his eyes, the blinding force washing over him so fierce it raised goosebumps on his flesh. He squinted through his fingers and caught a glimpse of Julia where she'd been similarly cast aside by the explosive energy. The angel looked as startled as Morgan felt.

Few powers on Earth could physically move one of their kind against their will.

Morgan's breath caught in his throat.

The war demons were disintegrating, their monstrous bodies crumbling to fiery cinders where they floated in the sky.

Resonance exploded inside Morgan's soul when he finally saw the being in their midst. Cassius's eyes shone with divine wrath as he glared at the remains of the enemy who had attacked him. His body was cocooned in a maelstrom of sheer, crackling radiance that pulsed with immense power.

But it wasn't the fact that he had just demonstrated the true extent of his abilities that shocked Morgan. It was the snow-white wings sprouting from his back and the sword wreathed in Heaven's Light in his hand that captured Morgan's stunned gaze.

Cassius's feathers slowly returned to their black and

crimson colors as the last of the war demons fell to the ground in a shower of dark ash. He turned and swooped north, his face radiating anger and determination, oblivious to Morgan and Julia's presence in his rage.

Startled cries rose in the darkness. Someone shouted a warning.

The cops fired on the angel.

Morgan reacted instinctively.

Wind roared as he shot across the park, his powers enclosing Cassius in a violent storm that deflected most of the bullets. The next volley of shots bounced off the whirling gale surrounding the dark-winged angel.

Julia's voice boomed in the night. "*Stop!*"

She glared at the cops where she hovered in mid-air, her face aglow with the luminescence that characterized her kind.

The officers kept firing, panic clouding their minds.

Julia cursed and cast out a wave of seraphic energy. The cops yelled in alarm as their weapons crumpled in their hands, the earthborn metals reacting to the angel's Terrene powers.

A disturbance at the north end of the park drew Morgan's tense gaze.

Bailey and Charlie had tackled a man to the ground near a tennis court. The orb of defensive magic the wizard wielded made the air shimmer violently as he countered the fallen sorcerer's black-magic globe. Charlie chanted an incantation, a focused frown on his face where he stood behind Bailey's shield. The sorcerer went limp a moment later, his mind befuddled by the enchanter's dark spell. Though akin to black magic, dark enchantments were allowed to be used exclusively by magic users working for one of the supernatural agencies.

Morgan headed for Cassius. The angel's features grew clearer as the tempest enclosing him faded. He was wearing a grim expression.

"What the hell took you so long?!" he snapped at Morgan.

Relief flooded Morgan, so intense he almost sagged where he hovered above the park. He clamped down on the storm of emotions swirling inside him from all he had just witnessed.

"Are you okay?!"

Surprise flashed in Cassius's eyes.

"Yeah," he muttered, his tone a fraction less cool.

Morgan drew closer to the dark-winged angel. "You're not hurt?"

He moved around Cassius and scanned his body for injuries.

Cassius raised an eyebrow. "Those bullets barely made an impression."

"I meant the war demons."

"Oh. My wounds have already healed."

Morgan studied him for a moment before blowing out a sigh. "You're a trouble magnet, you know that?"

Irritation wrinkled Cassius's brow. "Yeah, well, it takes one to know one." His scowl faded as he looked past Morgan to the south. Concern replaced the ire darkening his eyes. "Joyce."

He turned and flew toward the cream-colored house.

13

ADRIANNE STARED AT THE CRATER IN THE MIDDLE OF the playground. "What the hell happened?"

Julia and Morgan exchanged tense glances.

"We should avoid talking about this here," Julia said guardedly.

Adrianne frowned. The place was packed with cops and Argonaut agents. Already, a slew of reporters hovered on the periphery of the park, their cameras trained on the playground.

"Like bloodhounds scenting a kill," Zach said darkly.

Bailey came over from where a team of Argonaut officers were lifting the unconscious and heavily shackled black-magic sorcerer into the back of an armored vehicle.

"He took some kind of pill before we got to him. Looks like he's gonna be out of it for a while."

"Have Lucy tend to him," Morgan told the wizard curtly as he crouched on the lip of the depression.

Bailey dipped his chin. "Already on it. Charlie and I will stay with him until we get to the agency, just in case he wakes up and tries anything funny. I'll let you know what Lucy makes of the drug he took."

Lucy Walters was a Level Two medical mage working for the Argonaut Agency. If anyone could identify the poison the sorcerer had ingested and heal the bastard, she would.

Morgan clenched his jaw. The fact that the man had been willing to die rather than fall into the hands of the Argonaut Agency spoke volumes about their enemy's intentions.

"That guy really used a summoning staff?" Adrianne asked Julia skeptically after Bailey and Charlie had left.

"Yes." Julia frowned. "He conjured war demons from the Nine Hells to attack Black. The staff wasn't on him when we arrested him. He probably accessed it through some kind of portal."

"It's a miracle Cassius got rid of those creatures so quickly," Zach said uneasily. "It should have taken at least five angels or demons to dispose of that large a number of those monsters."

"I can see why Strickland holds him in such high regard." Julia looked in the direction where Cassius had disappeared, her frown deepening. "Where is Black, by the way? Is still at Joyce Almeda's house?"

"He went home," Morgan said.

The others stared.

"He's a key witness to a crime, Morgan!" Adrianne protested. "Like, the second one in twenty-four hours!"

"He's not going anywhere, Adrianne." Morgan rubbed the scorched earth between his fingers. He could smell Hell's acrid odor all over it. "And he fully intends to cooperate with us."

Adrianne's eyes widened at that. "Wait. You mean he agreed to take on the case?!"

Morgan rose, a muscle jumping in his jawline. "Although I wish it were under different circumstances, yes. Cassius will work with us until we get to the bottom of who's behind these human sacrifices and Joyce Almeda's murder."

Cassius's face rose before Morgan's eyes.

By the time they'd made it back to the house, Joyce Almeda had already taken her last breath. Cassius's haunted expression when he'd seen her had made Morgan's chest tighten with pain and fury. In that moment, he'd wanted nothing more than to take the angel in his arms and share in his sorrow.

He knew Cassius would have lashed out at him had he followed his instinct. The agony and rage trembling off the dark-winged angel had made the air shiver where he'd stood in the dining room, above the still warm body of the old woman. Cassius had murmured a few words to her neighbor before storming out of the house, the demon cat on his heels.

Morgan had found them mounting the black and silver motorbike parked outside.

"We need to talk about what happened here tonight," he'd told Cassius in a hard voice.

Cassius's stormy gaze had swept over him like a scourge. For a moment, Morgan had thought the angel would lose his temper.

Cassius had taken a long, shuddering breath before nodding curtly. "I'll be at my place."

Morgan had sighed. "I meant we need your statement."

"Then I'll come to the agency first thing tomorrow,"

Cassius had grated out between clenched teeth. "I want to look at your case notes anyway."

Hope had flared inside Morgan at the angel's words. He'd masked it behind a neutral expression.

"Does that mean you're gonna take Strickland up on his offer?"

"Yes," Cassius had said bitingly. "After everything that happened tonight, I want to find these bastards as much as you guys do."

Morgan had hesitated before laying a hand on Cassius's shoulder. "You know Joyce's death wasn't your fault, right? That sorcerer was here before you arrived at the property. He didn't follow you, Cassius."

Cassius had gone rigid at his words. The demon cat had meowed anxiously where it sat between Cassius's thighs, its yellow gaze swinging warily between the two angels.

"I couldn't protect her."

Surprise had flashed through Morgan at Cassius's bitter words. His stomach had clenched all over again at the tortured light that flared in Cassius's pupils.

"She died because I couldn't protect her."

Morgan had frowned at that. "You and I both know that's a pile of bull—"

The rest of Morgan's words had been drowned out by the roar of Cassius's Vincent Black Shadow. Morgan had stepped back and watched wordlessly as the angel vanished in the night, the red taillights of his motorbike winking out when he took a corner and exited the cul-de-sac.

"I wonder if there's a link between Cassius and what's happening in the city," Adrianne muttered, bringing Morgan back to the present. She sighed at Morgan's scowl. "I'm not saying I suspect him of being behind the murders. I'm just stating facts. We need to find out why this sorcerer went after Joyce Almeda."

"Well, the only thing that connects Joyce to Cassius is the cat," Zach said as they headed up the slope. He shrugged at their expressions. "Hey, I'm just stating facts too."

Morgan pondered the demon's words as they reached the tree line. He hadn't sensed anything out of the ordinary from the cat bar the fact that it was a demonic spirit.

Forensic vans from Argonaut were pulling up to the curb when they exited the park. Adrianne stopped and spoke to the lead technician.

"Focus on that crater and the bridge over the playground," she told the witch. "And be careful. The ground is tainted with black magic."

Maggie Briggs nodded. "Gotcha." She started to turn away and paused. "By the way, are we still on for girls' night out this Friday?"

Adrianne glanced guiltily at Julia. "Hmm, yeah."

Julia narrowed her eyes at the sorceress as they left the techs behind and headed across the road. "How come I'm not invited to girls' night out?"

Adrianne sighed. "You know very well why. None of us has a chance of scoring when you're around."

"Bailey's heart would shatter into a million pieces if he could hear you right now," Zach said drily.

"Yeah, well, Bailey had his chance and he blew it," Adrianne grumbled.

Adrianne and Bailey's on-off relationship was the stuff of legend at the agency. The sorceress and the wizard had known each other since they were at the magic academy and had advanced through the ranks of the Argonaut

Agency together. It had seemed inevitable that they would end up together.

Whatever Bailey had done to anger the sorceress and end their relationship, she had never made it public.

Julia opened her mouth to protest.

Adrianne interrupted her. "Look, I know it's not your fault the guys flock to you." She paused and chewed her lip thoughtfully. "Tell you what, you can come as long as you promise to wear some kind of hideous outfit."

"I don't own any hideous outfits," Julia said.

Adrianne scowled at the angel. "I'll buy you one."

❧ 14 ❧

Cassius stared into the bottom of his third glass of whiskey.

He didn't feel in the least bit inebriated. He knew the reason for this was the traces of core power that still remained in his veins.

"Shit," he mumbled, raking a hand through his hair. "I really want to get drunk right now."

Joyce Almeda's pale, lifeless face swam before him for what felt like the hundredth time that evening. Cassius closed his eyes and dropped his head back on the couch, remorse twisting his belly all over again. He knew Morgan was right. It wasn't his fault the old lady had been targeted by that sorcerer. Still, he couldn't suppress his guilt at having failed to save her.

If only I'd gotten there a couple of minutes earlier.

Cassius clenched his jaw, frustration gnawing at his insides. The demon cat meowed next to him. He opened his eyes and studied the creature with a faint frown.

"I really need to give you a name."

The cat yawned and propped its head on its paws, its yellow gaze locked attentively on him.

"How about Beelzebub?" Cassius suggested.

The cat's tail flicked agitatedly, showing its discontent.

"Little Satan?"

Something that resembled a sigh whooshed out of the cat.

"Lucifer?"

The cat glared at Cassius.

"Okay, not Lucifer." Cassius pursed his lips. "How about Loki, then?"

The cat raised its head, its tail swinging with interest.

"You like Loki?"

Cassius reached over and scratched the creature under the chin. The demon cat's eyes shrank to slits of pleasure. It licked his fingers, a deep rumble echoing from its chest.

"You look like a Loki," Cassius murmured. "All trouble and mischief."

"Just like its owner," someone drawled behind him.

Cassius looked over his shoulder. Morgan was standing in the doorway of his apartment.

Cassius narrowed his eyes. "I really wish you'd stop treating my place like an open house."

A smile curved Morgan's lips. "I brought Chinese." He lifted the carrier bag in his hand in a conciliatory gesture. "Permission to enter?"

Cassius's stomach grumbled. He flushed. "Permission granted."

Morgan's smile widened at his grudging tone. The smell of takeout filled the apartment when he came inside. He put the bag on the coffee table, went over to Cassius's kitchen, and rummaged around in the refrigerator. By the time he returned to the couch with two cans of beer,

Cassius was already nose-deep in a carton of sweet and sour beef.

"What?" he said defensively in the face of Morgan's amused expression, chopsticks held aloft.

"You've got sauce on your chin."

Morgan reached over and wiped Cassius's skin with his thumb.

Cassius stiffened.

The air sizzled between them.

Morgan's pupils dilated. His gaze moved to Cassius's mouth.

Cassius's breath caught at the expression in Morgan's eyes. It was clear the Aerial was hungry for more than just food. Morgan hesitated before lowering his hand from Cassius's chin, his face guarded and his movements carefully controlled.

Cassius swallowed as he watched Morgan remove a couple of food cartons and place them on the table. The sexual tension filling the air gradually faded. Cassius dug into his meal again, troubled by how edgy he felt in Morgan's presence.

It was as if a live wire connected them, amplifying their reactions and desire for one another. Morgan had made it clear he wanted him. And Cassius couldn't deny that he craved what the Aerial's gaze and touch promised.

A surprisingly comfortable silence fell between them as they ate the food and drank the beers, Loki earning several morsels of Cassius's beef and Morgan's Kung Pao chicken. Morgan got rid of the trash after they finished and made coffee, the angel moving around Cassius's penthouse as if he lived there.

Cassius let him be, too pleasantly drowsy from the

food and booze to put up much of a resistance. The whiskey and beers were finally kicking in.

"Does Strickland know?" Morgan asked lightly as he brought over their drinks.

"Does Strickland know what?"

Cassius accepted the coffee gratefully and nearly groaned when he took a sip. Morgan had made it just the way he liked it.

"That you're an Empyreal?"

Morgan's quiet words echoed loudly in the hush that fell across the apartment. Loki got up and sauntered in the direction of the bedroom.

Cassius carefully put his cup down on the table, his pulse accelerating. "Yes, he does."

He met Morgan's gaze steadily. He'd known this conversation was coming ever since Morgan had witnessed his fight with the war demons. He'd hoped to avoid it for as long as he could, but it seemed Morgan wasn't going to be as patient as he'd hoped he would be. Cassius was just glad they were having this discussion in the privacy of his apartment rather than an interrogation room at the Argonaut Agency.

Morgan observed Cassius with an inscrutable expression. "Is that how you defeated Tania Lancaster?"

Cassius hesitated before nodding, not sure what he was reading in Morgan's eyes.

Most people who found out he was an Empyreal and witnessed his powers usually had the fear of God carved into them from the experience. That had been the case for nearly all the angels, demons, and magic users who had been present at Tania Lancaster's death, bar Victor Sloan, Francis Strickland, and a few others.

It was one of the reasons why everyone who'd survived

that battle had been sworn to secrecy on pain of death. It was also why certain factions in the four agencies had engaged in a deliberate campaign to smear Cassius's reputation in the decades following the incident that brought down Tania and her sect in London.

Not all angels and demons who had fallen to Earth five hundred years ago had special abilities like Morgan and his crew. Of those who did, Aerials were among the most powerful class. Only one rank stood above an Aerial and that was a Fiery, an angel or demon capable of wielding Heaven or Hell's Fire.

Victor Sloan was the only Fiery who had fallen to Earth. Though no one retained memories of their past life, his skills on the battlefield had long marked him as someone who had once commanded armies. As such, Victor was deemed to be the most powerful Fallen on the planet today.

But there was one echelon higher still. One that stood far above the Fieries and the Aerials. One that few humans knew of, but that all angels and demons had engraved in the very depths of their subconscious.

An Empyreal. An angel who could wield Heaven's Light or a demon who could manipulate Hell's Darkness and Chaos, the most formidable of all divine and accursed abilities. An entity whose powers were nearly equal to those of a God. No Empyreal demons had fallen to Earth. And, as far as the world knew, neither had an Empyreal angel.

"Does it scare you?"

Morgan blinked at Cassius's question. "What?"

"Does it scare you?" Cassius lifted his chin challengingly. "The fact that I'm an Empyreal?"

Morgan was silent for a moment. "No." He frowned. "I was just thinking about something."

"What were you thinking about?" Cassius said curiously.

"I was thinking that you're a goddamn saint."

It was Cassius's turn to stare in surprise. "What?"

Morgan frowned. "It's clear the four agencies have deliberately slandered you so that the world holds you in contempt. After all, what better way is there to crush a powerful enemy than to make them loathed by an entire planet?"

Cassius scratched his cheek, embarrassed. "I'm not a saint."

Morgan rose and paced the floor, as if he hadn't heard Cassius.

"And the fucking gall of the bastards. After all that bullshit about you being some kind of dangerous criminal who should be avoided at all costs, the first one they run to when they can't solve their goddamn problems is you!" He whirled around and glared at Cassius. "You should have told them to shove it where the sun doesn't shine!"

Cassius couldn't help but laugh then.

Morgan paused and flushed. He ran a hand through his hair, clearly mortified by his outburst.

Cassius fought the urge to go over and kiss him. He arched an eyebrow instead. "So, are you saying I should tell Strickland to shove it?"

Morgan narrowed his eyes at Cassius's teasing tone. "No way are you getting out of the promise you made to me."

"I don't recall making any promises to you," Cassius drawled, now more than a little amused.

He hadn't realized taunting Morgan could be so much fun.

"You're really enjoying this, aren't you?" the Aerial said stiffly.

Cassius grinned. "I am."

Morgan's gaze dropped to Cassius's mouth.

The mood changed in a flash. Cassius's breath stuttered as the air in the apartment oozed with sexual tension once more.

"We should go to bed," he mumbled. "We have an early start tomorrow."

Morgan took a step toward Cassius, his eyes darkening. "Is that an invitation?"

Cassius swallowed as Morgan closed the distance between them. "No."

Morgan leaned down, one hand on the backrest of the couch. "Are you sure?"

Cassius did his best to stay still. Morgan stopped inches from his mouth.

"Pretty damn sure."

His pulse thundered wildly as Morgan's heat and the heady scent of his arousal wrapped sultrily around him. It was taking everything Cassius had to keep his hands to himself.

Morgan smiled. "Liar."

His breath tickled Cassius's lips.

Shit.

Cassius's mouth parted in hungry anticipation. He edged forward, lust tightening his belly.

"You're right." Morgan straightened. "We should call it a night."

What the—?!

Cassius scowled as the Aerial whistled a low tune and headed for the front door.

Morgan looked over his shoulder and chuckled at Cassius's outraged expression. "I would do something about that erection if I were you."

Cassius flushed, conscious of his raging crotch.

"You're such an asshole!" he snarled at the laughing angel's departing back.

15

Cassius fluffed his pillow for the tenth time, buried his head in it, and closed his eyes. A frustrated sigh left him a moment later.

He couldn't sleep.

Morgan's face rose before his mind's eye. Cassius scowled.

Next time that bastard wants to kiss me, I'll make him grovel on his hands and knees!

It dawned on Cassius that he was being somewhat presumptuous about Morgan's interest in him. There was a good chance Morgan might not want to ruin their future working relationship by entering into a physical one, despite the clear attraction between them. Office romances rarely worked out for the best, especially where it concerned angels and demons. Being a quasi-immortal meant grudges and bad feelings stuck around for centuries rather than years.

Cassius's stomach tightened as he thought back to Morgan's kiss the day before. Despite his frustration at the Aerial, he could not deny that he most definitely wanted a repeat. Even if it were just to confirm that the kiss had been as wickedly good as he recalled.

He'd finally fallen into a light doze when he felt the mattress dip slightly next to him. Cassius blinked fuzzily at the dark room, his pupils adjusting to the lack of light.

"Loki?"

An irritated sound left the cat from its spot near Cassius's feet.

Cassius stared. The one climbing into his bed was Morgan.

I must be dreaming.

Morgan noticed his shocked look.

"I can't sleep," he said by way of explanation.

Cassius gaped. *Why, the nerve of this asshole!*

He scowled, sat up, and switched the night lamp on. "What the hell does that have to do with you climbing into my bed in the middle of the night?!"

Morgan arched an eyebrow, unfazed by his outburst. "You're the one who banned me from having sex every night, remember? The least you can do is be my bed partner."

Cassius opened and closed his mouth, too speechless to speak for a moment.

He told his interested dick to calm the fuck down and glared at the Aerial. "Are you insane?!"

Loki hissed and jumped down from the bed. The demon cat slipped through a gap in the bedroom door and vanished into the darkness, displeasure reflected in every line of its body.

"Don't worry, I'm not planning to have my wicked way with you," Morgan drawled. "I just like having someone to hold."

"Then get a goddamn pillow buddy!" Cassius snapped.

He gasped as Morgan looped a strong arm around his waist and pulled him down on the bed. The Aerial turned off the light and tucked Cassius against him, his chest flush against Cassius's back and a powerful leg slipping between Cassius's knees.

"Goodnight," Morgan murmured.

Cassius's heart slammed heavily against his ribs. "Like I'm gonna be able to sleep with you plastered up against me!"

"You're grumpy when you're tired."

"Shut up!"

Morgan chuckled softly.

Cassius cursed under his breath, acutely conscious of every delicious inch of Morgan's hard body where it touched his. Luckily, the Aerial was wearing a T-shirt and sweatpants. Cassius chewed his lip, not sure whether it was disappointment or chagrin he was currently experiencing. He hesitated before wriggling slightly. He sucked in air when he felt the thick shape of Morgan's dick against his butt.

Morgan groaned, his breath tickling Cassius's nape. He squeezed Cassius lightly, his arm hot against his midriff. "Please tell me you're not doing that deliberately. I'm already finding it hard enough as it is not to rip your clothes off and ravish you right now."

Cassius's vision filled with a rush of torrid images. He registered the blatant sexual frustration in Morgan's voice with an inane jolt of elation.

"I am not!" he protested weakly.

"You really are a bad liar," Morgan said drowsily.

The way Morgan relaxed against him a moment later told Cassius the Aerial had drifted off. He ignored the foolish feeling of happiness still dancing through him and closed his eyes, Morgan's alluring scent wrapping him in a warm cocoon that soon lulled him to sleep.

LIGHT DANCED WARMLY ACROSS MORGAN'S EYELIDS AS he surfaced from a heavy slumber. He stirred, feeling more rested than he'd felt in years. Something weighed him down as he shifted against soft, cotton sheets. Morgan froze and carefully opened his eyes.

Cassius was lying with his head tucked against Morgan's heart and an arm and leg thrown carelessly across Morgan's body. The angel's slow breaths skittered across Morgan's T-shirt and arm, soft and warm. His long eyelashes were motionless where they rested against his cheeks and his beautiful face looked boyishly young in sleep.

Surprise jolted Morgan as he glanced at the daylight streaming into Cassius's bedroom through the glass wall overlooking the terrace. Seagulls whirled in the clear blue sky beyond, white wings almost blinding under the sun.

He could tell it was past seven o'clock. Morgan frowned.

He couldn't recall ever dozing off as quickly and as deeply as he'd done last night. He normally struggled for hours when he was on his own and usually needed the physical demand of sex to tire himself out enough to surrender to sleep. He stared at Cassius.

Then again, maybe I shouldn't be so surprised.

Something stirred inside Morgan as he beheld the angel's sleeping form. Something that had been gnawing at him since the day before.

An image of Cassius in his Empyreal form danced

before Morgan's eyes. With it came an all too familiar flood of emotions. The same emotions that had filled him to the brim yesterday at the park. The wretched feelings that woke him almost every night since he'd fallen to Earth, a silent scream on his lips and his heart thundering in his chest.

Fear. Pain. Rage. Longing.

Although no one who'd plummeted to Earth five hundred years ago retained any memories of their identities and past lives, Morgan's fragmented dreams had been with him since the first year of the Fall. And in all the centuries that he had been plagued by nightmares he couldn't make sense of, only one thing remained true. And that was the response they always engendered.

Unease swirled through Morgan as he gazed at Cassius.

He could not deny the connection that existed between them. Just as he knew it wasn't only physical attraction that made him yearn to touch the man in his arms.

There was a resonance between them. A twisted bond that linked their soul cores. Which suggested that they had known each other before the Fall. Had possibly known each other for a long, long time.

Yet, despite the unsettling feeling knotting his stomach, Morgan couldn't help but feel that the thing that connected him to the Empyreal was something sacred. Something divine. Something as beautiful as the being who'd haunted his dreams for as long as he could remember. The creature who made him feel things he'd never felt before. The fair angel with the shimmering, white wings and armor covered in blood and ash. The one with the blade bathed in light who'd plunged through the tear in the Nether alongside him five hundred years ago, their bodies broken and their consciousness fading as they drifted through clouds tainted with smoke and screams.

The one who bore a startling resemblance to Cassius in his Empyreal form.

Is he who I've been searching for all these years?

The question burned through Morgan as he listened to Cassius's steady breathing. He was pondering whether Cassius would prove to be the key to unlocking the mystery behind his nightmares when the angel stirred.

❧ 16 ❧

A POWERFUL DRUMMING ECHOED IN CASSIUS'S EARS AS consciousness returned. He made a soft sound and snuggled deeper into the bed, seeking more of the hypnotic beat that had soothed his soul while he slept.

Except his bed was harder than he recalled it ever being. And it was moving rhythmically, in sync with his own breathing.

Cassius blinked his eyes open.

"Good morning," Morgan drawled where he lay beneath him.

Cassius stared. The memories of last night came flooding back.

Heat burned his cheeks when he realized he was draped wantonly across the Aerial. He scuttled backward and stiffened as a powerful arm looped around his waist, locking him in place.

"Where are you going?" Morgan said lazily.

Cassius's mind tried to frame a sharp retort.

Unfortunately, his body was preoccupied by all that it could sense. The addictive scent of the angel holding him in his arms. The solid frame that was all muscle and sinew plastered against every inch of him. The thick cock digging into his belly. Lust stormed Cassius, quickening his pulse.

Morgan smiled, seemingly oblivious to the filthy thoughts raging through Cassius. "Thank you."

Cassius did his best to focus on their conversation. "For what?"

"For a good night's sleep." Morgan stretched an arm above his head before tucking it behind his neck, a sigh tumbling from his lips. "This is the first time in ages I've sleep so well without...you know." He shrugged. "Sex."

Cassius swallowed as he observed the Aerial's beautifully toned muscles bunch up and relax. "Great. Now, how about you let me go and get the hell out of my apartment?"

Morgan raised an eyebrow at his stilted tone. "Shouldn't we do something about that first?"

"What do you mean?" Cassius mumbled.

He gasped as Morgan flipped him onto his back. Cassius blinked dazedly, shocked at how easily the Aerial had trapped him beneath his body and at how familiar it felt.

It was almost as if they'd played this game many a time before. That they'd laid in each other's arms, just like this, on countless occasions. That they'd shared a bed for thousands of nights, in another time and life.

That insane notion was still sinking into Cassius's bewildered mind when Morgan rose on all fours above him. The Aerial's eyes shifted to a deep aquamarine as he looked down Cassius's body.

"I meant we should do something about your erection." A sinful smile stretched Morgan's mouth as he stared at the unmistakable tenting in Cassius's pajama bottoms. "It looks...painful."

Cassius silently cursed his treacherous body. His thoughts scattered to the winds when Morgan trailed a lazy knuckle up and down his aching length. He bit his lip, his belly contracting with pleasure.

God, that feels good!

Morgan's smile widened to a sexy smirk.

Cassius fought the urge to yank him close and kiss him hard.

"How about we help each other?" Morgan murmured.

Cassius shivered as Morgan slipped a hand inside his pajamas, too far gone to resist. His breath locked in his throat at the first touch of Morgan's fingers on his naked cock. He punched his hips instinctively and bit back a groan when the motion caused his shaft to rub enticingly against Morgan's hot palm.

Morgan pushed Cassius's pajamas down his hips and freed his erection. He started rubbing Cassius's stiff length briskly, his touch masterful and his fingers applying just the right amount of pressure to make Cassius's toes curl. He nudged Cassius's chin up with his nose and pressed his mouth against his throat, his heavy pants telling Cassius he was just as turned on as he was.

Morgan kissed and licked and sucked his way up and down Cassius's quivering flesh before biting down on the pulse at the base of his neck with enough force to make Cassius shudder but not enough to break the skin, his hand tightening punishingly on Cassius's dick at the same time.

The dual pleasure-pain had Cassius writhing on the bed. "Shit! That's—!"

Morgan's gaze blazed as he lifted his head and stared

into Cassius's eyes, his fingers busy on Cassius's cock, his palm growing slick with Cassius's precum.

"Touch me," he ordered gruffly.

Cassius's heart raced as he gazed at Morgan's flushed face and dilated pupils. He danced his hands down Morgan's torso and rock-hard abs, liking the way Morgan twitched and tensed at his touch. Morgan cursed as Cassius slipped his fingers inside his sweatpants, his chest shuddering with his breaths.

He groaned and dropped his head onto Cassius's shoulder when Cassius released his raging erection. Cassius's hands trembled as he tentatively explored Morgan's shaft, learning his shape by touch. Morgan's dick was silky smooth and deliciously veiny where it rose proudly from a nest of trimmed pubes.

"Fuck!" Morgan thrust his cock through Cassius's hungry hold, his jaw tense. "*More.* Touch me more!"

Cassius licked his lips and stroked a thumb across the thick head of Morgan's cock, the scent of Morgan's precum filling his nostrils as he spread the sticky evidence of his arousal all over his hard length. He couldn't wait to find out what Morgan tasted like.

Morgan's low growl danced down Cassius's spine as he punched his shaft seductively through Cassius's hands. The bright burn in Morgan's eyes and the harsh pants and grunts rising from his throat made whatever misgivings Cassius still clung to evaporate in the sunlight. He surrendered to the passion blazing between them and sought Morgan's mouth with eager desperation, intent on fully enjoying this illicit encounter.

Waves of pleasure slammed into Morgan at the sweet friction of Cassius's hands on his dick. He couldn't believe how embarrassingly close he was to exploding just from Cassius's touch.

Cassius's eyes were liquid silver with desire as he danced against Morgan, his fingers busily stroking Morgan's erection while he thrust his own cock through Morgan's hand. He grabbed Morgan's nape, lifted his head off the pillow, and nipped at his chin with his pretty white teeth.

"Kiss me!"

The throaty command pushed Morgan's buttons in all the right ways. He took the angel's mouth in a torrid kiss and pressed his body down onto his.

Cassius welcomed Morgan's weight with a lustful sound, his tongue lashing eagerly against Morgan's as he frenched him. His heart thudded rapidly against Morgan's chest as they moved against one another, writhing and rubbing their bodies together, their hands dancing briskly on each other's straining dicks.

Cassius made a frustrated noise before spreading his legs and wrapping his thighs around Morgan's hips, as if he couldn't get close enough. Morgan growled in approval, the motion allowing him to sink deeper into the cradle of Cassius's body. Cassius's heels found Morgan's lower back. He anchored himself to Morgan and rolled his hips sexily, mimicking the act of lovemaking.

Morgan's balls tightened and grew heavy. Delicious tension stiffened his spine and pooled in his belly, heralding his orgasm. Cassius grabbed the pillow above his head in a white-knuckled fist as Morgan's stroking motion accelerated on his cock, his cries of pleasure swallowed by Morgan's hungry lips, his glazed eyes locked on Morgan's.

Morgan let go of Cassius's mouth and sank his teeth in the angle of his neck. A savage sound erupted from his chest as the first wave of his climax crashed over him. He circled his thumb across the sensitive head of Cassius's cock and was rewarded by a loud shout.

Cassius's back bowed off the bed and the tendons in his neck corded with tension as he came with sweet violence, his cock exploding and filling Morgan's hand with hot cum. Morgan groaned and cursed as he convulsed against Cassius, his own dick making a sticky mess of Cassius's fingers and belly as he ejaculated. He took Cassius's mouth in a scorching kiss as they rode their orgasms, drinking in the angel's lustful gasps and moans.

It was a while before they stopped shuddering with aftershocks of pleasure. Their pants echoed across the bedroom as they slowly relaxed against one another, Morgan's body heavy on Cassius.

A fuzzy feeling swept over Morgan as he breathed in the musky smell of sex filling the air and experienced the comforting thump of Cassius's heart against his chest. Even though he made love to someone practically every night, he hadn't felt this physically sated in a long time.

I was right. He really is perfect for me.

Morgan sighed and lifted his head from Cassius's shoulder.

"If it weren't for the fact that we need to be downtown in about thirty minutes, I would seriously go for another round right now," he told Cassius in a chagrined voice.

Cassius tensed. "What do you mean, we need to be downtown in thirty minutes?"

Morgan grimaced and rose up on an elbow. "Oh. Didn't I tell you? We have an appointment with Strickland at eight."

Cassius narrowed his eyes. "No, you didn't tell me!"

He shoved Morgan off him, climbed down from the bed, and marched into the bathroom.

Morgan walked in in time to see Cassius strip out of his clothes. He bit back a groan, his dick stirring with a fresh wave of arousal as he took in Cassius's toned, athletic build and flawless skin.

He was debating going down on his knees and sinking his teeth into Cassius's perfectly formed ass when he caught Cassius's disgruntled expression. The angel was wiping off the evidence of their recent mutual gratification from his groin and belly. He balled up his T-shirt, threw it in the laundry bin, and twisted around to turn on the water. He stiffened when Morgan came up behind him.

Morgan trailed a finger down Cassius's spine and smiled at Cassius's shiver. *Not so angry after all.*

He brought his lips to Cassius's right ear, knowing he was playing with fire and not really caring.

"Should we shower together?" Morgan breathed, dropping his voice an octave.

His move had the desired effect.

Cassius shifted closer, head angling to give Morgan better access to his neck. Color stained his cheeks when he realized what he'd unconsciously done.

He pulled away and gritted his teeth. "There's a perfectly fine bathroom in your apartment! Why don't you reacquaint yourself with it?!"

Morgan grinned as Cassius stepped under the hot spray, the angel's half-hard length belying his stern words. He had a feeling he was going to enjoy finding out all the little things that turned Cassius on. He leaned in to steal a kiss.

Cassius grabbed his shampoo and glared at him, the bottle held defensively between them.

"Hmm." Morgan inhaled deeply. "That's a nice fragrance, but I gotta say, I like your scent better." He grabbed Cassius's wrist and tugged him close, heedless of the water pounding his head and the makeshift weapon wedged between their chests. He pressed his lips softly to Cassius's. "I can't wait to taste you."

Cassius's mouth parted and his eyes glazed over slightly at the sultry promise in Morgan's voice.

"I'm gonna savor it all," Morgan said huskily. "Your dick. Your cum. Your sweet, little ho—"

Cassius scowled and bit Morgan's lower lip.

17

"What happened to your mouth?" Adrianne said curiously.

Morgan raised a finger to his lip and rubbed the small cut. "A mosquito attacked me."

The 'mosquito' frowned at him from the other side of Strickland's office. Morgan smiled faintly. He could heal the wound anytime he wanted to. He just got a kick out of watching the dark-winged angel glance at it guiltily from time to time.

"It's mosquito season already?" Bailey said where he leaned against the couch Cassius, Julia, and Charlie sat on. The wizard looked at Adrianne, concerned. "Make sure you sleep with your windows closed. You bruise like a peach."

Adrianne narrowed her eyes at him.

Bailey shrugged at the sorceress. "I'm just saying. Remember that time that mosquito bit you on your tushy? I had to buy you a hemorrhoid ring before a mage could heal—"

Luckily for the wizard, Strickland walked inside his office before the sorceress could kill him.

Despite Cassius claiming it would be faster for them to fly downtown, Morgan had driven them to the office. He preferred having a normal mode of transportation during regular working hours. Besides, he suspected news about Cassius's presence in San Francisco would soon spread like wildfire, as would the angel's involvement in the incident at the park in Mission District and Joyce Almeda's murder.

Considering their otherworldly abilities, angels and demons were prohibited from using their powers outside approved situations or unless they were under extreme duress. Morgan saw no need to contribute to the unsavory rumors that were bound to circulate if Cassius were seen blatantly contravening the rules that governed the Fallen and flying around town without strict permission from Argonaut.

A frown wrinkled Morgan's brow as he thought back to last night's incident. *That definitely fell under the 'extreme duress' category. Thankfully, the humans who witnessed the war demons' attack don't know what an Empyreal is.*

"Is that a hickey?" Julia asked Cassius in a low voice as Strickland took his seat.

Cassius raised a hand to his neck. "No."

He tugged his collar up, a telltale redness warming the tips of his ears.

Morgan met the angel's irate glance with a steady expression. The fact that he was the one who'd marked Cassius didn't at all weigh on his conscience. He wanted the world to know he intended to claim the angel as his.

Julia's shrewd gaze landed on Morgan. "Those damn mosquitoes are everywhere, huh?"

Strickland leaned back in his chair and studied them coolly. "Report."

Morgan gave the Argonaut director a breakdown of the incident that had taken place in Mission District the night before, his tone neutral and clipped. Cassius grudgingly recounted his own version of events from when he'd called upon Joyce Almeda to the moment Morgan and his team had turned up at the park.

Adrianne took notes while Charlie used a recording spell to put their conversation on file.

"You've never seen that man before?" Strickland asked Cassius.

"The sorcerer?" Cassius shook his head. "That was the first time our paths crossed."

"The guy's fingerprints have been erased by acid, so we can't trace him in any agency's database" Julia said. "The fact that even his face hasn't come up during our searches means he's likely had plastic surgery too."

Strickland observed them broodingly before directing a sharp stare at Adrianne. "Any news from Lucy?"

Adrianne's expression turned solemn. "She stopped the poison from completely destroying the guy's heart, but he's still unconscious. She said he would have been a goner had we gotten him to her ten minutes later."

"Any idea what he used in the suicide pill he ingested?" Cassius asked. "It might give us a clue as to the identity of his friends."

"She thinks it was a cocktail of Glitterfang, Nightshade, and—" Adrianne paused, "a third poison she hasn't been able to identify yet," she finished reluctantly.

Surprise danced through Morgan at that.

A frown marred Strickland's brow. "Lucy can't identify the poison?"

Morgan shared the director's concern. Lucy was one of the best medical mages in the country. She knew her poisons inside out.

"If she doesn't know what it is, then it's not from this world," Cassius said.

All eyes turned to him.

"You mean it's from one of the realms?" Adrianne said, troubled. "Like Glitterfang?"

"Probably," Cassius replied calmly.

Unease swirled through Morgan. The tear in the Nether had done more than just bring the Fallen to Earth five hundred years ago. It had ripped inter-dimensional doorways between Earth and the planes where the other-worldly existed, including the Nine Hells. Gods, angels, spirits, demons. Many could access the rifts and tread the Earth if they so wished. That most chose not to had to do with their distaste for the earthly realm and the fact that the portals were notoriously unstable.

Unlike the official, concealed gates between the worlds that were only accessible to a select few, one could easily get lost between the dimensions when using the volatile doorways that had opened at the time of the Fall. Those who did often ended up in the Abyss, the forgotten space beyond the Nether from which there was no escape.

But many dared to make the treacherous passage. Trade between the realms had grown strong in the centuries since the Fallen had arrived on Earth. Rain Silver, Dark Blight, and Glitterfang were but a few of the poisons and medicinal concoctions that had made their way into the human world in exchange for the manmade goods the otherworldly desired, for all that they disliked humankind.

"If we find out which one it came from, we might be

able to figure out what it is and get a lead on who bought it." Cassius grew pensive. "We should also check if that poison was used in the rituals. Fracturing a human soul takes more than just Dark Blight, blood, and spells. It could be an important element of the process."

"I agree," Morgan said. "We should have Lucy and Maggie take another look at the bodies of the victims."

"Do that." A muscle jumped in Strickland's jawline as he gazed at Cassius. "We have another, more pressing problem," the director said bitterly. "Someone filmed your fight with the war demons last night."

Morgan straightened in his chair, his pulse spiking. "What?!"

Cassius's knuckles whitened where he sat on the couch.

"The video is already circulating online," Strickland continued in a hard voice. "I'm afraid we won't be able to keep your secret for long, Cassius."

"What secret?" Bailey asked, nonplussed.

Adrianne's gaze turned suspicious.

"You guys never did explain what exactly happened last night at the park," the sorceress said slowly, frowning at Morgan and Julia. "All I got from the cops was incoherent babbling about some kind of bright light."

Julia sighed. "That's because it wasn't something we could talk about without touching base with Strickland first."

"Stop the recording," Strickland told Charlie grimly.

Charlie hesitated and glanced at Morgan.

"Do it," Morgan ordered.

Charlie swallowed and ended the recording spell.

A tense hush fell over the office.

Adrianne blew out a frustrated sigh. "Will someone kindly explain what the hell is going on?!"

Julia cocked a questioning eyebrow at Strickland. The director nodded his silent permission.

"Cassius is an Empyreal," Julia said.

Confusion washed across Adrianne's face. Bailey and Charlie looked similarly puzzled. Zach paled slightly.

"He's an Empyreal?!" the demon mumbled.

"What the hell is an Empyreal?" Adrianne snapped.

"It's the highest-ranking angel or demon in Heaven and the Hells," Morgan said quietly.

Adrianne blinked. "I thought Fieries were the top dogs among your kind."

"As far as humans are concerned, they are," Julia said sedately. "Victor Sloan is considered to be the most powerful Fallen on Earth, by virtue of being a Fiery. There are some Aerials who match his abilities." She glanced at Morgan. "But few humans know of the Empyreals. The class of angels and demons whose powers exceed those of the Fieries and the Aerials."

"As far as we know, Cassius is the only one of his kind who fell to Earth," Strickland said somberly.

"There weren't many Empyreals around, even before the wars between Heaven and the Nine Hells," Julia said pensively. "They are a rare breed indeed. And a highly dangerous one. Even Heaven and the Hells were wary of the battle skills of the Empyreals. They were considered to be on par with the Gods."

Adrianne and Charlie blanched.

"Gods?!" Bailey mumbled.

Cassius grimaced as he became the focus of a battery of wary stares. "It's not as if I had a choice in the matter."

"You're not just an Empyreal, though," Julia stated quietly.

Cassius went still, his expression turning inscrutable.

"What do you mean?" Strickland said.

Morgan studied the Terrene angel with a frown. It seemed Julia had picked up on the same thing he had.

"Your soul core. It's different." Julia met Cassius's enigmatic stare unflinchingly. "You're not *just* an Empyreal," she repeated.

A stunned silence fell across the room.

"Is that true?" Strickland said, more than a little shocked.

Cassius hesitated before nodding.

"What are you then?" Adrianne asked.

"I...don't know." Cassius raked a hand through his hair. "I can't remember a thing before the Fall."

"I'm old enough to recognize that your abilities far surpass that of an Empyreal," Julia said quietly. "And your soul core *is* unique. I have yet to sense one like it in all the time I've walked the Earth."

"Just how old is Julia?" Charlie whispered to Bailey.

The wizard shrugged.

"Is that why your wings are different?" Adrianne asked Cassius brusquely.

Zach winced. "Jeez, way to be subtle."

Adrianne bristled. "Cassius is part of our team. We need to know this kind of shit, so that we can better protect each other."

Cassius narrowed his eyes at the sorceress. "I never said I was joining your team. This case is a one-off collaboration."

"Oh, please," Adrianne scoffed. "It's clear something's going on between you and Morgan. You guys can't keep your hands off one another."

Strickland stared from Cassius to Morgan and back again. "Wait. You guys have a *thing?*"

"No," Cassius stated vehemently.

"Not yet," Morgan replied steadily.

Strickland's expression turned thunderous.

"Relax, Francis," Morgan said. "It's not as if we're gonna have sex in the bullpen."

Cassius glared at Morgan. "Who said I'm gonna have sex with you at all?!"

Morgan's slow grin had Cassius gritting his pretty teeth.

"Poor you." Julia patted the irate angel's knee. "Zach and I are here if you want to talk about our uncouth leader."

"Hey!" Adrianne protested. "How come I'm not included in this little advisory group?"

"Yeah," Bailey added, similarly outraged. "I can give him tons of love advice."

"I somehow doubt that." Julia grimaced. "You two are not doing so hot in that category yourselves."

18

Victor Sloan gazed at them steadily across the video call. "No."

Strickland clenched his jaw. "You are one hundred percent certain no summoning staff has gone missing from the vault in London?"

"Yes, I'm sure." Victor's gaze shifted to Cassius, concern darkening the stone-blue depths. "Are you okay? I heard what happened."

Cassius nodded, unsurprised at that fact. Cabalista had eyes and ears in every city on every continent, including the branch agencies they were meant to collaborate with. He shifted in his chair, acutely conscious of Morgan's sharp stare from where the Aerial leaned against the wall to his right.

Cassius, Strickland, and Morgan were the only ones in the director's office, Strickland having asked the other members of Morgan's team to leave, much to their chagrin.

Cassius swallowed a grimace as Morgan's laser-like gaze burned into the side of his face. Having the man he was currently interested in in the same virtual space as the one he'd ended a relationship with several months ago was more awkward than he'd thought it would be.

Though Victor's expression remained diplomatic, Cassius could tell he'd picked up on the vibe between him and Morgan.

A lingering remorse twisted Cassius's chest as he observed his former lover. He still had mixed feelings about his breakup with Victor. The light in the depths of Victor's eyes told Cassius he shared those sentiments and more.

Cassius had been more than a little surprised when Victor had first asked him out. It had happened shortly after their battle against Tania Lancaster, when Europe was still reeling from news of the downfall of the sect that had terrorized it for decades. Cassius had refused Victor's offer at first, certain the Fiery was only interested in him because of his newly revealed status as an Empyreal. It was only after Victor had confessed that he'd been captivated by Cassius for a long time that Cassius had capitulated. After all, he'd been similarly interested in Victor for years, though he'd never admitted it to the demon.

There had been a spark between them since the day their paths first crossed, a century after the Fall. It had taken that long for humans to stop distrusting the angels and demons who had crashed onto their world and inadvertently destroyed their cities, killing thousands upon thousands of their unsuspecting citizens. The Hundred Year War that had followed had been even more destructive for mankind. Though their magic had put a dent in the numbers of Fallen, it couldn't compare to the untold number of humans who had lost their lives during those acrimonious conflicts. It had taken several concerted attempts by a determined group of angels, demons, and magic users to finally bring peace to the world once more. Victor had been part of that alliance and Cassius one of their hired guards.

Like all the Fallen, Victor was stunningly attractive. Cassius would have had to be dead not to be drawn to him. But there had been more to the chemistry between them than just the pull of physical attraction. Cassius had long assumed he was the only one who felt it and that Victor was straight. Having the Fiery reciprocate his interest had come as a pleasant shock.

Despite his reputation as a cold and forbidding demon, Victor had proven to be an incredibly attentive and kind lover. Their friendship had flourished almost as fast as their physical relationship, and sex between them had been as satisfying as Cassius had suspected it would be. Victor had made no secret of his growing feelings for Cassius over the years; he had even wanted to make their relationship official. But something had always stopped Cassius from fully surrendering his heart to the other man. Something he couldn't explain.

He liked and respected Victor. But he couldn't love him.

The day Cassius had told Victor he wanted to break up, the resignation in the demon's eyes had made Cassius suspect he'd been expecting it for some time. They had parted ways amicably, Cassius moving out of Victor's home and into his own place in London before he finally decided to leave the city and move continents.

Disquiet clouded Victor's gaze. "Things are going to get bumpy once news spreads that you're an Empyreal."

A wry smile curved Cassius's mouth. "Bumpy is a polite

word. I can already feel the world hating me even more than it already did."

A grimace twisted Victor's mouth. "You've survived worse. This too shall pass."

"I know," Cassius said, grateful for the quiet strength in Victor's voice and eyes.

He knew the demon would always have his back, whatever happened.

"How come you're so sure no summoning staff has disappeared from the vault of the Cabalista headquarters?" Morgan said coolly. "Have you checked it personally?"

Strickland cast a warning glance at Morgan. Cassius frowned faintly. The Aerial was making no effort to hide his distrust of the demon.

"I don't need to," Victor replied. "There's tracking magic on all seven summoning staffs we confiscated from the warlocks who made pacts with the Nine Hells. If one of them left the vault, the director of every branch of Cabalista in the world would get a personal alert."

"Still, it would make sense to check," Strickland said guardedly.

"I will gladly do that, if only to reassure you, Francis," Victor said. "I'll also be sending a couple of my trusted agents your way shortly. The presence of a new summoning staff is a serious matter. Have you informed the other agencies yet?"

Strickland's face grew guarded. "No. The incident is still under investigation by Argonaut."

Cassius could tell from Morgan's rigid posture that news of Cabalista potentially joining their investigation was as welcome as a Stark Steel bullet in the gut.

Victor frowned faintly. "Take my advice, Francis. Talk

to Brianna and Reuben. I'll let Jasper know what's going on."

Cassius masked a grimace. Jasper Cobb was the Terrene demon in charge of the San Francisco branch of Cabalista. He was one of the many demons who had made it inherently clear over the years how much he detested Cassius. His reaction when Victor had made him aware of Cassius's relocation to San Francisco had only served to confirm his long-held opinion about the angel.

Strickland opened his mouth to protest.

Victor raised his hand. "I know what you're going to say, but this is bigger than Argonaut. From what I've learned, it appears someone in your city is fracturing and stealing human souls." His expression turned hard. "We all know what Tania intended to do with the souls she took. We cannot take the risk of that happening again. It would be best if everyone pooled their resources to try and get to the bottom of this before we are all visited by untold tragedy."

A muscle jumped in Strickland's jawline.

Cassius felt some sympathy for the mage. But he had to agree with Victor on this matter. The only way they'd managed to defeat Tania Lancaster in London was when they'd stopped bickering with one another and cooperated.

"Alright, I'll talk to them," Strickland said grudgingly.

"Good." A warm smile lit Victor's face. "I'm coming to San Francisco in the next week. It would be nice if we could grab dinner."

Strickland's face relaxed. "Sure."

Strickland and Victor had maintained a close friendship after their battle with Tania Lancaster.

"Will you join us?" Victor asked Cassius.

"Okay," Cassius murmured.

Victor looked over at Morgan. "Mr. King is cordially invited to attend too, if he so wishes."

Morgan frowned at Victor's diplomatic tone. "Why not? The more the merrier."

Cassius sighed. Strickland scowled at Morgan.

Victor's smile widened, ever the suave politician. "Great."

19

Bailey dropped down into the sewers after Cassius.

"What's gotten into him?" the wizard muttered, staring after Morgan.

Adrianne followed Bailey's gaze to where Morgan was talking to an Argonaut agent farther along the tunnel, irritation painted in every line of his body.

They'd returned to Bayview Park, at Cassius's suggestion.

"I don't know. Maybe it's to do with that conversation with Victor Sloan we weren't privy to." She looked pointedly at Cassius as they started up the passage after Morgan. "You know, the one we were forcibly kicked out of Strickland's office for." The sorceress released a frustrated sigh. "And why the hell did he insist on Charlie casting a soundproof enchantment spell on his office?"

"Maybe because he knew you were planning to spy on the call?" Julia suggested drily.

Zach smiled.

Adrianne scowled, not bothering to deny the accusation. "I hate being kept in the dark. I mean we're the ones investigating this damn case, aren't we? So why all this cloak-and-dagger bullshit?! No one is even willing to tell us what it was exactly Tania Lancaster intended to do with the fractured souls of the people she killed thirty years ago! That would go some way toward helping us figure out who's behind—!"

"She was going to tear the Nether open," Cassius said.

Morgan rocked to a stop up ahead. He whirled around to face Cassius, his voice a low growl when he spoke. "I thought you were strictly forbidden from talking about what happened in London!" The Aerial glanced around. The tunnel was empty bar for their group, the Argonaut agents guarding the crime scene having fallen back. "Charlie, cast a—"

"Yeah, yeah," the enchanter said morosely.

He made a movement with his hand and murmured a spell. A soundproof bubble formed around them.

Cassius narrowed his eyes at Morgan. The Aerial had been acting like a giant ass since they'd left the agency's bureau a short while back.

"You knew?" Cassius said grimly. "And the secrecy spell doesn't work on me."

A muscle jumped in Morgan's jawline. "About what Lancaster intended to do? Yeah."

"How?" Cassius snapped.

"I have a source." Morgan arched a defiant eyebrow in the face of Cassius's glare. "One I have zero intention of telling you about."

"Tania Lancaster was going to open the Nether?" Julia said in a deadly voice.

A soft glow lit the tunnel as the Terrene angel unconsciously drew on her powers in her rage, her skin radiating divine light. Zach looked similarly furious, crimson gleaming in his eyes and around his body.

"Are they talking about what happened five hundred years ago?" Charlie asked Bailey.

The wizard nodded, troubled.

"Why would she do that?" Adrianne said, aghast. "Wouldn't it bring about another Fall?!"

Cassius strode angrily past Morgan and started up the tunnel. "We still don't know why Tania wanted to create a breach in the Nether. Some people thought it might have something to do with the Nine Hells."

The others fell into step around him, Morgan in the lead.

"But she did figure out something no one on Earth had grasped before," Cassius continued bitterly as they made for the confluence chamber where the remains of the ninth victim had been discovered two nights ago.

"Which is?" Bailey asked warily.

"That a human soul contains its own inherent magic, irrespective of whether or not the person is a magic user," Morgan replied in Cassius's stead. "And that that soul can be fractured in such a way as to open a doorway between the realms." He sighed at Adrianne and the other two magic users' shocked expressions. "It's why they call it selling your soul to the devil. Demons from the Nine Hells have used human souls as portals to travel to Earth for eons. But no one has ever tried to combine dozens of fractured souls to attempt something bigger."

Cassius shared a grudging glance with the Aerial, impressed despite himself. "You came to that conclusion on your own?"

"I'm not just a pretty face," Morgan muttered.

Cassius's lips twitched despite himself.

"I doubt Tania found this out on her own, however clever she was," Julia said in a steely voice.

"You're right," Cassius said. "We've long suspected someone else was pulling the strings behind the scenes."

"And you never discovered who that person was?" Zach asked with a frown.

"No. He's a clever bastard, whoever he is."

Adrianne stared. "How do you know it's a man?"

"Because the last word Tania Lancaster screamed before I killed her was 'Master.'"

ॐ

MORGAN SENSED ADRIANNE AND BAILEY'S NERVOUSNESS and Charlie's dread as they gazed at the dark-winged angel. Even Julia and Zach looked wary.

Still, Morgan felt no fear. He knew Cassius was incredibly powerful. Just as he knew that the Empyreal would never maliciously hurt anyone. He was far too soft-hearted for that.

Strickland was right. Cassius wouldn't raise a hand to another being unless it were in self-defense or to protect others.

Irritation swarmed Morgan all over again. He could only guess how lonely and forsaken Cassius must have felt all these centuries of being shunned by the world and his own kind. His only sin was that his wings looked different from those of the other Fallen and that he possessed powers he had never wished for.

A fiercely protective feeling tightened Morgan's chest. He would not let anyone hurt Cassius. Not as long as he had breath left in his body.

He slowed for a moment, stunned by the forceful emotions roiling inside him. It only confirmed what he'd suspected all along. That what existed between Cassius and him was more than just physical attraction. Morgan clenched his teeth.

He could no longer deny what he wanted.

And that was to own Cassius.

Morgan wished to stamp his mark all over the angel. To make him his in the eyes of this world and every other realm. And he knew from Victor's eyes that the demon craved the exact same thing. Whatever relationship had existed between Victor and Cassius, the demon hadn't given up on claiming it back and more.

"How long are you intending to be grumpy for?" Cassius asked in an exasperated voice, oblivious to Morgan's dark thoughts. "It's getting difficult to breathe down here with all your negative energy."

"I'm not grumpy," Morgan protested.

"Liar," Julia muttered.

"Considering we're going to have to cooperate with the other agencies on this case, the truth about what Tania Lancaster intended to do was bound to come out sooner or later," Cassius told Morgan.

Adrianne rocked to a halt. "Wait. What's this about other agencies and our case?"

Morgan grimaced at his team's unhappy expressions. "Victor told Strickland he should get Cabalista, Rosen, and Hexa on board. Though I hate to say it, I agree with him. This is too big for any one agency."

Cassius stared at Morgan.

"What?" Morgan said defensively. "I changed my mind."

"He normally doesn't," Adrianne told Cassius blithely.

"Wait." Julia frowned heavily. "Does this mean we're gonna have to deal with Jasper Cobb?"

"Yes," Morgan muttered.

"But he's such an asshole," Julia protested.

Cassius grimaced. "I hear you."

"I take it Reuben and Brianna will be in on this too?" Zach said coldly.

Reuben Fletcher was the Aerial angel in charge of San Francisco's bureau of The Order of Rosen. He was known to be a stickler for the rules and had little patience for people who didn't toe his line.

Brianna Monroe, the director of the local Hexa bureau, was a Level One witch with a strong affinity for transformation magic and a hard woman to get a handle on.

Zach had crossed paths with all three bureau heads in the past. Although he'd never gone into the details, he'd clearly come away with a sense of distaste for their practices. Considering how mild-mannered the Aqueous demon was, that was saying something.

Lights cut through the gloom up ahead. They came out of the tunnel and into the chamber Cassius had discovered with Loki two nights ago.

The area had been temporarily drained by the city's public utilities agency at the request of Argonaut. The remains of the dead man were long gone and the bitter scent of black magic imbuing the air had disappeared. Only forensic markers remained, along with the odor of sulfide that pervaded the sewers.

Cassius stepped down into the basin and headed over to the altar.

"You finally gonna tell us what it is we're back here for?" Morgan said curiously. "Our techs have been all over this place several times already, as have we."

Cassius climbed onto the stone dais. He walked across the complex pattern of runes carved into the rock and headed to the center, not bothering to avoid the Dark Blight staining the surface. A silvery residue now covered the black lines.

The powder was a carefully prepared concoction of Glitterfang and Blossom Silver. Used by white-magic users in their rituals and potions, Glitterfang was made by the Nereids and was poisonous to demons and black-magic users. Blossom Silver, a medicine concocted by the Naiads, could heal non-fatal injuries caused by demonic weapons or black magic.

When combined in a very specific way, the two neutralized the deadly effects of Dark Blight, the black liquid made by shadow alchemists from the heart of a Dryad.

"This place gives me the creeps." Bailey glanced nervously at the tunnels radiating off the chamber. "That poor guy must have been terrified when they brought him down here."

"He was probably unaware of what was happening to him." Cassius took out his Colt, removed a bullet, and stood the slug in the middle of the altar. "Most of Tania Lancaster's victims were under the spell of her enchanter by the time they became part of the ritual. A soul crying out in terror is not as useful a weapon as a sedated one."

Morgan frowned as Cassius removed his dagger and unleashed his Stark Steel sword.

"I'd step back if I were you guys," Cassius said.

"Wait." Julia stiffened as a pulse of power blasted across the chamber. It was coming from Cassius. "What are you doing?"

A look of intense concentration came over Cassius. "Summoning a Reaper."

Surprise jolted Morgan a second before a wave of

divine energy washed across his skin. Light exploded inside the chamber. The Aerial raised a hand to his eyes, his heart quickening. The brilliance slowly faded.

Adrianne gasped.

Cassius's wings almost touched the walls of the confluence chamber where he hovered above the altar, his brilliant, white feathers fluttering with small bursts of power that made the air tremble. The Empyreal gripped the blade sheathed in Heaven's Light in both hands and slammed the pointed tip into the Rain Silver bullet, splicing it neatly in half.

20

THE CARTRIDGE EXPLODED WITH A VIOLENT SHOCKWAVE. Adrianne and Bailey cursed as they tumbled backward. Zach grabbed Charlie by his jacket before the enchanter could go flying into the concrete wall of the basin.

"A warning would have been nice!" Julia yelled above the gale sweeping the chamber.

The angels and the demon had barely budged from their positions.

"I did say to step back!" Cassius shouted.

Morgan released some of his powers and formed a protective barrier around the three magic users. He exchanged a tense glance with Julia and Zach.

Summoning a Reaper usually required runes made from animal blood and a complex spell that only high-level magic users could perform. Opening a doorway between the Earth and the Nine Hells took an incredible amount of power and was authorized under exceptional circumstances by Argonaut and the other agencies. As far as Morgan knew, this had happened a handful of times since the Fall.

He'd never seen a Reaper being invoked in the manner Cassius had just done, using only Rain Silver and his powers. Judging from Julia and Zach's troubled expressions, neither had they.

Does this mean Cassius can access the other dimensions at will?

The Empyreal focused on the pool forming on the altar, heedless of their concerns. Light danced brightly across his body and his blade where it had half disappeared into the stone.

Morgan's belly clenched with a different kind of tension as he gazed upon Cassius's radiant form. *He's beautiful.*

The turbulence rippling the shiny surface the Rain Silver bullet had created gradually died down, as did the tempest whirling around them.

An expectant hush fell across the chamber.

The silver darkened as the portal formed. A sharp stench of camphor preceded the ominous shape that slowly emerged from the inky doorway.

"Oh hell," Bailey muttered, pale-faced.

The Reaper stood nine feet tall when he fully materialized, his spectral form wreathed in shadows and a sharp scythe glinting in one bony hand. Crimson eyes flared under the hood covering his skeletal head. The apparition drew himself to his full height as he registered his surroundings, an angry, black aura warping the air around him.

"*Who dares summon me from the Nine—?*" the Reaper roared. "Oh." He paused, aura fading and tone turning affable. "Hello, Cassius."

"Hi, Benjamin," Cassius murmured.

Bailey and Charlie gaped. Morgan and the others stared.

"The Reaper has a *name?!*" Adrianne hissed sideways at Morgan once she'd recovered from her shock.

The apparition narrowed his crimson-glowing orbs at the sorceress. "Of course I have a name! All anthropomorphic manifestations have one." He cocked his scythe at Morgan and his team. "Who are these people?" he asked Cassius irritably. "It is clear you have not brought me here to harvest their souls." He glanced at Adrianne. "Although, I am willing to make an exception and take hers if you so wish."

"Hey!" Adrianne protested.

Cassius rolled his eyes. "No one's soul is getting harvested. I wanted to talk to you about what happened here a couple of nights ago and the other strange murders that have been taking place across the city in the last two months."

Morgan frowned, puzzled. Considering the nine victims' souls had been stolen, a Reaper wouldn't have been present at the time of their demise.

So, why has he summoned one?

"Ah." Benjamin rested his scythe on the altar and propped his chin atop the weapon with a bony clunk. "It is the damnedest thing, really," he muttered, tone somewhat piqued. "Us Reapers have been talking about it for weeks now."

Morgan shared a startled glance with his team.

"Wait. You guys were aware of the stolen souls?!" he asked the Reaper.

"Do you know who's behind the rituals?" Julia said sharply.

"Oh, no." Benjamin waved a skeletal hand dismissively.

"We are only present at the time of the impending passage of a human soul to the afterlife. Their affairs are no concern of ours."

Disappointment shot through Morgan.

"In that case, why have you and your, er, Reaper colleagues been discussing the spate of murders we're investigating?" Zach asked.

"We were puzzled by the numbers missing from our tally, is all." Benjamin's pupils contracted to tiny red circles. "It is our solemn duty as Reapers to ensure that all human souls go to the afterlife." He paused. "I must admit, this incident bears a close resemblance to that time thirty years ago, when that sorceress started stealing human souls. It left quite the void in our accounts."

Morgan stiffened. *The Reapers know about Tania Lancaster?!*

"Benjamin indirectly helped us find her," Cassius explained at their confused expressions, confirming Morgan's suspicions. "We had a Hexa mage place a timed spell bomb on the soul of a black-magic sorcerer we captured at the time. We allowed the man to escape shortly after. He didn't know about the spell he was carrying and ran straight back to Tania's hideout through a portal, like we'd suspected he would. When the soul bomb detonated, I followed Benjamin to the dying man's location and alerted the others."

Adrianne gasped, the color draining from her face. "You went through a Reaper's portal?!"

Cassius didn't reply. Morgan clenched his teeth.

I guess the answer to my prior question about him being able to traverse the dimensions is a yes.

A gruff, rhythmic sound echoed around the chamber.

The Reaper's shoulders trembled. Morgan realized Benjamin was laughing.

"The soul of the sorceress was so twisted and delicious," the Reaper chortled. "So were those of her acolytes. They made a handsome meal indeed for me and my friends. We were loath to regurgitate them in the Nine Hells. Why, those cursed souls were almost as delectable as this Rain Silver you have gifted me with."

Charlie gagged and slammed a hand over his mouth.

"That one is weak-stomached," Benjamin chuckled.

"Is that true?" Bailey asked Zach, horrified. "Our souls get eaten by Reapers when we go to the afterlife?!"

The demon grimaced and scratched his cheek.

"Yeah. It's not a well-known fact, for obvious reasons," he muttered. "It's not like they digest them or anything," he added hastily when Bailey's face took on a distinctively green tinge. "They just, you know, keep them in their bellies until they know where they need to spit them back up again."

"Like birds and their throat pouches," Julia contributed helpfully.

"That's disgusting," Adrianne mumbled. "I'm never gonna die."

Cassius sighed.

"The Dark Blight painted into this altar," he asked the Reaper, "can you smell it? It has a pretty unique undertone."

Benjamin squatted down and sniffed the stone. "Hmm. You are correct. It is very faint."

"Is it anywhere else in the city?" Cassius asked insistently. "There can't be many places around carrying this smell."

Oh. Morgan stared at Cassius. *That's what he's after!*

"Give me a moment."

Benjamin scraped off a layer of the dried, black liquid with the tip of a bony finger and disappeared into the portal.

Silence fell across the confluence chamber.

"Where did he go?" Charlie said hoarsely.

"To search the city with the other Reapers," Cassius replied. "A Reaper's sense of smell is the best in all the realms," he explained in the face of their stares. "Benjamin can probably tell what you had for dinner last week."

"So, you're pals with the Reaper?" Julia said in the awkward silence that followed.

Cassius's ears reddened self-consciously. "He's...a friend, yes."

Emotion brought a flush of color to Adrianne's face. She sniffed before glaring at Morgan. "Don't you dare break Cassius's heart!"

Morgan scowled. "Where'd that come from?"

"That poor guy has to resort to being friends with Reapers," Adrianne mumbled. "He must be so lonely."

Cassius grimaced at her look of pity. "You're making me sound like a total loser."

Zach smiled.

Benjamin returned. "These are the places where we've picked up a trace of this particular Dark Blight."

The Reaper rattled off a list of addresses.

"Damn." Julia exchanged a stunned glance with Morgan. "Those are the locations where the other victims were found!"

"We could have used this information weeks ago," Zach said in a frustrated voice.

"You wouldn't have been able to save them," Cassius remarked. "This spell would only have activated at the time of their deaths." He studied Benjamin with a frown. "Those are the only places you and the other Reapers have identified as carrying this particular taint?"

Benjamin's eyes flared. "There was one more location where one of our brethren thought he detected an infinitesimal trace of it. Someone was murdered a week ago, in a back alley behind a bar. The Reaper who collected the dead man's soul didn't detect anything suspicious at the time. He revisited the scene just now and explored it more thoroughly for this scent."

"And?" Morgan said impatiently.

"He caught a whiff similar to this Dark Blight on the ground close to where the body of the victim was found."

Cassius narrowed his eyes. "What's the name of the bar?"

"*Occulta.*"

21

Adrianne ended the call and put her cellphone away. "Jerry Carneiro. That's the name of the wizard who died behind *Occulta* a week ago."

"Who's the lead agent on the case?" Morgan asked as they made for their parked SUVs.

"Zakir Singh."

Bailey grimaced. "Spit Guy?"

Cassius recalled the man with the scar from the bullpen yesterday. He frowned faintly.

Christ, has it only been thirty hours since I was arrested and taken to the Argonaut bureau? It feels like a lifetime ago!

"I really should have picked another city," he muttered under his breath.

Morgan flashed a sharp look his way.

Then again, I wouldn't have crossed paths with Mr. Sexy Grump over there.

Cassius ignored the way his chest tightened at that thought.

"Talk to Singh and see where his case is at," Morgan told Julia.

Julia grimaced. "He's not going to like us interfering in his investigation."

"We're not going to interfere. We just need to know what he has on the victim and any potential leads he's come up with." Morgan glanced at Cassius, his expression turning guarded. "We should keep what happened with the Reaper to ourselves for the time being," he said curtly. "Strickland must already know, since he was involved in the battle to take down Tania Lancaster."

Cassius noted his bitter tone with a pang of guilt.

"Any more secrets you want to share with us?" Zach asked Cassius.

"My lips are sealed," Cassius murmured.

This earned him a battery of incredulous stares.

"Wait. You mean there *are* more secrets?!" Morgan said, incensed.

"Believe me, it's best if you never find out about them," Cassius stated firmly.

"I'll check in with Lucy and Maggie, see if they have anything new on our victims' bodies," Adrianne said while Morgan scowled at Cassius.

"Do that," Morgan grumbled.

Bailey rocked to a halt. "Shit."

The wizard was staring at something on his phone.

"What is it?" Morgan asked irritably.

Bailey turned his cell around so they could all see the screen.

"This just came up as an alert," he said grimly. "Looks like Cassius made the news."

Cassius's heart sank as he watched the video playing out on a national broadcast channel. Though the recording was jumpy, it clearly showed him in his Empyreal form. He clenched his teeth.

Damn that sorcerer!

A hand landed on Cassius's shoulder, startling him. He turned his head and met Julia's solemn gaze.

"Don't worry," the Terrene angel said quietly. "We won't let anything happen to you."

"You only did what you had to do," Zach added, his face unusually serious. "If it weren't for your actions in that park last night, we would never have gotten our hands on that sorcerer and a solid lead on this case."

Cassius flushed as he clocked the others' similarly determined expressions.

Adrianne smiled and poked an elbow in Cassius's ribs. "I told you, we've got your six."

Zach, Bailey, and Charlie headed off to Joyce Almeda's house and the park where they'd taken down the sorcerer to check in with the forensic agents still on site. Morgan dropped Adrianne and Julia at the bureau before heading back to his and Cassius's apartment building.

"You're being awfully quiet," the Aerial said after a while.

Cassius stared broodingly out of the passenger window. They were coming up to South Beach. San Francisco Bay glittered brightly to their left as Morgan navigated the Friday afternoon traffic on the Embarcadero.

"It's strange."

Morgan glanced at him. "What is?"

"That you guys are so willing to trust me, when you barely even know me. Most people find it hard to overlook my unsavory reputation."

"Damn. Cabalista really did a serious job on you, huh?" A muscle twitched in Morgan's jaw. "We're not like them, Cassius. You can trust us."

"That's what everyone always says, before they get

what they want from me," Cassius retorted, unable to disguise the bitterness in his voice. "After that, they all invariably—"

The rest of his words were cut off, Morgan yanking the steering wheel to the right and jerking to a sudden stop on the hard shoulder of the freeway. The seatbelt dug sharply into Cassius's chest, ripping a curse from his lips.

"What the—?!"

Morgan leaned across the console, curled a hand around Cassius's nape, and pulled him in for a hard kiss. Cassius sucked in air, stunned by the smoldering anger in Morgan's eyes. Morgan's mouth gradually softened on Cassius's, a different kind of heat darkening his gaze.

"Do you believe this is fake too?" he murmured against Cassius's lips, his tone harsh despite the gentle way he was touching him. He took Cassius's hand and pressed it to his chest. "That this, right here, is all made up?"

Cassius shuddered at the feel of Morgan's heart drumming under his fingers. It was beating as fast as his.

"Do you really think I would touch you because I intend to manipulate you for my own gains?" Morgan asked grimly.

Cassius swallowed. "No."

A frustrated sigh left Morgan. He dropped his forehead against Cassius's. "I'm going to be frank with you. I want you. Not just for one night." Morgan stared hotly into Cassius's eyes. "I know you can feel it too. This thing between us? It's more than just lust. Our soul cores react to one another whenever we touch."

Cassius flinched as Morgan pressed a scorching hand to his belly. An echo of resonance danced between their bodies, a dark thread of twisted fate that hinted at a long-forgotten past.

"Tell me you want this, too, Cassius. Tell me you believe me."

A sound that was half a moan left Cassius when Morgan nipped gently at his lower lip. Fire flared through him where Morgan touched him, slowly melting his body and mind.

"Tell me, Cassius!" Morgan growled.

"I do." Cassius buried his hands in Morgan's hair and sought his mouth, succumbing to the flames burning between them. "Now, kiss me, damnit!"

Morgan obliged him with a groan full of need, tongue slipping inside Cassius's mouth to lash seductively against Cassius's trembling tongue.

A horn honked next to Morgan's SUV.

"Hey, assholes! Go make out in your own home!" an irate driver yelled at them.

Morgan reluctantly lifted his mouth off Cassius's.

Cassius blinked dazedly, his erection throbbing between his thighs.

Morgan's eyes blazed. He grazed the stiff length with his fingers, making Cassius shudder all over again and bite his lip on another moan.

"Should we do something about this when we get back to your apartment?" Morgan said, a sultry smile stretching his mouth.

"Stop teasing and drive!" Cassius ordered hoarsely.

Morgan chuckled and pulled out into the traffic.

Cassius's penthouse was regrettably occupied when they got there. The contractors hired by the Argonaut Agency to repair the damages caused by the tactical team the day before were busy drilling out the broken front door and replacing the terrace's glass panels.

"We'll be done in a couple of hours." The guy in charge

glanced from Cassius to Morgan, evidently picking up on the tension between them. "Your cat's in the bedroom."

"Wanna come over to my place?" Morgan asked Cassius.

Cassius hesitated. Though they'd both wanted to touch and kiss each other on the elevator ride up, they'd had company in the shape of two elderly women who'd chatted non-stop, oblivious to the sexual chemistry sparking the air between the silent men on either side of them.

The brief reprieve had given Cassius time to cool off. Though he wanted nothing more than to relive the pleasure he'd found in Morgan's arms that morning, a voice deep inside him was warning him not to rush into things.

"Can I take a raincheck?"

Morgan's calm expression didn't change. "Sure. I'm next door if you want me."

Cassius felt a pang of disappointment when Morgan walked out of the penthouse without a backward glance. He'd thought the Aerial would put up more of a fight.

The sun was setting by the time the contractors finished up and left.

Cassius showered and changed into black jeans and a red T-shirt. He checked the address for *Occulta* on his cellphone while he shrugged into his leather biker's jacket, putting food and water out for Loki and grabbing his helmet.

The cat's mournful meow rose behind him as he headed for the front door. Cassius stopped and turned. Loki ran up to him and slinked his body between Cassius's legs.

"I can't take you where I'm going, so be a good kitty and wait here."

Loki sat on his haunches and stared at him, yellow eyes faintly accusing.

Cassius felt like a complete cad as he closed the door on the demon cat. He took the elevator to the garage, climbed on his motorbike, and headed downtown.

Housed in the basement and first two floors of an old, redbrick warehouse to the west of the busy Union Square bar scene, *Occulta* was a popular hangout for the magic users and supernatural entities in the city. Cassius parked on a side street one block from the address and headed for the alleyway that backed onto the place.

A couple hugged the wall next to a red, metal door, their mouths glued together as they humped through their clothes. Cassius caught a hint of crimson in the woman's eyes when she looked lazily at him over her partner's shoulder, her hand busy on the panting guy's cock.

The taint of sulfur and sex oozing from the demon identified her as a succubus.

Cassius headed past the pair and the fire escape rising from the basement, conscious of the succubus's faintly annoyed stare when she realized her presence did nothing for him.

Few were completely immune to the irresistible allure of her kind, even among angels and demons.

The muted scent of human blood and an echo of magic fluttered across Cassius's senses when he neared the dumpsters farther up the dimly lit passage. He stopped next to the middle one, squatted, and traced a spot on the ground before bringing his finger to his nose. He narrowed his eyes.

The unique Dark Blight taint and the bitter black magic he'd picked up in the sewers under Bayview Park that first night and this morning were just about detectable. His gaze moved to a maroon stain on the asphalt a few feet to his right.

This must be where Carneiro died.

"Why am I not surprised to find you here?" someone said above him.

Cassius looked up, his heart in his mouth.

Morgan dropped down from the fire escape rising up the back of the building and landed nimbly next to Cassius. Cassius rose, his mouth dry and his pulse now racing for a whole other reason.

Morgan's crisp, white T-shirt accentuated his broad chest while his dark jeans showed off the hard muscles of his thighs. Metal studs gleamed in his wine-red leather jacket and belt, and his hair was still damp from the shower.

Morgan stilled as he raked Cassius with his gaze, his pupils flaring.

"You look nice." He leaned in and inhaled. "And you smell good enough to eat," he murmured in a voice that went straight to Cassius's dick.

Morgan's scent wrapped around Cassius, an intoxicating blend of ozone and evergreen that made him want to strip the Aerial naked and lick him from the top of his head to his toes. Cassius swallowed.

I am screwed.

Morgan's seductive smile told Cassius he could sense his growing arousal.

So, SO screwed.

"Shall we go check out the place?" Morgan drawled.

22

FIVE MINUTES LATER AND MORGAN'S MOOD HAD darkened considerably. The noise of a busy Friday night crowd washed over Cassius and him as they entered the vestibule leading to the bar. The stiff set of Cassius's shoulders told Morgan the angel was already on his guard. Morgan frowned.

I can't blame him.

The doorman's face had hardened with recognition when they'd approached the front door of *Occulta* amidst the low murmurs of the patrons loitering outside for a smoke. From the wary look in everyone's eyes, it seemed most of the magical and supernatural community knew Cassius was in town. Even the few humans among them had appeared frightened when they'd recognized the dark-winged angel.

For a second, Morgan had thought the doorman would refuse them entry. The man had finally relented after an awkward pause.

"I don't want no trouble," he'd grumbled as he

unclipped the red, velvet rope from the stanchions guarding the doorway.

Judging from the scent of Frankincense oozing from the guy, Morgan guessed he was a Level Four wizard.

"Neither do we," Cassius had said calmly.

Something that looked a lot like fear had flashed in the magic user's eyes. That was when Morgan had realized the truth.

Cassius's recently revealed status as an Empyreal meant that anyone who would have openly challenged him in the past was now too scared to do so.

The fact that this did little to please Cassius didn't surprise Morgan. Cassius wasn't the kind of man who would take pleasure in his superior strength and his quasi-God-like status. If that had been the case, he would have declared his rank centuries ago and exerted his powers for his own benefit. There was one simple truth Morgan had learned after knowing the dark-winged angel for two days.

He just wanted to be left alone.

Irritation swirled through Morgan all over again. He wasn't sure if he would be able to show the degree of tolerance and mercy Cassius displayed toward those who ostracized and openly insulted him.

He really is a saint.

Morgan looked around curiously as they slipped through the throng of people occupying the first floor of the bar. Though he'd been in the city for a good ten years, he wasn't heavily into its night scene. When he did choose to go out, he liked to patronize the stylish jazz clubs in the Theater District, where he could enjoy a leisurely drink and intelligent conversation. It was where he picked up most of his lovers.

The interior of *Occulta* delivered on its promise and

more. The false, vaulted ceiling with its exposed metal beams gave the bar an open, airy look, while the Victorian gas lamps and chandeliers cast a muted light that projected an intimate feel. Black and red leather booths complemented the hardwood floor and the walnut tables and chairs opposite the bar. The walls were exposed brickwork alternating with rich wallpaper and wood paneling, all of them dotted with an eclectic collection of iron signs and period posters that completed the steampunk feel of the place.

Despite the number of magic users and otherworldly beings mingling with the humans crowding the place, the atmosphere didn't reek of their scents. Whoever owned *Occulta* was using a powerful air-purifying spell to keep the smell of the bar's preternatural patrons under control.

They were halfway to the counter when the hubbub died down noticeably. Morgan clenched his jaw as he and Cassius became the focus of scores of leery stares. The noise of the crowd resumed once more, an added note of urgency underscoring it.

A pretty woman with pink and white hair observed them steadily when they came up to her. She was one of three barkeeps manning the main drinks counter.

"What will it be, gentlemen?"

"Whiskey on the rocks," Morgan said.

"Same," Cassius murmured.

She took their payment, brought their drinks over with practiced ease, and leaned over the counter.

"Don't mind these assholes." She cocked her head at the suspicious gazes being directed at them. "Their bark is worse than their bite. And they don't know a good thing when they see it."

Cassius blinked. "Hmm, thanks. I think."

The woman smiled. "You're even more handsome than my mom said you were."

Cassius stared. Recognition dawned on his face.

"Are you related to Stephanie Keller?" he asked, surprised.

Morgan glanced between the woman and the angel, a puzzled frown wrinkling his brow. "Who's Stephanie Keller?"

"She was one of the witches who helped take down Tania Lancaster," Cassius murmured, troubled.

Alarm darted through Morgan. The woman grimaced at their expressions.

"Mom has early Alzheimer's. She didn't mean to spill the secrets she was meant to keep." She shrugged. "If it's any consolation, she only said she'd met you and that you'd saved her life. The Cabalista sorcerer who turned up when the secrecy spell broke agreed to let her be."

Sadness oozed from Cassius. "Please give her my regards when you see her."

"Will do. I'm Suzanne Myers, by the way. You can call me Suzie."

She offered her hand to Cassius. Cassius grasped it and paused for an instant.

A faint smile curved his lips as he slowly shook the woman's hand. "It's nice to meet you, Suzie."

Suzie's eyes twinkled with admiration. "You really are as good as mom said you are."

Morgan stared, conscious something had just passed between the two but uncertain what it was.

Something drew Suzie's attention. "I think your friends are calling you."

She pointed past their shoulders. Morgan and Cassius turned.

"*Yoohoo!*" Adrianne shouted, waving a hand wildly from where she occupied a circular booth with Julia and two other women.

The Terrene angel moved her cocktail glass deftly out of the sorceress's way.

Morgan was wearing a scowl by the time they made it to their table. "What the hell are you doing here?"

"It's girls' night out," Adrianne said with an unrepentant grin, scooting over to make space. "We thought we could kill two birds with one stone and check out this place for hot, shady people."

Julia shrugged at Morgan's accusing stare as he slipped onto the leather-upholstered seating with Cassius. "It was her idea, not mine." She introduced Cassius to the woman beside her. "This is Maggie Briggs, head of forensics at Argonaut."

The brunette dipped her chin, her intelligent stare swinging between Morgan and Cassius.

Julia indicated the redhead next to Maggie. "And this is Lucy Walters, Argonaut's senior medical mage."

A saccharine smile stretched Lucy's mouth as she studied Morgan and Cassius for a moment.

"So, he's your type, huh?" she asked Morgan, indicating Cassius with a tip of her glass. "I can't say I blame you. I would lick that guy like a lollipop if I had the chance."

Cassius choked on his whiskey.

Morgan patted the coughing angel on the back and rolled his eyes hard.

Julia arched an eyebrow at Lucy. "I thought you and Don Quixote were still doing the dirty?"

"Do I even want to know who Don Quixote is?" Morgan groaned.

"Donnie Mancha," Adrianne said. "He's a fireman Lucy

hooked up with at a karaoke bar a month ago. That guy is hung like a horse."

Morgan grimaced. Cassius took a large gulp of his whiskey.

"Alas, Donnie and I parted ways a while back." Lucy shrugged. "He was interested in exploring parts of my plumbing I wasn't so keen on having explored with his, er, horse-like ding dong." She paused. "He would *definitely* lick Cassius like a lollipop."

"Jesus," Cassius muttered under his breath.

Morgan studied Julia's garish Hawaiian shirt. "Adrianne picked that out for you?"

"Yeah," Julia said. "She found it in a thrift store."

Morgan clocked the interested stares half the male clientele and many of the women in the bar were directing at the Terrene angel. "I don't think it's working."

Julia smiled faintly. "I know."

"It's a good thing we're friends," Adrianne grumbled, stirring her drink viciously with her straw. "I haven't had sex in months thanks to you."

"What are they talking about?" Cassius muttered to Morgan.

"It's a long story," Morgan replied, taking a sip of his whiskey. "One we should only hear after more drinks."

"You've gone out several times without me and still not pulled," Julia pointed out to Adrianne. "I actually think you don't want to hook up with anyone."

Lucy and Maggie nodded wisely.

Adrianne bristled. "And what's that supposed to mean?"

"I reckon someone still has feelings for a certain wizard," Julia said.

"Yeah," Maggie murmured.

"Yup," Lucy said. A grin curved the mage's mouth as she looked past Adrianne's shoulder. "Speak of the devil."

Julia stared. "Oh. The whole gang is here."

Adrianne stiffened when she turned and saw the men who'd just entered the bar.

A nervous-looking Charlie stuck close to Bailey at the head of the group. Zach trailed behind them, the demon acknowledging several acquaintances with nods and smiles.

"What the hell is he doing here?" the sorceress muttered, glaring at Bailey.

"That should be obvious." Julia sipped her cocktail and smiled. "He's here to cockblock you."

23

THEY SQUEEZED AROUND THE BOOTH TO MAKE SPACE FOR Charlie, Morgan's thigh pressing against Cassius's leg. Cassius concentrated on his whiskey, the heat emanating from Morgan a distraction he could have done without.

Bailey and Zach returned with a round of drinks and pulled a couple of spare chairs over to the booth.

"So, how's girls' night out going?" Zach asked, taking a sip of his beer.

Adrianne frowned. Lucy grinned. Maggie sighed. Julia took another sip of her cocktail, her expression smug.

"That bad, huh?" Bailey said with blatantly fake concern.

Cassius hid a smile in his glass.

"Why are you guys here?" Morgan asked Zach gruffly.

The demon shrugged. "Probably the same reason you all are. We're casing the joint."

Charlie glanced anxiously across the bar. "Is it me, or are we drawing a lot of attention?"

"It seems everyone and their dog knows about Cassius now that that damn video went viral," Bailey muttered.

Cassius didn't have to look around to be aware of the stares being directed at their group. Having suffered the same kind of scrutiny for centuries, he was immune to them. The others were obviously not used to being observed this closely.

"By the way, did Strickland get in touch with you about that news broadcast?" Julia asked Morgan.

"We spoke this evening."

Cassius looked at the Aerial, surprised.

Julia arched an eyebrow. "And?"

"The heads of the four agencies are having a meeting about it tonight," Morgan admitted grudgingly, not meeting Cassius's eyes. "Strickland and the other three local directors are also taking part."

Cassius's grip tightened on his glass. The fact that Morgan hadn't mentioned this to him didn't bode well.

"Wait. Does this mean they don't all know about what went down in London?" Zach asked with a frown.

"Yes," Morgan grunted. "The secrecy spell Victor Sloan imposed on everyone who was present at the time bar Cassius was absolute. Now that Cassius's identity as an Empyreal has been revealed, Strickland and Victor are bringing the others up to speed on the Lancaster case."

Adrianne's troubled gaze danced between Cassius and Morgan. "What does that mean for Cassius?"

"I hope they're not thinking of doing something stupid like arresting him," Zach said grimly.

Despite the disquiet that had been with him ever since he'd found out about the video, Cassius couldn't help but feel grateful for the Argonaut agents' concerns. He frowned faintly as he stared into his drink.

Fear was a powerful emotion. It led many astray, causing them to do things they would never contemplate doing were they sound of mind. And most of those actions turned out to be mistakes they would regret for the rest of their lives.

Adrianne and the others' apprehensions were not unfounded. There was a good chance the agencies could decide Cassius was too powerful for their peace of mind.

Unfortunately for them, Cassius had meant every word he'd said to Strickland yesterday, when he'd first been brought to the bureau. Just because he hadn't fought back before didn't mean he couldn't or wouldn't. And he knew the world would come to regret it if he were to use his powers to defend himself against an all-out attack.

"They won't," Morgan said darkly. "Not if they know what's good for them."

Cassius stared at Morgan, not quite certain if he understood the meaning behind the Aerial's words correctly.

"It's been ages since I've tested myself in battle," Julia mused, downing her cocktail. "I could do with the practice."

"Same," Zach drawled.

Cassius's pulse raced as he gazed at them.

"We told you we had your back," Adrianne reminded him.

"You'll make a lot of enemies if you choose to stand at my side," Cassius said slowly.

"We don't abandon our friends," Bailey stated firmly.

"One for all and all for one," Zach said wryly, lifting his beer in a toast.

The rest of Morgan's team nodded, adamant.

Cassius's chest tightened. He blinked, lost for words.

"Why do I get the feeling we're getting roped into something we don't even understand?" Lucy muttered to Maggie.

Adrianne brightened. "Speaking of which, Lucy found traces of that poison in the bodies of the victims. It's just as Cassius suspected."

"It was in their blood and on the runes that were carved into their flesh," Lucy confirmed. "I thought it was Dark Blight at first, but I re-analyzed the samples and compared them with what I found in the sorcerer's bloodstream following Pretty Boy's suggestion. The trace was faint but definitely there. It seems they only used tiny amounts of it for fear of killing their victims before the rituals."

"How's our prisoner?" Morgan asked. "Any sign of him waking up yet?"

"Nope." Lucy shrugged. "Whatever this thing is, it's suppressed his metabolism and brain activity. The guy is practically in a coma."

Cassius shared Morgan's frustration at this piece of news. The sorcerer was their best chance of finding out who was behind all of this before any more victims fell prey to their dark scheme.

"I looked up the central Argonaut archives for any unknown poisons from other crime scenes over the past five years," Maggie said. "There was a single instance when forensics failed to identify a substance they discovered on the remains of a victim. It was a Lucifugous demon killed a year ago, during a magic hunt in the Redwoods State Park. I'm waiting for a specimen from our Santa Cruz branch."

Surprise jolted Cassius. "A Lucifugous?"

Maggie nodded. "Yes."

Morgan stared at Cassius. "What is it?"

"There was a Lucifugous in the sewers, the night I went looking for Loki," Cassius mumbled, his mind racing.

Could there be a connection between what's happening and the Lucifugous demons in the city?!

Morgan frowned. "You never said anything about finding a demon in the sewers."

"I didn't think it was relevant at the time," Cassius replied slowly. "I just presumed he was attracted by the dead body."

"What happened to it?" Adrianne asked.

Cassius clenched his fist below the table. "I...killed it. It attacked me."

"There were no signs of any other bodies down there," Bailey said, puzzled.

Cassius remained silent.

Zach grimaced. "Let me guess. This is one of those secrets you can't tell us about?"

"I'm sorry," Cassius murmured guiltily.

"What did Singh say about Carneiro's murder?" Morgan asked Julia, the look he gave Cassius indicating this conversation was far from over.

The angel frowned. "He wasn't particularly forthcoming with information. All he said was that Carneiro was a Level Three wizard working on ad hoc contracts for Hexa and that the guy got drunk and picked a fight with someone he shouldn't have behind *Occulta*. There were no witnesses to the crime. He still hasn't gotten any leads on a potential suspect."

"This place has security cameras," Cassius said.

Charlie blinked. "It does?"

He studied the empty metal supports and beams above them.

Adrianne frowned thoughtfully at a spot high up on their left. "Hmm."

"Those are pretty well concealed," Zach mused.

Bar brick and metal, there was nothing visible to the naked eye. Only a powerful magic user or otherworldly would be able to detect the sophisticated security system currently tracking everyone's movements in and outside the building, and this only if they knew where to look.

"Whoever's spell this is, they are good," Bailey said grudgingly.

Cassius's gaze flicked to the woman behind the bar. "That she is."

The others exchanged startled glances.

"Suzie Myers is responsible for the magic imbuing this place?" Morgan said with narrowed eyes.

"She's a witch," Cassius murmured. "A powerful one."

Adrianne observed the pink-haired woman behind the bar with a skeptical frown. "You could tell, just by being close to her?"

Cassius hesitated. "I also sensed her soul core when we shook hands."

Surprise widened Lucy and Maggie's eyes.

"Wait. He can *sense* people's soul cores?!" Lucy hissed sideways at Julia.

"Yeah," Julia murmured. "It's one of his party tricks."

"Singh mustn't know about the cameras," Bailey said.

"That, or he didn't find anything useful when he examined them," Zach hazarded.

"I'm willing to bet it's the former." Julia turned to Cassius. "Have you checked the back alley for the Dark Blight you picked up in the sewers?"

Cassius frowned and dipped his chin. "It was just as we were told." He glanced around the bar. "One of the people here could very well be our black-magic killer. Or someone here could know of them."

The rest of them followed his wary gaze.

"Can't you just sniff out their soul cores, like you did with us?" Bailey asked in a hopeful voice.

Adrianne made a face. "You're making him sound like a dog."

"Sorry."

"Suzie's magic is pretty good," Cassius said. "She's masking the auras in this place, so the only way for me to pick up traces of Dark Blight or black magic would be to get real close to people."

Julia arched an eyebrow. "Should we mingle?"

"Alright," Cassius said reluctantly.

"We'll take a raincheck," Lucy said. "Maggie and I have an early start tomorrow. Have fun."

The two women slipped out of the booth and took their leave.

To Cassius's surprise, Morgan and the others formed a subtle cordon around him as they headed into the crowd, Julia fighting off interest from scores of admirers, much to Adrianne's chagrin.

They spent the next half hour exploring every corner of *Occulta*, Cassius seeking out traces of Dark Blight and black magic with subtle pulses of his power. He detected several illegal magical substances and Class A drugs when they passed the restrooms on the second floor, but nothing that matched what he was looking for. They were coming back up from the basement when someone knocked into Cassius at the top of the stairs.

"Hey, watch it asshole!" the guy slurred as he whirled around.

The men with him sobered when they clocked Cassius's face.

"What?" The guy glanced from his companions'

cautious looks to Cassius. Recognition dawned in his alcohol-glazed eyes. His expression turned ugly. "Why, if it isn't Victor Sloan's little cocksucker."

24

THE NOISE LEVEL AROUND THEM DROPPED. RAGE BURST inside Morgan, bringing forth a flurry of his powers. Wind fluttered his clothes and hair as he took a step toward the guy who'd jostled Cassius, intent on giving him a piece of his mind and a taste of his fist.

"Don't." Cassius grabbed Morgan's hand and stayed his motion, his face calm. "He's not worth it."

He turned and started walking away.

The guy seized Cassius's arm. "Hey, I'm not done talking to you!"

Morgan closed his fingers on the man's wrist and squeezed. Hard.

"Yes, you are," he growled. "Now, back off!"

The closest *Occulta* patrons exchanged troubled murmurs as they watched the unfolding drama. Morgan reckoned news of the incident would spread across the bar within a minute.

The guy tugged violently on his arm and glared at Morgan. "Who the fuck do you think you are, asshole?!"

Morgan squeezed harder. It took him another second

to wrench the man's hand from Cassius's flesh, which confirmed his gut feeling. The bastard was an other-worldly. A human magic user would have caved under Morgan's sheer physical strength by now.

The guy snarled and swung his other fist at Morgan, a crimson glow flaring in his pupils. Morgan blocked the attack and forced him back until he was up against the banister.

"Hey, Gary, just let it be," one the demon's friends said anxiously, glancing at the stormy expressions on the faces of the rest of Morgan's team.

"What's going on here?" someone said briskly behind Morgan.

Morgan looked over his shoulder. Suzie appeared through the crowd. A frown wrinkled the witch's brow when she saw them. She looked past Morgan to the demon.

"Valencia, I thought I told you I'd ban you if you kept looking for fights in my place," she said flintily.

The demon sneered at Suzie. "Don't tell me you're part of this man-whore's harem too?" He glowered at Cassius. "This guy is just a loser. He should have died when he fell from the Nether!"

Cassius flinched. Fury burned Morgan.

The demon's face twisted with savage delight. "Hey!" he shouted across the bar. "I just got an idea! Why don't we rid the world of this worthless bastard right here, right now?! I'm sure we'll be rewarded generously for it. In fact, I bet we'll go down as heroes in history if we kill Cassius Black!"

Suzie swore as a wave of magic surged across the bar, overwhelming her aura spell.

"Morgan," Julia warned, reaching for her dagger.

Moran clenched his jaw. "I know."

He drew his knife and released the Stark Steel sword within. Metal hummed next to him as Zach unleashed his blades.

The three of them formed a vanguard in front of Cassius, their eyes focused on the people pressing in around them. Orbs of magic exploded in Adrianne and Bailey's hands where they'd taken up the rear, rune-covered daggers gripped tightly in white-knuckled fingers. Charlie started murmuring the beginning of a dark enchantment spell under his breath, perspiration dotting his brow.

Agitated voices rose from the crowd. The people inside *Occulta* were looking at one another and around the bar with fearful expressions.

"That magic isn't coming from them," Cassius said grimly.

Suzie startled. "What?"

Morgan glanced at the angel in surprise.

A muscle danced in Cassius's cheek. "Whoever's casting this is good, but I can taste the underlying essence of the spell." He took out his knife and released his sword, a pulse of power flaring from him and momentarily brightening his skin. "This is black magic. The same kind I detected in the sewers."

Suzie's shock turned to anger. She scanned the bar. "Can you tell where it's coming from?"

The room was starting to clear, a steady stream of patrons heading for the exit amidst a muted roar.

Cassius's tense gaze roamed the large space. "No. The spell isn't complete yet." The angel frowned. "I think he's shielding his location."

An irate voice reached them from the direction of the

entrance. "Goddammit, Julia! I thought I told you guys to stay out of my investigation!"

Zakir Singh barged through the flock of escaping people and headed briskly their way, seemingly oblivious to the panic thickening the air.

Adrianne groaned.

Suzie grimaced. "That guy is such a chump."

"Now is not a good time, Singh!" Morgan snapped. "Can't you see we have a situation?!"

Singh slowed, his contemptuous gaze finding Cassius before shifting to Morgan. "The only situation I see is that you brought an unsanctioned outsider to an active crime scene. Wait until I tell Strickland about this. He'll—"

The air trembled as the dark spell finally took form. Shadows burst into life across the bar. Morgan tensed.

Singh stiffened. "What the hell?!"

"*Warlock!*" Cassius barked.

Morgan cursed, his pulse thumping rapidly in his veins. Even he could smell the sulfurous taint suffusing the air.

Alarm widened Suzie's eyes as several humans screamed and fell to the ground, flesh blackening with purple, pustulant lesions. They scratched and clutched desperately at their throats, as if fighting for breath. Panicked shouts erupted from the rest of the crowd. Everyone made a mad dash for the exit.

Dazzling brilliance exploded next to Morgan.

For a moment, the Aerial thought Cassius had released his powers.

The light faded to pure-white orbs that pulsed violently above Suzie's palms. The witch squatted and slammed her hands on the ground, her expression furious. Bright lines humming with magic spread out across the hardwood floor from the point of contact. They merged to form complex runes that snaked up the walls of the building.

Morgan exchanged a surprised glance with the others. He could tell they'd grasped what he'd just sensed.

Suzie Myers was a Level One witch.

"Help me!" Suzie yelled at Bailey.

The wizard startled. He strode forward and dropped low next to the witch, a scowl darkening his face. Brightness flared across his fingers as he placed his hands on the floor, his defensive magic melding seamlessly with hers.

The odor of sulfur faded slightly and the shadows started to abate.

"Get these people out of here!" Suzie yelled at the doorman who'd come running inside the building. "You two, give him a hand!"

This she directed at the barkeeps crouching behind the counter.

The wizards nodded, their fearful gazes sweeping the group next to the witch before they picked up several humans writhing on the ground and carried them bodily outside. Some of the otherworldly and magic users were creeping back into the building to rescue more of the fallen humans.

A pulse of seraphic power throbbed across the chamber, making the chandeliers tremble and the lights flicker. Morgan blinked, recognition jolting him. He whirled around.

Cassius was studying the back of the bar with a frown, his black and red wings unfurled and his hands fisted tightly at his sides. His skin was aglow with the divine energy that heralded his Empyreal transformation.

"Show yourself!" he yelled. "I know you're here!"

Something flashed in the gloom. A knife darted out of

a pool of shadows and sailed across the bar in the blink of an eye.

Julia stopped the blade an inch from Cassius's heart.

"Don't!" Cassius barked when Morgan made to grab it. "It's coated in Dark Blight and poison!"

Julia's eyes blazed with light as she struggled to contain the weapon. The knife screamed, desperate to evade the Terrene angel's powers, the bloodlust of its wielder turning the air around it dark with malice.

"This thing is made out of Stark Steel!" Julia said, frustration underscoring her words. "I can't crush it!"

The world trembled and brightened as Cassius finally let his powers free.

Many of the humans and the magic users who had yet to escape the building fell to the ground retching, faces twisting in agony, unable to withstand the sheer pressure of Cassius's Empyreal form. The otherworldly among them froze, hands rising to shield their eyes from the incandescent light. Terror and awe widened their gazes when the dazzling glow faded and they finally saw the white wings flaring from Cassius's back and the crackling radiance wreathing his body.

Suzie paled. "Bloody hellfire."

"Shit," Adrianne mumbled, her legs trembling as she fought to stay upright.

Bailey gritted his teeth and stumbled over to the sorceress. "I've got you!"

He braced his body against her side and grabbed her waist.

Charlie swayed and would have dropped to his knees had Zach not caught him.

Cassius was oblivious to it all, his focus on the cursed knife attempting to pierce his heart. The lightning enveloping his Empyreal form flared around his hand as he wrapped his fingers around the handle.

"*No!*" Morgan grabbed Cassius's wrist.

"It's okay." Cassius met his gaze, his own deadly calm. "It can't hurt—"

Blinding whiteness filled Morgan's vision as his and Cassius's soul cores connected with violent resonance. He sucked in air.

Cassius gasped, his aura flickering agitatedly.

Images danced before Morgan's eyes. He blinked, struggling to make sense of the rapidly shifting snapshots. His heart thudded painfully against his ribs when he finally grasped what he was looking at.

Memories! These are memories!

Agony filled his head in the next instant, a living vice that gripped his skull and threatened to crush his brain. He groaned and let go of Cassius, nausea roiling his stomach, bringing a rush of acid to the back of his throat.

Cassius shuddered, his gray eyes reflecting the same pain. He shook his head as if to clear his thoughts, his aura gradually stabilizing. The Empyreal clenched his jaw and concentrated on where he still gripped the cursed, Stark Steel knife. Light flared as he destroyed the spell, the air trembling with power.

The evil aura enclosing the weapon slowly evaporated.

The blade clattered to the floor when Cassius released it. His vivid gaze locked on the fading shadows at the far end of the bar. A cloaked figure appeared from behind a black-magic shield. It swore and darted toward the back of the building.

"Found you, asshole!" Cassius hissed.

The Empyreal moved, his figure blurring in a burst of dazzling light.

❧ 25 ❧

THE WARLOCK CAST A BURST OF MAGIC OVER HIS shoulder as he bolted toward the corridor that led to the alley behind the bar, the hood of his outfit casting his face in shadows. Cassius batted the dark globe away with his sword.

Morgan cursed as it narrowly missed his head and smashed into the ceiling, melting metal and bricks.

"Sorry!" the Empyreal shouted over his shoulder before disappearing into the passage.

Morgan and the others followed, Suzie at their side.

The witch flashed a frown at Morgan. "Argonaut had better pay my repair bills after this!"

"Argonaut will give you a goddamn medal after tonight!"

"Medals are for fools," the witch scoffed. "I prefer cold, hard cash!"

Zach laughed at that. "A woman after my own heart."

The witch smiled at the demon despite their dire situation.

The bitter stench of dark magic and the sulfurous taint

of the warlock's powers slammed into them as they rushed through the back door and emerged into the alleyway.

"Watch out!" Julia barked.

She deflected a destructive spell with her blade. Morgan and Adrianne blocked the ones that followed.

Suzie and Bailey joined forces, their magic fusing to form a shield around them. Dumpsters blew up on their left and several craters formed in the asphalt and the opposite wall as a volley of dark spheres bounced off the defensive barrier.

Morgan scowled at the hooded sorcerers surrounding them. It was clear they intended to stop him and the others from following Cassius where the angel chased after the warlock to their right.

"We're going to have to drop our shield if we want to help him!" Suzie warned.

"Do it!" Morgan ordered.

The barrier vanished as Suzie and Bailey retracted their defensive spells.

Ozone and magic saturated the air as they engaged their attackers. It didn't take long for the Aerial to realize that their enemies were all Level Two and Three magic users.

Adrianne's offensive magic brought a sorcerer to his knees. The man snarled as Charlie's enchantment spell covered him in a dark haze. He dropped to the ground, semi-conscious.

Suzie sent a sorcerer flying toward the fire escape above her head, her eyes and hands aglow with magic. The man's scream ended abruptly as he smashed into metal.

Bailey and Zach fended off a double attack to the witch's back, the wizard's rune-covered blade humming with defensive magic while the demon cast a wave of water that lifted the sorcerers off their feet and sent them crashing into the wall across the way.

Morgan unfurled his wings and rose on the updraft, his heart thundering in his chest and his gaze locked on Cassius and the warlock. Metal glinted as he flew over a line of sorcerers. He rolled and twisted, avoiding the poison-coated daggers aimed at him. Startled shouts sounded as he shoved his attackers into the ground with a violent burst of wind. The asphalt cracked and rose around the sorcerers as they tried to rise, Julia using her Terrene powers to entrap them in a prison of rock.

A tide of sinister energy blasted into Morgan's body, slowing his flight. He swore and angled his wings to maintain his position in the air. He didn't have to look far to locate the source of the evil power he was sensing.

Blackness was pooling in the air next to the warlock where he'd stopped short of the alley's end. He ignored the sound of the police and ambulance sirens rising from the road behind him, low words tumbling from under his hood as he uttered an incantation. Morgan's eyes widened.

An inky shield was protecting the man from Cassius's attacks.

A frown darkened the Empyreal's face as he repeatedly smashed the ever-shifting wall of shadows that separated him from the warlock with his sword. Though the blade chipped the barrier, it couldn't penetrate it.

Dread twisted Morgan's belly.

Julia's wings thrummed the air with powerful beats as she came to a hover to his right. "What the hell is that?"

"I don't know."

Zach appeared on Morgan's left, his expression grim. "It has to be something out of this world to be stopping Cassius in his Empyreal form."

The warlock barked something at Cassius before reaching inside the shadowy portal next to him and extracting something from within.

Julia swore.

"Oh shit," Zach said hoarsely. "Is that—?!"

"A summoning staff!" Morgan growled.

They surged forward, knowing they had but seconds left before the warlock achieved his goal.

The hooded man bit down on his finger and smeared his blood on the ebony wood. He slammed the summoning staff on the ground, flashed a wicked smile at Morgan from under his hood, and raised a hand toward him.

A gossamer wall of shadows exploded in front of Morgan and the others. It rapidly extended above and below, curving to form a translucent sphere that enclosed the distal end of the alley where Cassius and the warlock faced off against each another.

Morgan smashed into it with a grunt and rebounded sharply backward. Julia and Zach cursed when the same thing happened to them.

Julia scowled. "What the everliving fuck is this?!"

She shot forward again. The barrier repelled her once more.

Water wrapped around Zach's blade as he unleashed his Aqueous powers, forming a coating as sharp as diamonds. The demon stabbed the insubstantial wall with his sword, putting all of his strength behind the attack. Sparks erupted on the blade's tip.

The barrier held.

Several bright balls smashed into the wall beneath them, to no avail.

"Damnit!" Adrianne panted as she slowed to a stop.

She lowered her hands and flashed a frustrated scowl up at Morgan. "This isn't magic!"

Morgan glanced over his shoulder. Adrianne and the others had incapacitated the rest of the sorcerers with Suzie's help. Charlie was staying put near the bar's exit, his attention focused on keeping their prisoners under his enchantment spell.

Suzie walked up to the barrier and placed her palms on it. She frowned, magic pulsing off her in powerful waves.

The warlock glanced her way and curled his hand into a fist. The barrier throbbed with a violent burst of dark energy. Suzie cried out, her palms reddening as the wall burned her skin. Bailey grabbed her shoulder and yanked her back.

Ice filled Morgan's veins as he watched the inky pool forming at the warlock's feet. He sensed the same dread echoing across the rest of them as they gazed helplessly at Cassius.

The Empyreal was trapped on his own inside the ethereal sphere.

26

MORGAN CAUGHT MOVEMENT AT THE MOUTH OF THE alley behind the warlock. Singh and the *Occulta* doorman turned the corner of the building housing the bar and rocked to a halt.

"Clear the road, Zakir!" Morgan ordered. "And call for back up!"

Singh nodded shakily as he stared at Cassius and the warlock, the fear widening the Argonaut agent's eyes telling Morgan all thoughts of berating them had fled his mind.

"Stay back, Samuel!" Suzie barked at the wizard doorman as he took a step forward.

A group of men and women appeared behind Singh and Samuel, guns and daggers drawn. Morgan recognized the insignias of Rosen, Hexa, and Cabalista on their jackets.

"What the hell?!" one of them gasped.

A Hexa agent cast his magic at the shadowy barrier. The pale sphere exploded harmlessly against the ethereal wall.

"Don't bother!" Adrianne shouted. "You can't get through this!"

Startled cries left the agents and Samuel when they saw what emerged from the portal the warlock had opened.

"*Go!*" Morgan yelled, his gaze locked on the skeletal figures rising from the living darkness that now connected this world to their realm. "Get as many people away from this place as you can!"

The men and women retreated.

The war demons came quietly, their leathery wings unfurling with faint cracks as they tasted the air with their forked tongues.

"Shit!" Julia growled, her hand fisting on her sword.

Morgan gritted his teeth. There were at least fifty of the creatures.

From Cassius's account, the sorcerer who had killed Joyce Almeda had only managed to summon fifteen war demons at the park. Even one of those monsters was more than enough to challenge the average angel or demon.

The war demons' crimson eyes found the Empyreal who'd shot up to hover above them.

"Kill him!" the warlock ordered.

"*No!*" Morgan screamed.

He moved back some dozen feet before rushing forward and smashing his shoulder into the barrier.

Morgan gnashed his teeth and cursed the Hells as the insubstantial wall resisted his attacks over and over again, blood soaking his T-shirt where his skin broke. Julia and Zach joined him, blades sparking off the gossamer barrier and fists striking the shifting shadows until their knuckles bled.

They didn't even put a dent in it.

Cassius's figure blurred as he engaged the war demons on the other side, his body wreathed in dazzling radiance.

A maniacal bark of laughter left the warlock where he stood watching the battle, his bloodlust making the barrier throb with malevolence.

Black blood stained Cassius's blazing sword as he sliced and carved at the enemy, the gore evaporating off the blade as quickly as it coated it. His features radiated holy wrath as he deflected the claws and fangs coming at him from every direction, his wings occasionally obscured by the enemy horde surrounding him.

The war demons' attack was relentless, as was the Empyreal's defense. Still, Morgan knew Cassius couldn't keep this up for long.

A claw cut through the protective barrier shielding the Empyreal seconds later, drawing blood on his right arm. Fangs raked his left thigh in the next instant. Cassius kicked and stabbed the war demons who'd wounded him, his face full of unwavering determination.

Despair formed a heavy knot in the pit of Morgan's stomach. He dug his fingers into the barrier and summoned all of his powers as he attempted to pry it open. The tempest that exploded around him pushed Julia and the others aside some ten feet. Adrianne cursed as her body was inexorably forced backward on the ground.

"Morgan!" she yelled, her voice full of fear.

Morgan barely felt his nails snap. He clenched his jaw.

More! I need more power, damnit!

Cassius cast an alarmed look his way.

Something darted through the air from the warlock's direction.

A gasp escaped Cassius. He froze, shock flaring across

his face and a sliver of blood bursting from his lips. He looked down dazedly.

Morgan stopped breathing.

A thin, jagged spear of pure, writhing darkness had left the warlock's hand and pierced the Empyreal's body straight through his back.

"*NOOOO!*" Morgan bellowed.

The war demons swallowed the wounded Empyreal.

A cry left Adrianne's lips. Bailey gripped the sorceress's shoulder, his face pale, an equally ashen Suzie standing helplessly beside them.

Julia cursed and rammed her shoulder repeatedly into the barrier, Zach mimicking her desperate actions.

"*I will KILL you!*" Morgan screamed at the warlock, smashing the wall with his bloodied fists. "*I swear on everything that I am, I will—*"

Brightness filled the world.

The war demons shrieked and fell back, clawed hands rising to shield their monstrous faces and wings spreading to block the divine light even as it consumed them and turned their bodies to fiery ash.

Morgan's pulse stuttered, his wings growing limp in shock. The being who floated above the alley was one he knew all too well.

It was the angel from his dreams.

Shimmering armor covered Cassius's body from the neck down. His hair had brightened to the palest gold and his eyes burned with Heaven's Light.

The warlock stumbled back at the end of the alley, his hood shifting briefly to expose part of his pale face, his mouth a rictus of fear. He cursed, gripped the summoning staff, and called forth another wave of war demons.

Cassius frowned at the fresh surge of monsters

crawling out of the portal. He closed his left hand around the weapon embedded in his bleeding body and turned his head, his bright gaze locking with Morgan's across the ethereal wall.

In that moment, Morgan knew he was looking at someone else.

Someone Cassius used to be.

"Lend me your strength, Ivmir," the angel said calmly, his voice so powerful it cracked the walls of the alley.

The name he spoke flared through Morgan's consciousness and made his heart throb with an echo of remembrance. The Empyreal stretched his right hand out toward the barrier. A pulse of seraphic energy arced from his fingertips. It shot through the air and slammed into a point directly opposite Morgan, the reverberation smashing the windows of nearby buildings.

A fracture appeared in the sphere of shadows.

Morgan scowled, slipped his fingers into the crack, and wrenched it open inch by slow inch. He managed to squeeze his hand through the gap he'd created just as the war demons swarmed the Empyreal once more.

"Cassius!"

Morgan gasped. Heat exploded deep inside as his soul core connected with Cassius's across the distance that still separated them. He had little time to fathom the why and how, his entire being filling with a power that threatened to break his bones and shatter his mind. To his everlasting surprise, his body reacted instinctively to the forceful flood, channeling it as if it had done so many times before.

A ball of black wind exploded around Morgan's hand.

He stared at it, stunned.

"Now, Ivmir!" Cassius roared, his holy blade carving

through the war demons crowding him in lightning-fast moves, seemingly oblivious to his bleeding wound.

Morgan scowled. He knew what he needed to do.

He drew his hand back sharply and smashed his dark, storm-wreathed fist into the barrier. Once. Twice. Three times.

The wall warped and cracked with a thunderous sound.

Morgan, Julia, and the others rushed through it even as it shattered around them.

"*No!*" the warlock shrieked.

A spell tumbled from his lips, the fury of his dark magic making the air throb. Another portal opened next to him. He gripped the summoning staff and stepped toward it.

Anger burned Morgan where he slashed and stabbed the war demons surrounding Cassius.

He's going to get away!

Suzie scowled. "Oh no you don't, asshole!"

The warlock cried out as a sphere of the witch's white magic struck his left leg, breaking it with a loud snap. He vanished in the next instant, the doorway closing behind him with a whisper.

The black wind around Morgan's hand extended to engulf his sword. The war demons screeched as they succumbed to his and the others' blades, Morgan felling twice as many as the others, his movements lightning fast and deadly.

Cassius finally emerged from the war demons' dying midst.

The angel met Morgan's gaze just as the last of the monsters thudded to the ground, a grateful light in his beautiful eyes. The brightness engulfing him faded, his armor disappearing and his wings slowly returning to their black and crimson colors.

Morgan caught him around the waist as he started to fall.

"What do I do?" the Aerial mumbled, staring helplessly at the spear of dancing darkness that still pierced the angel's body. "Tell me what to do!"

Cassius swallowed, his face turning ashen as the last of his Empyreal powers faded.

"Destroy it!" he gasped in a voice full of pain. "I know you can."

Morgan nodded, his vision blurring with tears. He carefully lowered Cassius to the ground, held him in his arms, and took a gentle hold of the spear. Power flared from his soul core as he concentrated.

A black tempest exploded around his fist.

The weapon screamed, a high-pitched sound sure to shatter Morgan's ear drums. He gritted his teeth and squeezed his fingers. The jagged spear slowly disintegrated in his grip, a low whine escaping it as it succumbed to the dark wind.

Cassius shuddered when it finally vanished from his body. He blinked at Morgan. His face softened. He raised bloodied fingers and caressed Morgan's cheek shakily.

"Don't cry."

Morgan turned his head and kissed the angel's hand. Cassius's arm fell and thudded limply onto the ground.

"Cassius?" Horror widened his eyes as he stared at the angel's unmoving form. "*Cassius!*"

27

"THAT THING MISSED YOUR SOUL CORE BY AN INCH," Lucy gushed, her eyes bright with unconcealed excitement.

Cassius grimaced where he lay on the bed, hand rising to touch the bandage around his midriff. Whatever it was the black spear had been made of, it had resisted his ability to heal himself. It was only thanks to a large amount of Blossom Silver and Lucy's magic that the wound had finally closed. He winced as he sat up and swung his legs over the edge of the bed, too restless to stay still.

"Don't," Morgan chided, rising from the chair beside him. "She just patched you up." The Aerial narrowed his eyes at the medical mage. "And you? Do you have to sound so morbidly happy about the fact that he nearly died?!"

Lucy grinned as she finished healing Suzie's hands, her mage magic and arcane staff redolent of Juniper. "What I'm saying is, Cassius's soul core deflected the weapon at the very last second. It was as if his body knew what the spear was and protected itself by sheer instinct. Which is pretty amazing, if I may say."

Cassius stilled and stared at her, shocked by this latest piece of news. Morgan frowned.

"After everything that went down in that alley, nothing would surprise me," Julia muttered.

The angel glanced irritably at the medical mage tending to her. Though her fists and the wounds she'd incurred while battling the war demons had healed, Lucy had insisted everyone get checked over, in case the warlock's magic had tainted their bodies.

Zach was taking things more easily where he lay on his bed, the demon enjoying the attention of the pretty mages crowding around him.

Adrianne observed him with a faintly disgusted grimace where she sat putting a cold compress on Charlie's forehead. The young enchanter had used up a significant amount of his soul-core magic to maintain his control over the sorcerers they'd captured, only retreating when another Argonaut enchanter had arrived on the scene to take over. The result was a fever Lucy predicted would last a couple of days.

The frosted-glass, sliding doors at the end of the room opened. Bailey appeared with two carrier bags.

"I got Skittles, Hershey's, Snickers, Reece's Peanut Butter Cups, Milk Duds, and M&M's," the wizard said briskly.

Julia raised a hand. "Snickers, please."

"Milk Duds," Zach said.

Bailey threw them a couple of sweets each and dropped two packets of M&M's next to Adrianne.

"Here, eat," the wizard told the sorceress. "We both know how grouchy you get when you have low blood sugar."

Adrianne narrowed her eyes at him.

Cassius caught the Hershey Bailey threw him, tore the wrapper, and bit into the confection. The fastest way to replenish soul-core energy was to consume a lot of food. Protein was best but chocolate and sweets were everyone's emergency backup, since they were easier to keep on one's person.

Zach caught Suzie's amused smile as he opened a carton of Milk Duds under the mage's disapproving frown. "What?"

"You don't look like a Milk Duds kinda guy," the witch said.

"You shouldn't judge a book by its cover," the demon drawled, popping a sweet in his mouth.

"I can see that," Suzie said.

Julia glanced curiously between them.

Lucy arched an eyebrow. "Is it me, or is there some kind of chemistry between the demon and the witch?"

Zach sighed. Suzie rolled her eyes before looking around the medical bay, a trace of unease dancing across her face.

They were on the top floor of the San Francisco Memorial Hospital, in a private ward reserved for magic users and the otherworldly. If Cassius had to guess, the witch wanted out of there and pronto. He didn't blame her.

Her newfound fame as a Level One witch wasn't something Suzie desired and she'd made that clear by keeping a low profile all these years. Regret danced through Cassius as he observed her.

Suzie caught his stare. Her face softened. "I know what you're thinking, but this isn't your fault." She shrugged. "It was going to happen sooner or later. I'm just glad I was there to help."

"Thank you," Cassius murmured.

Suzie's expression hardened slightly. "I can handle the agencies."

Morgan frowned. "You saved a lot of lives back there, including my team's. That has to count for something."

"Still, they are going to want her to register with one of them," Adrianne told Morgan. "A Level One witch walking around doing her own thing isn't something any of the agencies will abide."

Cassius fisted his hands at that, remorse twisting his belly all over again. He'd landed Suzie in a thorny position without meaning to.

Suzie straightened where she sat, her tense gaze leveled at the muted channel playing on the TV on the far wall. It showed a crowd of reporters outside the main entrance of the hospital in the top left of the screen, while the live broadcast from the news helicopter circling *Occulta* took up the main display, the flashing lights of the fire engines and police cars blockading the road bright in the darkness. Cassius clenched his jaw at the sight of the damage to the alley behind the bar and the nearby buildings.

He had no memory of what had happened when he'd transformed into the armored angel. Morgan had told him about it when he'd woken up half an hour ago. The Aerial's expression had grown troubled when he'd realized Cassius couldn't remember any of it.

All Cassius recalled was coming around to find the dark spear still embedded in his body, the war demons dead, and the gossamer wall of shadows that had separated him from Morgan and the others gone.

According to Morgan, their soul cores had resonated when Cassius was in his armored angel form, unleashing a power the Aerial wasn't even aware he'd possessed from the very marrow of his body. It was that black wind that had given Morgan the ability to break the warlock's barrier and destroy the spear impaling Cassius.

No one knew what energy the warlock had used to create the weapon and the wall of shadows. Like Adrianne had stated at the time, it hadn't been magic. But whatever it had been, Morgan's new powers had managed to defeat it, though not without taking a toll on the Aerial.

Though he'd grumbled about getting checked over, the dark circles of exhaustion under Morgan's eyes made it clear his soul-core energy had been depleted by the battle. It was only after he'd drunk the rejuvenating concoction Lucy had made for him that some color had returned to his face.

Cassius was conscious it wasn't just fatigue that had Morgan looking so haggard. He recalled the tears in Morgan's eyes before he'd fainted and the pain pulsing from the Aerial's heart and soul core across the bond that connected them.

The prospect of losing Cassius had taken Morgan to a dark place and Cassius couldn't help but feel sorrow at that realization.

I've hurt him again.

Cassius blinked, startled by the words that had come unbidden to his mind.

"You okay?" Morgan said.

Cassius swallowed and nodded, unease swirling through him. *Where did that come from?*

A commotion outside the bay drew his gaze. The sliding doors opened. Strickland stormed in, his face thunderous. Cassius stiffened.

Jasper Cobb, Reuben Fletcher, and Brianna Monroe walked in behind him, their expressions equally unhappy.

28

Morgan fisted his hands. He'd hoped they would have at least the rest of the night to themselves before the directors demanded to talk to them.

"Leave us," Strickland ordered Lucy and her mages.

Lucy frowned, her irate gaze sweeping over the trio behind Strickland.

"Go," she told her staff.

The mages glanced worriedly at the four directors as they hurried out of the bay.

"You too, cupcake," Jasper sneered.

Lucy straightened to her full five foot three inches. "These agents are my patients. I will leave when I damn well please, demon!"

Reuben sighed. "We don't have time for this."

Lucy gasped as wind wrapped around her, clamping her arms to her sides and lifting her off the ground. Morgan jumped to his feet.

Zach got to Lucy before him.

The windows vibrated as the demon unleashed his

Aqueous powers, forming a lasso of writhing water that stripped the bands holding Lucy captive. Morgan caught Lucy as she landed unsteadily on the floor.

Adrianne and Bailey were on their feet, magic flaring at their fingertips and scowls darkening their faces. Julia rose, her skin brightening with a pulse of seraphic power. Charlie sat up weakly, a frown on his feverish face.

"Don't," Brianna told them coldly.

"What the hell do you think you're doing?!" Strickland barked at the Rosen director.

"Disciplining your unruly subordinates," Reuben replied irritably. "No one in my agency would dare demonstrate that kind of lip in front of me."

"You and your agency can go fuck yourselves, asshole!" Zach hissed.

Morgan blinked, surprised by the animosity in the Aqueous demon's voice.

Strickland frowned at Zach. "There is no need to be rude, Mr. Mooney."

The demon dampened his powers. "I'm sorry, sir. I meant Mr. Fletcher and his agency can go indulge in sexual intercourse with themselves, *sir*."

Suzie bit her lip, shoulders shaking slightly as she muffled a snort.

Julia smiled at Zach. "You tell him."

Strickland's frown deepened.

"It would be better if you left, Lucy," Morgan told the medical mage. "If only to protect yourself." He looked over at Suzie. "Thanks for everything you did tonight."

A grateful expression flashed in Suzie's eyes. Morgan had created an opening for her to leave quietly. She took Lucy's arm.

"Come on, let's go."

A muscle twitched in Lucy's cheek as the witch dragged her away. She hesitated before dipping her chin curtly at Strickland and taking her leave, her cold stare lingering on Reuben. The doors hissed closed behind them.

A hush fell inside the bay.

"Should we really have allowed that witch to leave?" Brianna said. "Not only is she an important witness, we need to decide what to do about her."

"My agents will take her statement in the morning," Strickland said dismissively. "As for Suzie being a Level One witch, I've known about it for some time. She is Stephanie Keller's daughter and under the protection of my agency."

Morgan exchanged a surprised glance with Cassius and the others. *Strickland knew about Suzie?!*

Brianna stared. "She's Stephanie's daughter?"

"Yes."

The witch's expression turned thoughtful. "Hmm. I understand why you decided to take her under your wing, Francis. Still, as the director of Hexa, I would have expected the courtesy of a phone call to put me in the loop."

"The witch can wait." Jasper indicated Cassius with a jerk of his head. "We should start by interrogating that mongrel. After all, he's the reason we're in this mess in the first—"

The rest of the demon's words ended on a choked gasp. Everyone froze.

Morgan glared at Jasper where he held him up by the throat against the far wall, black wind swirling around his fingers. He'd moved before the demon had completed his sentence, the power within him rising at his furious command. It was becoming easier for him to control it. And it seemed it wasn't just strength it had gifted him with.

He'd never moved as fast as he had just done.

"I dare you to say that again!" Morgan growled at Jasper.

"Morgan," Strickland warned.

"Get a hold of yourself, Aerial!" Reuben snapped.

Morgan ignored them, his gaze locked on the demon writhing in his grip, crimson eyes filled with loathing. The wall trembled as Jasper started to unleash his Terrene powers.

"Get your hands off him." This time, Reuben's voice was ice.

The air trembled with a burst of the Rosen director's Aerial powers.

"It's okay, Morgan," Cassius said quietly. "Let him go."

Morgan clenched his teeth and slowly lowered the demon to the ground before releasing him.

Jasper coughed and wheezed, hand rising to his bruised throat. "You bastard!" He glared at Morgan. "You'll pay for that!"

"No, he won't," Strickland said in a steely voice. "I thought we'd all agreed to be civil when we decided to come here after our meeting. Antagonizing Cassius, Morgan, and everyone else in this room is not going to get you anywhere."

"Hey, why don't you turn into your Empyreal form and sock him one?" Adrianne hissed sideways at Cassius.

Julia cracked her knuckles. "We'll even pin him down for you."

"Cassius doesn't need to be in his Empyreal form to beat up that asshole," Zach scoffed.

"Yeah, he can do it with a hand tied behind his back," Bailey said.

Cassius made a face at their show of confidence.

Jasper glowered at them. "I find it hard to believe Black is as powerful as you people are portraying him to be." He looked over at Strickland. "Isn't it possible he employed an enchanter to cast some kind of twisted memory spell on you and the group who fought Tania Lancaster?"

Brianna frowned. "Victor Sloan is immune to enchantment spells. If he said that's what happened in London thirty years ago, then it happened, Jasper."

"Brianna is right," Reuben told Jasper tersely. "There's no point going over this again."

Jasper's expression grew ugly. "Sloan was Black's lover." He sneered at Morgan. "And it seems everyone's favorite dark-winged angel has tricked someone else into taking his side since coming to San Francisco."

Morgan took a step toward the demon, fury making his blood boil. "Why you—!"

Light flared across the medical bay. The air trembled with subdued seraphic power.

Cassius sighed where he stood by his bed in his Empyreal form, his white wings grazing the ceiling.

"We have more important things to discuss right now than who I'm sleeping with," the angel said, ignoring the stunned stares of the three bureau directors. "This should be enough to convince you, Jasper," he told the pale-faced demon, his tone hardening and a pulse of energy making the windows vibrate. "Now, why don't we all sit down and have that civil conversation? We need to get to the bottom of who's killing non-magic-users in the city and stealing their souls, before they achieve their goal." Cassius frowned. "If the warlock we encountered tonight is anything to judge by, we have a formidable battle on our hands."

29

"HE KNEW YOU?" STRICKLAND SAID, SHOCKED.

Cassius nodded, his expression troubled.

Morgan stared at the angel where they sat opposite one another, as surprised as everyone else in the room.

They were in a conference chamber, back at the Argonaut bureau. Lucy had grudgingly signed their release forms from the hospital an hour ago, but not until she'd spent a good few minutes giving Strickland and the other bureau directors a piece of her mind about how Morgan and his team needed a good night's rest and not a goddamn interrogation.

A dull roar reached them from the bullpen down the corridor.

The incident at *Occulta* meant dozens of magic users and humans had showed up in the hours that followed the battle to report what had happened to them. More agents had been called in from home to help take down statements and join the multi-agency investigation team on site.

Julia leaned against the door of the conference

chamber to Morgan's right, Zach and Bailey framing the wall on either side of her. Adrianne stood behind Cassius, her posture equally watchful as she studied the three bureau directors sitting with Strickland at the head of the room. Only Charlie was missing, the enchanter having been discharged home with strict instructions to rest for the next couple of days.

Reuben drummed a hand on the table. "What did this warlock say exactly?"

"That I deserve to die for what I did." Cassius hesitated. "I don't believe the attack tonight was planned. He was far too angry and out of control. I think he reacted out of rage when he realized I was at the bar."

Understanding dawned on Julia's face. "That would explain a few things. How we only felt that dark energy after the demon who picked a fight with you shouted your name across the room."

"I agree," Morgan said. "I doubt *Occulta* was the setting for the next sacrificial ritual." He clenched his jaw, recalling the warlock's furious actions in the alleyway and the eerie bloodlust underscoring his attacks on Cassius. "Do you have any idea what he was talking about?"

Cassius shook his head. "None."

Jasper scowled at Strickland. "Victor was right. You should have told us what was going on weeks ago, Francis!"

Strickland sighed. "I realize that now. And I am truly sorry. It was presumptuous of me to assume Argonaut could deal with this case on our own."

Though Strickland's words smarted, Morgan had to grudgingly agree. They needed everyone in on this, especially now that their enemy had revealed the extent of their black-magic powers.

"What's done is done," Reuben said with a dismissive

wave of his hand. "If your suspicions are correct, then this warlock and his companions are intending to use human souls to tear the Nether open. We cannot let that happen." A muscle twitched in the angel's jawline. "Another Fall would be disastrous for this world."

A despondent silence fell across the room.

"What if this isn't just about tearing the Nether open and causing a second Fall?" Cassius said quietly.

This earned him a frown from Strickland and the other directors.

"The only instance we know of black-magic users stealing human souls is Tania and her acolytes," Strickland said. "We all arrived at the same conclusion when we examined their hideout. That they needed the power of fractured souls to do something nothing else on Earth could do. And that was to breach the Nether."

Cassius grimaced and rubbed the back of his neck. "I know that's what we all believed at the time. And I still think this concerns the Nether. But I don't think it's their final goal."

"There are some things we still can't explain," Morgan added. "Why they targeted Joyce Almeda, for instance."

"Is she the woman who was killed close to the park where you revealed your Empyreal form?" Brianna asked Cassius.

"Yes. She hired me the day before to find her cat."

Jasper sneered. "You've sunk so low as to hunt down cats for humans?"

"It's better than doing your agencies' dirty work," Cassius said levelly.

The demon bristled at that. Reuben and Brianna frowned.

"Maybe your client was their next intended victim," Strickland suggested.

Morgan shook his head. "Her murder doesn't match their modus operandi. All the other victims were snatched outside their homes and vanished without any evidence of a struggle, only for their remains to be discovered a week or so later, at the site of a sacrificial ritual."

"The sorcerer we captured in Mission District was after something else," Cassius added. "Something he thought Joyce Almeda had in her possession."

Adrianne frowned. "But we didn't find anything at her property or in her past to indicate a connection to magic users."

Brianna studied Cassius with a calculating expression. "What *do* you think their purpose is? You said you believe this concerns the Nether. Why else would they want to open it, if not to cause a Fall?"

Cassius's face grew distant. "There are many things we don't remember about the Fall or the Nether. Why the tear happened. *How* it happened. But one thing we do know about the Nether. It's a portal in itself."

Reuben narrowed his eyes. "Are you suggesting they want to use the Nether as a doorway?"

Cassius shrugged. "Possibly. It's just an idea."

"A doorway to where?" Julia said guardedly.

"My best guess? One of the Nine Hells." Cassius paused. "There are plenty of objects of power in those dimensions."

"Objects of power?" Adrianne said, puzzled.

"Weapons." Morgan frowned. "Divine and demonic artifacts left over from the various wars between Heaven and the Hells."

"What?!" Adrianne gasped. "And they're just lying around the place, like dirty laundry?!"

Zach sighed. "Your impression of the Hells is kinda inaccurate."

A knock came at the door.

"It's Maggie," a voice said outside.

"Let her in," Morgan said.

Julia opened the door. Maggie came in, a laptop in hand. She glanced at Strickland and the other bureau directors with a neutral expression, before focusing on Morgan.

"I have the video recordings from *Occulta* and that liquor store you wanted me to check out."

"Thanks, Maggie." Morgan grimaced. "And I'm sorry about the late hour."

Maggie shrugged and plugged the computer into the monitor on the wall. "I was up anyway." A faint smile stretched her mouth as she glanced at Cassius. "Looks like Lucy and I missed all the fun."

Cassius sighed. "I wouldn't exactly call what happened fun."

They watched the videos from *Occulta* first, the camera feeds arranged in neat rows across the screen showing the main entrance, back doors, and every level of the bar from several angles. No one spotted the cloaked figure of the warlock entering the building at any point.

Brianna leaned forward when Suzie manifested her powers and created a defensive spell to combat the effect of the warlock's dark magic.

"Interesting." The witch glanced at Strickland. "Her magic closely resembles that of her mother."

Tension filled the room when Cassius changed into his Empyreal form and went after the warlock, the video breaking up with static under the influence of his powers. Most of the battle in the back alley was missing, the spells used by both sides having destroyed Suzie's cameras or interfered with the recordings.

"Let's watch the one from the liquor store," Morgan said.

Maggie switched folders and brought up the feed from the camera located above the front door of the shop opposite *Occulta*. It gave them an angled perspective of the opening of the alley and had captured a partial view of the battle. Only Cassius and the warlock appeared in the frames.

"Mother of God," Reuben muttered when the war demons emerged from the portal. The angel had paled slightly. He glanced at Cassius. "You killed all those war demons by yourself?!"

"Keep watching," Morgan said in a hard voice.

Cassius's eyes widened with surprise when the armored angel he'd transformed into appeared amidst a storm of light. He straightened in his chair, his knuckles whitening on the armrests before he cast a questioning look at Morgan.

"That's really you," Morgan confirmed quietly.

Strickland leveled a stunned stare at Cassius. "You had another form?"

Brianna exchanged surprised glances with Reuben and Jasper. "You mean that's not what he looked like in London?"

"No." Strickland shook his head dazedly and sat back in his chair. "He only took on his Empyreal appearance then. He didn't have that armor and his hair didn't change color."

Remorse darkened Cassius's face as he watched

Morgan lower him to the ground and grab the spear of darkness impaling his body. Strickland and the three directors studied what happened next unblinkingly.

"That's the same black wind you manifested earlier, at the hospital," Brianna said thoughtfully.

Jasper touched his throat with a grimace. The demon's bruises were already fading.

"What is that black wind?" Suspicion darkened Reuben's eyes. "I've never seen an Aerial display that kind of power."

"I don't know." Morgan hesitated, wondering if he would come to regret his next words. "But it appeared after my soul core connected with Cassius's again."

Palpable shock reverberated around the room.

"Your soul cores connected?" Strickland mumbled.

"*Again?!*" Adrianne squeaked.

Julia and Zach traded troubled glances.

Morgan looked at Cassius and registered the silent permission in the gray depths opposite him. He took a shallow breath, conscious he was about to reveal something he would have preferred to keep between himself and the Empyreal. Alas, circumstances dictated that they make everyone else aware of the truth.

Besides, they might be able to help us figure out what this new power is.

"I think Cassius and I knew each other before the Fall," Morgan said quietly.

"He's right," Cassius said. "I've felt this too."

"There's more," Morgan said. "The final form he took in that video is one I've seen in my dreams almost every night since I came to Earth."

"What?!" Cassius gasped.

Reuben stared at Morgan in disbelief. "You dream of the Fall?!"

"Yes." Morgan rubbed the back of his neck awkwardly. "Although they are more nightmares than dreams." He met Cassius's unblinking gaze. "I always see the same thing. A fair angel with shimmering, white wings and pale armor covered in blood and ash, holding a blade wrapped in Heaven's Light. His face is always obscured. All I know is that we fell to Earth together."

"But—I was on my own when I came to!" Cassius said.

"As was I." Morgan observed the dubious looks aimed at him. "Our soul cores have resonated several times since we met a couple of days ago. Tonight's was the strongest connection yet." He faltered. "I'm pretty sure that's what awoke this new power."

Morgan fisted a hand and concentrated. Warmth flared in his belly and filled his veins. A shiver of black wind burst into life around his fingers.

"Wait." Julia frowned, unease darkening her eyes as she studied the phenomenon. "Are you saying this is a power you've always possessed?"

Morgan dipped his chin. "That's what it feels like. It's as if my body remembers how to channel it."

Tense silence followed.

"There's also the name Cassius addressed you by during that battle," Zach said slowly. "Like he knew who you were too, in your past lives."

"What name?" Strickland said, confused.

"Ivmir." Morgan gazed calmly at the angel opposite him. "Cassius called me Ivmir when he was in his armored form."

30

"Who the devil is Ivmir?" Brianna said, exasperated.

"I don't know." Morgan paused. "And judging from Cassius's expression, neither does he."

Brianna turned to Reuben and Jasper. "Does it mean anything to you?"

"Never heard it," Jasper snapped.

"No," Reuben said, his wary gaze dancing between Morgan and Cassius.

Cassius's heart thudded violently as he stared at Morgan. Though he didn't know who Ivmir was, there was no denying the vestige of familiarity the name evoked. He could feel it in the very marrow of his soul.

Ivmir was the name Cassius had known Morgan by in their other lives.

Cassius frowned, nails biting into his palms. It was as if his lost memories were teasing him, offering tantalizing peeks and morsels of his existence before the Fall and snatching them away just as quickly.

"I also have the video from the night Jerry Carneiro

died," Maggie said in a guarded tone, the tech looking ever so pale after the recent revelations.

"Play it," Morgan said.

Occulta was as busy as it had been tonight, the queue lining up to enter the place extending down the road for a good hour. There were no signs of the cloaked warlock inside the bar the entire time the place stayed open.

The recordings from the four cameras covering the back doors and the rear alleyway blacked out at exactly 00:05 for a period of twelve minutes, two hours before closing time.

Morgan frowned at Maggie. "Did the equipment glitch?"

"No," the forensic tech replied.

"That's a dark concealment spell," Brianna said in a hard voice.

"And a good one," Strickland muttered.

"Carneiro's time of death was estimated to be around 00:00-01:00," Julia said.

"Do we have a recording from the liquor store for that night too?" Cassius asked.

Maggie nodded and loaded the file. "We're lucky. The owner was going to erase it tomorrow."

She fast forwarded the recording to 23:55.

At 00:05, a black SUV pulled up the street and parked near the end of the alley. A couple of guys in suits with the distinctive bulge of guns under their armpits stepped out of the front seats.

The figure that climbed out of the rear was clearly a demon.

Jasper frowned. "That's a Lucifugous."

Cassius stared. Unlike most of his kind, this Lucifugous was wearing a suit.

Only a small number of the demons had managed to integrate into human society after the Hundred Year War ended. Although abhorred by mankind for their grotesque appearance, the Lucifugous had rapidly earned themselves a reputation for being brutal fighters. After spending decades as hired fists, they'd slowly carved out an empire for themselves in the shadowy underworld of most major cities in the world.

The Lucifugous removed a sports bag from the back-seat and stepped into the mouth of the alley behind *Occulta*. He stopped, as if waiting for someone.

A cloaked figure appeared a moment later from the direction of the bar.

Cassius clenched his jaw. "That's him."

The demon and the warlock spoke for a couple of minutes, the warlock's hood revealing the lower half of his face. The warlock extracted a pouch from under his cloak and passed it to the demon in exchange for the sports bag. The Lucifugous chuckled as he examined the contents of the pouch. He extracted a small, gleaming round shape from it.

It was a gold coin.

The demon bit down on it and nodded, expression satisfied.

The warlock looked in the sports bag, smiled, and shook the Lucifugous's hand.

Something drew their attention. The warlock looked over his shoulder. The Lucifugous frowned and said something to the warlock before returning to the SUV. The warlock whirled around and headed back into the alley, his mouth a grim line and a sphere of black magic bursting to life in his hand. He disappeared from view.

"Rewind the recording ten seconds," Strickland said in a shaky voice.

Morgan frowned at the director's dazed expression while Maggie wound back the video. "What is it?"

Strickland paid him no heed, his gaze focused unblinkingly on the screen.

"There!" the director barked. "Freeze that shot."

Maggie tapped pause. Cassius's eyes widened.

Strickland rose from his seat and went over to the display. "Zoom in."

The director traced the frozen, pixelated image of the warlock with his fingers. The man's profile had been exposed for the briefest instant when he'd turned to go back into the alley, presumably to kill the wizard who'd just stumbled upon his dealings with the Lucifugous.

"Eric," Strickland murmured shakily.

Alarm danced across Brianna's face. "Wait. Do you mean—?!"

"Eric Crawford." Reuben narrowed his eyes as he studied the warlock's profile. He glanced at Strickland. "Your former apprentice."

Cassius traded startled glances with Morgan and the rest of their team, his pulse racing.

"You know this guy?" Julia asked warily.

"Eric Crawford was a Level Two sorcerer who used to work for Hexa," Brianna said in a clipped voice.

Strickland stared blindly at the warlock's profile, his face ashen.

"I met him when I was in Europe, some twenty years ago," he said. "He was only fifteen at the time and already a Level Four magic user. I took him under my wing and trained him." He met their stares, his own dismayed. "He moved to the States with me and settled in Seattle, where he started working for Hexa."

"Crawford disappeared six years ago, under mysterious circumstances." Brianna frowned at Strickland. "I remember the case well. You moved heaven and earth to find him, but not a single trace of his whereabouts was ever found. It was as if he'd vanished into thin air."

"Isn't it a little too convenient that your former apprentice is now a black-magic warlock stealing human souls?" Jasper asked Strickland suspiciously.

"Strickland wasn't Crawford's only mentor," Brianna snapped. "The head of Hexa also took him under her wing, so mind your words, Jasper."

"We need to put out an APB on this guy to all law enforcement agencies across the country," Morgan said grimly.

"If he is as powerful as you say he is, then I doubt that would help." Reuben tapped a finger on the table, his expression thoughtful. "The Lucifugous might be a better place to start."

"I agree," Cassius said with a nod, his mind going back to the Lucifugous demon he'd come across in the sewers. "Whatever was in that sports bag was worth a lot of money. I'm willing to bet it has something to do with the rituals."

"I'll run the license plate on that SUV," Maggie said.

"Thanks, Maggie," Morgan murmured as the tech shut down her computer.

Strickland observed everyone's tired expressions, his own still haggard from the shock of finding out his former apprentice was the warlock who'd attacked Cassius. "Let's call it a night."

31

It was past two a.m. by the time Cassius unlocked the door to his apartment. He flicked the light on, entered the hallway, and was greeted by a loud meow.

Loki ran over from the lounge, alarm painting a faint, crimson aura around his body. He stopped abruptly when he got within a couple of feet of Cassius. He sniffed the air cautiously, tail frozen and whiskers quivering.

"I wonder if he can smell the black magic on you," someone murmured behind Cassius.

He turned around. Morgan had entered his apartment and was closing the door, looking for all the world like he lived there.

"What are you doing?" Cassius said. "Your place is the next door down."

"I'm sleeping here tonight," Morgan declared.

"I'm not in the mood for sex," Cassius stated in an adamant tone, doing his best to ignore the alluring way Morgan's T-shirt stretched across his chest as he shrugged out of his jacket.

"Who said we're having sex?" Morgan asked innocently.

Loki came closer and rubbed his body against Cassius's legs, marking him with his scent. The demon cat hesitated before doing the same to Morgan.

Morgan squatted and scratched Loki under the chin. "See, he doesn't mind."

The cat's eyes shrank to yellow slits of pleasure and a low rumble of approval echoed from his belly.

"Traitor," Cassius mumbled to Loki. He sighed. "I'm tired. I'm gonna have a shower and sleep. Do what you want."

He turned and headed into the bedroom, his mind full of all that had happened tonight, the thread of unease dancing through him unabating. He hated that he couldn't remember the final part of his battle with the warlock, when he'd changed into his armored form. He was also still reeling from the shock of having triggered a new power inside Morgan. One that tasted eerily familiar to his senses.

Cassius had just stripped out of his clothes and was unwrapping the bandage Lucy had tied around his midriff when Morgan came up behind him.

"Here, let me."

Cassius stiffened and turned. Morgan was naked, having disposed of his own clothes in the bedroom. A shiver raced through Cassius as Morgan gently peeled the dressing away, a small frown of concentration wrinkling the Aerial's brow. He cursed under his breath when he exposed Cassius's wound.

Only a pink pucker remained of the jagged perforation. Cassius knew it would be fully healed by morning.

He gasped as Morgan leaned down and pressed his lips against the injury.

"I really thought I'd lost you."

Cassius swallowed at the way Morgan's voice trembled slightly. His chest grew tight when Morgan straightened and gazed at him fiercely, his aquamarine eyes brimming with emotion.

"I never want to go through that again."

Cassius's breath hitched in his throat as Morgan kissed his forehead and took him in his arms. He stiffened before slowly relaxing in Morgan's hold, Morgan's heat and scent wrapping him in a peaceful cocoon. They stayed like that for a moment, their hearts thundering against one another.

Morgan turned the shower on and led Cassius under the hot spray.

He washed Cassius wordlessly, his hands tender as he stroked and rubbed him clean. Cassius hesitated before reciprocating, an ache igniting deep inside him. He explored Morgan's body curiously with his fingers, marveling at the broad physique and hard muscles so different from his own. A faint frown creased his forehead as he lingered on the pale scar that cut across the Aerial's chest.

Morgan sucked in air when Cassius leaned in and kissed the faintly puckered skin where it crossed his heart.

"Is this from the Fall?" Cassius murmured.

"Ah-huh." Morgan's hands danced down Cassius's back and cupped his butt, pulling him close. "I woke up with that wound after I landed on Earth. It's never healed fully."

"Hmm." Desire heated Cassius's blood at the sight of Morgan's raging erection where it poked his belly. He stroked the thick, hot shaft lightly and smiled at Morgan's soft curse. "I thought you said we weren't gonna have sex."

Morgan bucked his hips, his fingers clenching on Cassius's ass. "I lied."

Resonance sparked hotly between their soul cores, causing them to gasp. Cassius tightened his grip punishingly on Morgan's cock and chuckled at the Aerial's lustful groan.

"Maybe I should discipline you," he said against Morgan's throat before nipping the flushed skin delicately with his teeth, enjoying this new feeling dancing between their souls.

It made him feel wanton and hungry, like he wanted to possess Morgan and be possessed by him at the same time. There was no point denying what was about to happen between them. They both needed this after tonight.

"Fuck!" Morgan hissed as Cassius started stroking him.

He turned the water off, pulled Cassius out of the shower, and dragged him into the bedroom.

"Wait!" Cassius protested. "We're gonna soak the sheets!"

An "Ooof!" left him as Morgan pushed him down unceremoniously on the bed.

"Considering everything we're about to do, we'll be drenching these sheets with more than just water shortly."

Morgan dropped a hand to his erection and gave himself a brisk rub as he searched the nightstand. Cassius's mouth watered as he stared at Morgan's thick rod. All thoughts of getting a good night's rest had fled his mind. A shudder ran through him.

He couldn't wait to have Morgan inside him.

"No condoms," Cassius breathed just as Morgan grasped the box of foils.

The otherworldly and magic users couldn't catch STDs, so the protectives were just an option. Cassius spread his legs and bent his knees, one hand dipping down his body to caress his own rock-hard cock. Morgan followed his every move as if he were a starving man at a feast.

"I want you bareback," Cassius stated brazenly, his insides throbbing.

A growl left Morgan. He climbed onto the bed, cast a bottle of lube at the sheets, and crowded Cassius with his body. Cassius welcomed Morgan's weight with a moan. He wrapped his arms around Morgan's shoulders and gripped his hips with his thighs, anchoring their bodies together. They shivered at the electrifying buzz connecting their soul cores.

Morgan rested an elbow next to Cassius, tilted his chin with his hand, and took his mouth in a torrid kiss, his touch forceful where he held his jaw. Lust tightened Cassius's belly as their tongues met in a passionate mating dance. Morgan kissed Cassius for timeless moments before working his way down his body, his hands and mouth worshiping every inch of skin he came across.

Cassius's entire world narrowed to the man making love to him with fierce passion, his own lips open on throaty gasps and sultry moans.

Morgan squeezed and tugged Cassius's nipples with his fingers before swirling and flicking his tongue across the hardened, sensitive nubs. Cassius groaned and arched his back as Morgan sucked one nipple into his hot, hungry mouth. His hand found the pillow under his head and he bit his lip to stop from crying out, pleasure shooting to his core from where Morgan suckled him, his precum making a sticky mess of Morgan's belly.

"Don't." Morgan's gaze burned Cassius as he tugged his lip free from his teeth. "I want to hear every single sound you make. Your moans, your gasps, your screams." He kissed Cassius, his expression feral. "They're all mine!"

Morgan soon shifted his attention to Cassius's quivering abs and tight belly before settling in the cradle of his body. He hooked Cassius's legs over his shoulders, fixed his hips with strong hands, and looked up at him from under his lashes, his eyes a deep turquoise. Cassius trembled as Morgan's breath danced tantalizingly across his erection.

"Can I eat you?" Morgan growled.

Cassius took his aching cock in one hand and guided it feverishly to Morgan's mouth. "*Yes!*"

A guttural cry left Cassius as Morgan closed his lips on the head of his dick and gave it a languorous suck. His heels dug punishingly into Morgan's back when Morgan took his shaft deeper into his mouth, lips and tongue working Cassius's quivering length with expert slurps and strokes.

A buzzing noise filled Cassius's head, pleasure swamping him in waves that threatened to drown him. He started thrusting up into Morgan's mouth, a sob falling from his lips at the bolts of hot ecstasy stabbing through his body, his soul core shuddering. Sweat beaded his face and chest as Morgan took his time blowing him toward his climax, taking him deep into the tight confines of his throat before drawing back all the way to his quivering tip, repeating the torturous motion over and over again.

Cassius's balls rose and his belly contracted painfully as the first wave of his orgasm tightened his spine. He clutched Morgan's head and tried to pull him off his aching cock.

"I'm gonna come!" he gasped.

Morgan let go and gently nibbled the underside of Cassius's shaft. "Then come."

He held Cassius's gaze as he swallowed his cock all the way to the root and gave him the strongest suck yet.

Cassius's climax hit him like a freight train.

His voice echoed loudly around the bedroom as he cried out and danced on the bed, his dick pulsing deep in Morgan's throat. Morgan groaned and gulped it all down, his fingers biting into Cassius's hips where he held him.

Cassius collapsed on the sheets a moment later, his heart racing and his body limp with pleasure. He hissed when Morgan let go of his spent organ, his flesh over-sensitive.

Morgan rose, grabbed a pillow, and tucked it under Cassius's lower back.

Cassius's breath locked in his throat at the sight of Morgan's erection. He looked even bigger than before, the veiny shaft a ruddy red and glistening with precum. Morgan knelt between Cassius's thighs and opened the bottle of lube.

"Spread your legs, Cassius," he ordered, smearing his palms and fingers with lube. He took his dick with one hand and started rubbing himself, his grip slick. "Show me all of you."

Desire pooled inside Cassius's belly once more, stirring his cock afresh. He flushed before grabbing hold of the back of his knees and stretching himself wide, exposing the most sinful part of him to Morgan's hungry gaze.

A savage curse left Morgan when he saw Cassius's taint and hole. He clasped Cassius's calves and pulled his legs high up in the air, lifting his lower body clear off the bed.

"Morgan!" Cassius's eyes rounded as he grasped

Morgan's intent. He buried one hand in Morgan's hair and tugged. "No! Don't—*oh!*"

The first flick of Morgan's hot tongue against his opening sent dizzying tingles through his back passage and up his spine. Cassius's fingers clenched tightly on Morgan's head, his other hand taking the bedsheet in a white-knuckled grip. He sobbed and tried to twist away when Morgan repeated the action, the sensation too raw. Morgan's hands tightened on his legs, keeping him in place.

Cassius could only moan and gasp and writhe helplessly as Morgan rimmed him, softening his entrance with his lips and tongue, sending arrows of intense pleasure shooting up his hole and echoing through his soul core. An animal expression darkened Morgan's face when he lowered Cassius's legs to the bed moments later.

He took hold of Cassius's right knee, opened his thigh wide, and pushed a lubed-up finger inside Cassius's ass. Cassius groaned, body instinctively bearing down on the intruder. Morgan thrust in and out a few times before slipping a second finger inside him, spreading him open.

Cassius panted as Morgan fucked him with his fingers. Sweat splashed down onto Cassius's belly from Morgan's face. Cassius moaned and fisted his hands on the pillow behind his head, hips undulating to meet Morgan's thrusts.

"Good! That feels *so* good!" Cassius met Morgan's torrid gaze. "Don't stop!"

Morgan scissored his fingers and stretched him wide before driving a third digit inside him. Cassius hissed and arched his head back, eyes closing tightly as he breathed through his nose, forcing his body to relax. His insides felt deliciously full despite the sting and burn of penetration.

Morgan's fingertips drew a harsh cry from his throat when they bumped his prostate.

"You like that?" Morgan growled, repeating the move.

Cassius's answer was an incoherent sound.

An untamed snarl left Morgan as he withdrew his fingers from Cassius's body. Cassius blinked his eyes open in time to see Morgan grab his meaty dick and guide it to his hole. Morgan hooked Cassius's legs around his waist, pressed his hands on either side of Cassius's body, and punched his hips forward in a hard thrust, his gaze burning bright with desire as he locked eyes with Cassius.

Cassius cried out as Morgan entered him in one smooth glide, penetrating him all the way to the hilt. Morgan stilled when he was fully lodged inside Cassius's back passage. He gritted his teeth, giving Cassius time to adapt to his girth.

"Are you okay?" Morgan gnashed, knuckles whitening on the bed.

Cassius nodded shakily, thankful for the brief reprieve. Morgan's cock stretched him to the brim, filling him deeper than he'd ever been filled. He licked his lips as his body adjusted to Morgan's thick length, the hot prickling of Morgan's penetration slowly easing. An ache replaced it, hot and hungry.

Morgan swore as Cassius clenched around him.

"Move," Cassius begged breathlessly, dropping a hand to his own trembling erection.

Morgan obliged with a fierce grunt, hips drawing back before pumping forward again. Cassius groaned, his heels digging into Morgan's lower back as Morgan set an intense pace from the get-go, his cock impaling him over and over again. He rolled his hips, matching Morgan's thrusts, welcoming the savage give and take of their lovemaking as he stroked his aching dick briskly.

Morgan leaned down and took Cassius's mouth in a passionate kiss, swallowing his gasps and cries. He lifted a hand from the sheets and took over Cassius's fingers where he rubbed himself.

"Does it feel good?" Morgan mumbled against Cassius's lips, pupils dilated and eyes a brilliant blue-green as he moved above and inside him.

Cassius sucked in air when Morgan's cock nudged his prostate, sending stars exploding across his vision.

"Can't you tell?!" he gasped, his back passage spasming greedily around Morgan's shaft.

Morgan cursed and dropped his face against Cassius's shoulder, his fingers squeezing Cassius's cock.

"*Shit!* Your hole is so tight and hot!" he groaned. "You feel incredible!"

Tension pooled in Cassius's belly and spine as Morgan thrust in deep and hard. He raked Morgan's back with his nails and gripped his waist tightly with his thighs, chasing his pleasure with breathless pants.

The way Morgan's movements accelerated told Cassius he was close to climaxing too. Morgan rose above him, his pistoning hips driving Cassius into the mattress, his self-control slipping. The bed rocked rhythmically as he threw his head back and gave in to his animal side, his neck cording as he rutted with passionate savagery, his erotic grunts heightening Cassius's pleasure ten-fold.

Heat flashed between their soul cores, drawing a cry from both of them. Cassius met Morgan's dazed stare. His vision flickered and his breath locked as his orgasm hit, his soul core trembling with echoes of fire that only intensified his pleasure. Devastating ecstasy stormed him as he came in Morgan's hand and all over their bellies, making him lose all sense of time and place. The only thing that existed in that moment was the man taking him, their bodies mating with sweet abandon.

Cassius shuddered and shook as he rode the wild waves, trusting Morgan to guide him safely to the other side. Morgan went rigid and came on a feral shout. Hot wetness gushed deep inside Cassius, Morgan's cock pulsing and throbbing as he ejaculated.

Cassius whimpered, his back passage quivering with ripples of intense pleasure, his hole growing slick with Morgan's cum. He tugged Morgan down for a kiss as the angel continued thrusting inside him, welcoming the carnal sensation of being filled with his seed.

Morgan finally slowed, hips twitching and jerking as the final aftershocks of pleasure coursing through him died down. He collapsed heavily on Cassius, his heart thundering against Cassius's chest and his heated breaths washing across his throat.

"Damn," Morgan mumbled after a moment.

Cassius chuckled weakly. "That good, huh?"

They both groaned when the movement made Cassius's passage tighten around Morgan's dick where he was still wedged inside him.

"Give me a moment to recover," Morgan panted.

Cassius blinked. "Wait. You mean you want to go again?!"

Morgan lifted his head and studied Cassius with a tolerant expression. "Oh, my sweet little lamb. You have no idea what's in store for you."

Cassius flushed, recalling the hours of lovemaking he'd overheard coming from Morgan's bedroom in the last couple of weeks.

"You're a beast," he grumbled, not quite able to hide his excitement.

Morgan nuzzled his nose and traced his stirring cock with a light touch. "I'm *your* beast."

Cassius groaned before clutching his face and kissing him, hunger stirring inside him afresh as resonance trembled between their soul cores.

They'd just finished making love for the third time and were lying limply in each other's arms when someone knocked on the bedroom door.

❧ 32 ❧

Morgan rolled off Cassius, jumped down from the bed, and grabbed his blade from the floor.

"Excuse me," a familiar voice said from outside. "Are you two quite done?"

Morgan froze.

"It's okay." Cassius had propped himself up on his elbows. He dropped back down on the bed and rubbed his hands over his face, his cheeks and ears flaming with embarrassment. "Er, could you give us a second, Benjamin?"

He tugged a sheet over his lower body and sat up.

"The cat and I have been waiting for you to stop copulating for a whole hour," the voice said sullenly. "I guess a little more time will not matter."

Morgan stormed across the room and yanked the bedroom door open.

"What are you, the Peeping Reaper?!" he snarled at the tall, skeletal figure with the scythe.

Loki yawned where he sat by Benjamin's feet, exposing small white fangs.

"I do not peep," Benjamin protested. The Reaper drew himself up to his full height, his hooded head rising well above the lintel. "Besides, watching humans mate is not exactly entertaining. All that exchange of bodily fluids is quite frankly disgusting."

"This, coming from a guy who swallows dead people's souls," Morgan muttered. He wrapped a sheet around his waist while the Reaper ducked and came inside the bedroom.

"What's up, Benjamin?" Cassius said.

The Reaper inspected the bedroom with a curious, crimson stare. "I came to inform you that one of my kind has detected the Dark Blight you showed an interest in at another location."

Morgan stiffened before trading an alarmed look with Cassius.

"Where?" Cassius asked grimly.

"In the vault of a church, in the Richmond District. He went to collect a soul nearby and smelled it."

Morgan took his phone out of his jeans and dialed Adrianne's number. Loki coiled himself around Benjamin's skeletal feet, low purrs rumbling from his belly. The Reaper's red eyes narrowed as he studied the cat.

"He likes you," Cassius said.

"Hmm," Benjamin mused.

"What?"

"He is an imp," the Reaper said.

Cassius stared at Loki, surprised. "He is?"

"Yes. A powerful one. I did not sense it until he touched me. There are not many of them about in this realm."

Cassius frowned.

Adrianne answered Morgan's call with a mumbled, "What?"

"Get everyone except for Charlie," Morgan ordered curtly. "We have a fresh lead on our case."

A pause followed. Adrianne cursed. "It's not even four a.m.!"

"We can grab some rejuvenating potions from the Argonaut mage on duty," Morgan said ruthlessly.

The sky was starting to lighten to the east when they pulled up opposite the dark, hulking shape of a Presbyterian church in the Richmond District. A faint glow lit the immense, stained-glass window taking up half the facade of the redbrick building. There wasn't any sign of activity outside it.

Morgan and Cassius stepped out of the SUV with Adrianne and Julia. Zach and Bailey joined them from the second vehicle.

"Can you sense anything?" Morgan asked Cassius.

Cassius frowned faintly. "Not yet."

"Are those fresh hickeys on his neck?" Bailey hissed at Zach.

Cassius shrugged his jacket collar up, color staining his cheekbones.

"I bet the poor guy didn't get a wink of sleep," Adrianne told Julia sotto voce.

Morgan flashed them a dirty look before meeting Cassius's annoyed stare. "What?"

"You need to stop marking me places where others can see."

Morgan's dick perked up slightly at that. "Does that mean you're granting me permission to mark you in...other places?"

He arched an eyebrow, knowing full well Cassius would

understand exactly which parts of his delectable anatomy Morgan was referring to.

Cassius frowned. "You're such an ass."

Morgan smiled. "And you love it."

The telltale flush of Cassius's ears made Morgan's smile widen. A pang of regret shot through him; he'd really been looking forward to making out with the Empyreal until daybreak.

"If you guys have finished flirting, maybe we can get on with what we came here to do?" Julia said drily.

They entered the church through a side door, Bailey using a spell to manipulate the lock open. Silence greeted them when they emerged into the nave.

Oak beams curved above their heads, forming arches that merged into a shadowy, vaulted ceiling. Rows of wooden benches spread out on either side of the central aisle that led to the altar gracing a dais on the eastern wall of the church. Votive candles flickered in shallow recesses flanking the seats, casting a soft light on the dark wood and the stained-glass window.

"Benjamin said there was a vault under this place," Morgan muttered.

A muscle jumped in Cassius's cheek as he headed up the central aisle. "It's this way."

Morgan frowned, knowing the Empyreal had finally picked up on the Dark Blight stain. They followed the angel past the altar and down the corridor leading off it, their guard up and their gazes sweeping the shadows for enemies. But it wasn't sorcerers they found in the basement Cassius led them to.

"Oh God," Bailey said hoarsely as Julia and Zach shone their flashlights around the gloomy chamber, the beams sweeping the walls and ceiling before focusing on their grim discovery once more.

Morgan clenched his jaw.

The badly mutilated bodies of a woman and a teenage boy lay in a bloodied pool on a stone altar covered in dark runes, in the center of the vault. Even Morgan could smell the Dark Blight in the black lines and symbols carved into the rock and the flesh of the two victims.

"This is a fresh kill," Adrianne observed in a hard voice.

She squatted and examined the crimson, congealing puddles around the altar.

Cassius walked over to the corpses and carefully peeled their eyelids open. "Their souls were definitely stolen."

"Call it in," Morgan told Adrianne grimly.

Adrianne straightened, her cell phone in hand.

A pulse of power made the air shiver. Everyone looked at Cassius. His skin lit up briefly, highlighting the fury painted across his face.

"They were related," he said in a voice that sent a shiver down Morgan's spine. "Mother and son."

Morgan glanced at the victims.

"How do you know?" Bailey asked hesitantly.

"Their scent." Cassius whirled away and headed for the exit, hands fisted at his sides. "And the fact that they managed to grab hold of one another as they were dying."

Morgan blinked. Cassius had seen what the rest of them hadn't clocked yet.

The woman and the boy's hands were wrapped tightly around one another.

Morgan headed after Cassius. He found him sitting on a bench in the church.

"Are you okay?"

"No. I'm angry!" Cassius snapped. "We need to find these bastards and stop them!"

Morgan sat down next to him. "We will."

Cassius chewed his lower lip. "If only I knew what Eric Crawford meant in that alley. It might lead us to him."

Morgan frowned faintly. "None of this is your fault, Cassius."

Cassius opened his mouth to voice a retort and paused. He sagged slightly before leaning into Morgan. "I know. I just—"

Morgan closed a hand around Cassius's fisted fingers. "That's one of the things I like and worry about when it comes to you. The world has given you plenty of reasons to hate it. Yet, you seem to hold its weight on your shoulders all the time."

Warmth bloomed inside Morgan as their soul cores connected, Cassius's feelings of gratitude echoing through him.

"I can't help it," Cassius mumbled. "It's a terminal condition."

Morgan tipped Cassius's chin up with a knuckle and pressed a soft kiss to his lips. "I'm sure I can find a cure."

Cassius's eyes darkened to a smoky gray.

"They are sinning in the house of God," Adrianne told Julia irritably where they'd appeared from the direction of the corridor leading to the basement.

Morgan sighed and released Cassius.

Adrianne's cell phone rang. She took the call. "Hi. What's up?" She stiffened as she listened. "Thanks, Lucy," she said in a steely voice. "We'll be there by daybreak." The sorceress's face radiated grim satisfaction as she ended the call. "Our guy from the park just woke up."

33

"What's your name and who do you work for?"

The sorcerer maintained an aloof silence, his gaze on the wall ahead.

Adrianne stepped inside his line of vision, leaned across the table, and stared him in the eye. "I said, what's your name and who do you work for?"

The sorcerer remained mute.

"Where is Eric Crawford?" Adrianne asked, relentless.

The sorcerer sneered at her.

Cassius clenched and unclenched his fists where he stood behind the mirrored window of the interrogation room. He wanted nothing more than to go in there and smash the smug look off the man's face. The image of the two victims from the vault under the church flashed before Cassius's eyes. He gritted his teeth so tightly his jaw ached.

It became clear after ten minutes of questioning that the sorcerer would continue to refuse to talk. Adrianne looked at the window and arched a questioning eyebrow.

Morgan stepped forward and pressed a button on the intercom.

"Do it," he ordered in a hard voice.

Julia straightened up from the wall she'd been leaning against to the sorcerer's right. She came up to the guy, stuck a gag in his mouth, and tied the ends behind his head.

"Bite down," she said coldly in his ear. "This is gonna hurt like a bitch."

She dipped her chin at Charlie and Adrianne and stepped back.

When he'd heard they would likely need an enchanter for the interrogation, Charlie had insisted on coming in despite his fever. Lucy had given him a rejuvenating potion to hold off the worst of it. Even so, the enchanter's face remained flushed and he shivered as he crossed the room and took the seat opposite the sorcerer.

Adrianne walked up behind the prisoner, hovered her hands on either side of his head, and concentrated. The man twitched as pale globes of magic exploded on her palms.

"Last chance," Adrianne warned.

The man spat out a garbled curse, his fingers clenching on the armrests of the chair he was shackled to.

Adrianne scowled. "It's your funeral."

The sorcerer screamed as the magic smashed into his skull and burned his mind, the sound muffled by the gag. He writhed and struggled violently in the chair, seeking to escape the offensive spell drilling into his brain. The metal restraints around his wrists and ankles bit into his skin, drawing blood.

Cassius narrowed his eyes. Although torture was not an interrogation tool the agencies sanctioned, Strickland had sought the agreement of the head of Argonaut to resort to it in this instance, if necessary.

Charlie waited until the man's eyes rolled back into his head and he was convulsing uncontrollably before casting his dark-enchantment spell.

The sorcerer groaned, a sliver of blood and spit dribbling down his chin.

Sweat broke out on Charlie's face after a minute.

"Something is resisting my magic!" the enchanter warned.

Cassius tensed.

Inky lines were spreading under the sorcerer's skin and darkening his flesh, giving it a parchment-like consistency and lending him a cadaverous appearance.

"Bloody hellfire," Bailey mumbled.

Morgan scowled and jammed a finger on the intercom button. "Stop!"

Charlie released his spell and sat back heavily in the chair, his chest heaving with his pants. Adrianne withdrew her magic, a muscle jumping in her jawline.

"There's black magic in his soul core," Cassius said in a deadly voice, his pulse racing at what he'd just sensed from the pale-faced sorcerer. "I think it's meant to kill him if he tries to reveal his secrets."

"Shit!" Zach muttered.

"Isn't there anything we can use to counter it?" Bailey asked in a frustrated voice.

Cassius hesitated before looking at Morgan, his heart full of misgivings. "The black wind. It might be able to destroy what's bound to his soul."

Morgan frowned. "Won't it kill him if I do that?"

Cassius swallowed. "That's a risk we're going to have to take."

Morgan's expression hardened. Cassius knew he'd registered his qualms.

"You'll have to guide my hand. I can't see soul cores."

The sorcerer lifted his head weakly as they entered the interrogation room. Fear widened his eyes when he saw Cassius.

"Hold him still," Cassius told Adrianne and Julia. "And remove the gag." He looked at Charlie. "Get ready. We will only get a slim window of opportunity for you to cast the enchantment spell."

Charlie swallowed and nodded.

The sorcerer's apprehension turned to angry confusion as Julia and Adrianne moved the table out of the way and fixed his body to the chair bolted to the floor.

"What the fuck are you assholes doing?!" he snarled, panic underscoring his words. "This shit is illegal!"

Cassius felt power pulse from Morgan as they stopped in front of the man. The sorcerer blanched at the sight of the swirling black wind that burst into life around the Aerial's fingers.

"What the hell is that?! No! *Get it away from me!*"

Cassius concentrated on where the man's bellybutton was. The sorcerer's dirt-gray soul core and the writhing, inky mass wrapped around it took shape a couple of inches behind it.

Cassius grasped Morgan's wrist and guided it to the man's abdomen. Heat flared inside him. "Here."

Morgan stiffened, surprise flashing across his face as his fingers slowly sank beneath the man's skin under the influence of Cassius's seraphic energy.

Julia and Adrianne's eyes rounded.

The sorcerer had gone rigid, terror painted in every line of his frozen body. "*No! Get it out of me! Get it—*"

He sucked in air and arched his back, his neck muscles cording.

Morgan grasped the sphere of shadows covering the sorcerer's soul core and clenched his fist. Darkness throbbed across the room when he yanked out the black magic. The air trembled as it disintegrated between his fingers, the shockwave shattering the window and light fixtures.

"*Now, Charlie!*" Cassius shouted.

Charlie murmured a rapid incantation, a focused frown on his pale face.

Blood burst from the sorcerer's mouth and dripped out of his nose and ears.

Cassius gritted his teeth. The black magic had eaten into the sorcerer's soul core. Now that they'd removed it, the erosion was opening up like a dam.

"Don't stop!" Cassius told Charlie as the enchanter faltered.

Crimson soaked the chair and dribbled onto the floor as the sorcerer started hemorrhaging from his lower gut. His eyes glazed over.

Charlie's enchantment spell had finally taken hold.

"Where is Eric Crawford?!" Cassius asked urgently.

"Secret!" the sorcerer gasped in a tortured voice. "No one knows but Master!"

Cassius exchanged a stunned look with Morgan and the others.

"Who's your master?" Morgan said grimly.

"Death," the sorcerer spluttered, blood frothing at his lips.

Cassius frowned. *Death could mean anything!*

"What is your Master after?" Morgan asked in a steely voice.

The sorcerer shuddered, his skin now as white as a sheet. "The Eternity Key."

He choked on another gush of his own blood, his eyes rolling back in his head.

Cassius knew the man was almost gone. He grabbed him by the shoulders. "What were you looking for at Joyce Almeda's house?!"

"The Keeper of the...Key," the sorcerer wheezed.

An ominous silence descended around them as he sagged lifelessly in the chair, the blood pouring out of him slowing as his heart stopped beating.

34

MORGAN'S NAILS BIT INTO HIS PALMS AS HE WATCHED the medical mages wheel away the body bag containing the sorcerer's remains, Cassius standing stiffly at his side.

"Shit," Adrianne mumbled, pale-faced.

She exchanged a troubled glance with Julia and Zach where they stood in the corridor. Morgan knew what was going through everyone's mind.

They'd never tortured someone to get a confession out of them before. It didn't matter that it was Morgan and Cassius who were ultimately responsible for the sorcerer's death. They'd all been in on it and would have to live with the consequences of that choice for the rest of their lives.

Strickland watched them broodingly while the cleaners mopped up the blood staining the floor of the interrogation chamber.

Bailey returned from the direction of the restrooms.

"Is Mr. Lloyd alright?" Strickland asked.

The wizard nodded. "Yeah. He threw up plenty, but he feels better for it. I've asked one of the medical mages to look him over."

Strickland observed everyone's grim expressions. "I know what just went down in that room wasn't pleasant for any of you. But we needed answers. This won't be much of a consolation right now, but that sorcerer was to be sentenced to death for the possession of a summoning staff."

Morgan stared at his right hand. He could still feel the heat of the sorcerer's soul core where he'd grasped it. The sensation had been uncanny, unlike any he'd experienced before. A single truth had echoed through him in that moment.

This must be one of Cassius's secret powers. The ability to locate and destroy a soul core.

Morgan didn't know whether to be scared or awed by that fact.

"I'm sorry."

Morgan looked at Cassius. "What for?"

Regret darkened Cassius's eyes. "For making you do that."

Morgan frowned. "You didn't *make* me do anything. It was my decision."

He could tell the Empyreal thought otherwise. He was about to berate the angel when Strickland spoke.

"Do you have any idea what the Eternity Key is?" the Argonaut director asked Cassius. "It's not something any of us have heard of before."

"No." Cassius sighed and raked his hair with his fingers, his expression tired. "But it wouldn't surprise me if it were an artifact of some kind."

"One from the Nine Hells?" Adrianne said.

Cassius nodded.

Strickland rubbed his chin thoughtfully. "It looks like whatever Eric wants to achieve, he won't be able to do it without this Eternity Key or its Keeper. You are certain there's nothing unusual in Joyce Almeda's background check?"

"Nothing," Julia said in a self-assured voice.

Footsteps sounded behind them. Maggie was walking rapidly up the corridor, Lucy on her heels.

"We found out what the poison is!" Maggie said excitedly. "The sample from Santa Cruz came in late last night."

Morgan straightened. "What is it?"

"Reaper Seed," Lucy announced grimly.

A stunned silence followed.

"Fuck," Zach mumbled.

Strickland narrowed his eyes briefly at the demon.

Morgan fisted his hands.

Reaper Seed was a banned substance and for good reason. It was a drug that could intoxicate most beings, including the otherworldly and magic users. It was fatal in high doses.

"That stuff was declared illegal on Earth over a hundred years ago," Strickland said, furious. "How the hell did these black-magic sorcerers get their hands on it?" The director frowned at Maggie. "Moreover, how did you figure out what it is?"

Maggie exchanged a guilty look with Lucy. "Hmm."

Lucy scratched her cheek and carefully avoided Strickland's gaze. "Let's just say I have a source who, er, knows his drugs."

Strickland's expression grew thunderous. "This source wouldn't happen to be a certain Dryad with a shop in Chinatown, would it?"

"Oh." Lucy blinked. "You know Brian?"

Strickland cursed.

"The Lucifugous," Cassius murmured.

They stared at him, puzzled.

"Reaper Seed might be dangerous to us, but it's a potent stimulant for Lucifugous demons," he explained. "The one I discovered in the sewers when I was looking for Loki may very well have been drawn there by the Reaper Seed on the ninth victim's body."

"Who's Loki?" Strickland asked, nonplussed.

"The demon cat Cassius rescued," Adrianne replied.

"The guy who met our warlock in the alley behind *Occulta* was a Lucifugous too," Julia pondered. "Who wants to bet that sports bag he handed over contained Reaper Seed?"

"That would make sense," Cassius acknowledged with a somber expression. "They would need a large amount for their runes and spells."

"Did you get any hit on that Lucifugous demon's number plate?" Strickland asked Maggie.

Maggie shook her head. "It was a fake. And I couldn't find anything about the guy when I ran his picture through our database."

Strickland scowled. "Damn it!"

"But I did find something interesting when the Santa Cruz specimen came in," Maggie said. "The Argonaut agent who sent it over included a copy of the incident report associated with the dead Lucifugous demon in Redwoods State Park. The body was picked up by another Lucifugous who wanted to give the dead demon his funeral rites. The name of that Lucifugous is Bostrof Orzkal."

A frown creased Julia's brow. "That thug?"

Cassius stared, puzzled. "Who's Bostrof Orzkal?"

"He's the top dog among the Lucifugous demons in the city," Strickland said unhappily. "He's also the rumored head of one of the largest crime syndicates on the West Coast."

"All the agencies in San Francisco have a tenuous agreement with him," Zach said in a hard voice.

"What kind of agreement?" Cassius said warily.

"The 'we scratch his back, he scratches ours' kind," Morgan replied in a steely voice. "We've overlooked many of his more minor crimes over the past few years in exchange for vital information on other important figures in the underworld."

He traded a guarded glance with Strickland. Knowing that Orzkal could be involved in this didn't please either of them one bit. Their past dealings with the Lucifugous had always ended up costing them more than they'd been willing to concede.

"He might be able to tell us who the other Lucifugous is," Cassius suggested. "The one who met Eric."

"And he might also know something about the Reaper Seed," Julia acknowledged grudgingly. "There's not a lot that escapes that asshole's attention when it comes to the grimy underworld of this city." She blew a heavy sigh. "Damn. Looks like we're gonna have to hunt a Lucifugous again."

Cassius frowned. Bailey and Adrianne startled. The wizard and the sorceress hadn't had any dealings with Orzkal yet.

Julia grimaced at their expressions. "I don't mean that kind of hunt. I mean laying out a trap so we can draw one out and have a little talk with them about where we can find Orzkal. You'd think the supposed head of a criminal syndicate would have a fixed abode, but this guy is like a ghost."

35

HAVING CONCURRED WITH MORGAN THAT IT WOULD BE best to wait until nightfall to lure out a Lucifugous, Strickland instructed everyone to catch up on some rest. The director offered to contact the lead historian at the Argonaut Agency's New York headquarters to delve into their archives for information about the Eternity Key and its Keeper.

"If he can't uncover anything, we may have to ask the other agencies to search their historical records," Strickland said grimly before Morgan and the others headed for the bank of elevators that would take them to the bureau's underground garage.

Morgan's gut instinct told him they wouldn't find any information on the Eternity Key or its Keeper. Only two people knew the truth. And that was Eric Crawford and the man he answered to.

The fact that the dead sorcerer had used the word 'master' had not escaped Cassius's attention, nor Strickland's when they'd reported what the man had revealed in his final death throes to the director. This case had too many echoes of London and their battle with Tania Lancaster. Morgan frowned.

Could Eric be a surviving member of Tania's sect?

A hush came over the bullpen when they reached the elevators. The agents gathered there eyed Cassius and Morgan warily. Though none of them had seen the video of the two angels fighting the warlock and his sorcerers last night, word of the battle had obviously spread from the people who'd been at the bar.

Morgan swallowed a sigh. *It must have been mentioned multiple times during the statements they took from the witnesses too.*

"Are you guys okay?" someone asked grudgingly.

Zakir Singh had risen from his desk and was crossing the bullpen toward them, a frown on his scarred face.

"Yeah," Morgan murmured.

Singh stopped in front of them.

"I'm sorry," he told Morgan gruffly. "About yesterday." Singh turned to Cassius. "And I apologize about what I said the other day. I was out of line."

He offered his hand to the angel.

Cassius shook it, unable to hide his surprise. "Um, thank you."

Morgan bit back a smile. He knew it would take the angel more time to accept that not everyone around him wanted him dead.

I'll just have to drill it into him, slowly and surely.

Thoughts of drilling other things inside Cassius made Morgan's dick twitch. He'd been interrupted making love with Cassius before he was fully satisfied last night.

Adrianne and the others boarded an elevator.

Cassius was about to follow them when Morgan grabbed his arm and tugged him toward the adjacent cabin. "Let's take this one."

Cassius gave him a puzzled look as the doors swished closed behind them. "There was space in the other—"

The rest of his words were lost on a gasp as Morgan crowded him against the wall and kissed him.

The way Cassius instantly melted in his arms made Morgan regret they were still in the Argonaut building. He wanted to strip the angel naked, lick him from his head to his delectable toes, and take him, right there and then.

Cassius blinked dazedly when Morgan reluctantly lifted his mouth off his.

"What was that for?" he said breathlessly.

"Just because," Morgan murmured, hands dipping down Cassius's back to squeeze his ass.

He pressed his lips to the pulse throbbing at the base of Cassius's throat.

Cassius shuddered and arched his body closer, a telltale bulge forming in the front of his jeans. "Just because what?"

Morgan raised his head and narrowed his eyes. "Do I need a reason to kiss and touch you?"

Cassius stared before bursting out laughing.

"What?" Morgan asked irritably.

"You're like a kid who's been told he can't play with his favorite toy," Cassius chuckled.

"Well, you *are* my favorite toy," Morgan grumbled.

Cassius's expression turned serious. "I am?"

Morgan stilled at the silent question in the gray eyes opposite him.

"Yes," he said quietly, dropping a soft kiss on Cassius's lips. "You are mine, just as I am yours."

Cassius sucked in air as Morgan pressed a hand against his belly, the resonance across their soul cores flaring hotly under his fingertips and Cassius's skin. He grasped Morgan's face and kissed him ardently, his body fairly vibrating with desire.

The elevator doors opened.

"Told you they were making out," Adrianne muttered to Julia. She narrowed her eyes at Cassius and Morgan as they reluctantly let go of one another. "We're meeting at eighteen hundred sharp. You guys better be there, fully clothed and bright and perky."

"Some parts of them are already perky," Julia observed.

Morgan and Cassius rode home in comfortable silence, Morgan's hand resting lightly on Cassius's knee and Cassius's fingers lying on top of it. They took the elevator without exchanging a word, their shoulders brushing and a slow heat charging the air between them.

Morgan had Cassius against the wall of the apartment hallway and his tongue down Cassius's throat the second Cassius closed the door. Cassius groaned, his hands clutching at Morgan's back, his lower body dancing sensuously against Morgan's, rubbing his erection against the solid thickness of Morgan's cock.

Cassius dropped a hand between their bodies and palmed Morgan's steely length. "I want to taste you!"

Morgan groaned as Cassius squeezed his cock lightly. Cassius pushed Morgan off him, whirled him around, and slammed him up against the wall.

A throaty chuckle left Morgan as Cassius nipped at his throat with his teeth. "I feel like my virtue is in peril."

Cassius licked and sucked the slight wound he'd made, his lips parting on a sultry smile. "I'm pretty sure it was my virtue that got plundered by *this*—" he grasped Morgan's dick tightly, drawing a curse from him, "—repeatedly last night."

Morgan shuddered as Cassius ran his hands under his T-shirt, exploring his chest and abs. Cassius leaned in and bit down on his left nipple, giving it a playful tug. Morgan hissed and bucked his hips, the pleasure-pain sending sharp tingles through his flesh.

A feverish expression washed across Cassius's face at the way Morgan responded to his touch. He unbuckled Morgan's jeans, drew the zipper down, and freed his erection.

"Fuck!" Morgan gasped, loving the feel of Cassius's hungry fingers on his shaft.

Cassius dropped down to his knees, grasped Morgan's meaty cock, and wrapped his lips around the broad head. Morgan gritted his teeth and fisted his hands on Cassius's shoulders while he suckled the oozing tip and whirled his tongue in light circles.

"*Jesus!*" Morgan rasped as Cassius licked him from the root of his cock all the way to the tip and back, his clever fingers working his shaft with strong strokes.

Cassius rubbed and teased Morgan to a frenzy before finally taking him inside his mouth on a lustful groan. Fire burned Morgan's veins as he watched Cassius's cheeks bulge with delicious tension, the angel swallowing him inch by slow inch, his heated gaze locked on Morgan's from under his lashes.

Morgan clasped Cassius's head with his hands and punched his hips forward.

Cassius gagged slightly, the motion driving Morgan deep into his throat. He panted through his nose and slowly relaxed his jaw, forcing his body to adapt to

Morgan's size. A hungry grunt left him as he gripped Morgan's thighs and started bobbing his head to and fro.

Morgan cursed and panted while Cassius blew him, pleasure slamming into him in forceful waves, his soul core resonating with Cassius's with sweet violence. It didn't take long for him to explode, Cassius's lips and tongue bringing him to his climax far sooner than he would have liked.

Cassius swallowed Morgan's cum like a starving man, color staining his cheekbones a bright pink and his eyes glazed with pleasure as he sucked Morgan dry.

Morgan hissed and carefully pulled his spent cock out of Cassius's mouth, Cassius chasing after him for a final lick of his sensitive tip.

"Come here," Morgan growled.

He pulled Cassius to his feet. Cassius smiled and kissed him.

Morgan locked his arms tightly around the angel, lust shuddering through him when he tasted himself on his tongue. He grabbed the back of Cassius's thighs, lifted him up, and hooked his legs around his hips as he carried him into the bedroom.

Loki raised his head from where he'd been sleeping on the bed. He jumped down and walked out, his tail flicking lazily in approval.

Morgan took Cassius into the bathroom, stripped them of their clothes, and crowded him under the hot spray of the shower. Cassius's trembling cock poked Morgan's belly as they kissed, their tongues lashing sensuously, their fevered stares locked under the pounding water. Morgan slipped a hand between their bodies and started stroking Cassius's shaft. Cassius moaned, hips canting to and fro as he chased his pleasure. Morgan worked Cassius's dick steadily, his heart thundering against his ribs and his mouth plundering Cassius's.

Cassius's scent. His heat. The stormy color of his passion-glazed eyes. The sounds he made. The musky smell of his precum.

All of it was a potent drug Morgan couldn't get enough of.

Cassius's breath hitched in his throat as he neared his climax.

"I'm gonna come!" he gasped against Morgan's mouth, his fingers clenching on Morgan's shoulders, clinging on for dear life.

Morgan stayed his hand.

"Morgan!" Cassius whimpered.

Morgan nuzzled his nose. "Ssshh. I'll make you come."

Cassius shuddered, his cock twitching in Morgan's grip. Morgan waited a full minute before slowing stroking Cassius's steely shaft once more, his movements feather light.

A groan of frustration left Cassius. Morgan brought him close to his orgasm before stopping again. Though Cassius protested, the wild look in his eyes told Morgan he was loving this game.

His climax would be all the stronger for being edged.

Morgan finally gave Cassius what he so desperately wanted. He dropped down on his knees, fixed Cassius's hips with his hands, and swallowed his cock all the way to the root.

Cassius exploded on Morgan's first suck, his throaty cries echoing against the tiles, his dick spurting powerfully inside Morgan's mouth and throat. Morgan drank most of it down with a hungry grunt.

Cassius shivered and shook when Morgan let go of his spent organ a moment later. Morgan clutched Cassius's waist and turned him around.

"Bend over and put your hands on the wall," he growled, taking a loving nip of Cassius's right butt cheek.

Cassius looked at him over his shoulder and did as he was told, his eyes bright with desire. He swallowed when he clocked Morgan's raging erection, his expression darkening with lust.

"Spread your legs," Morgan ordered gruffly.

Cassius obeyed wordlessly.

Morgan gave his rod a brisk rub, the sight of Cassius submitting to his every command making him shudder. He let go of his shaft, slipped two fingers inside his mouth, and coated them with the remains of Cassius's cum.

Cassius trembled as Morgan rose and parted his cleft, exposing the most intimate part of him, the water cascading down his back and down his ass making his hole twitch. He stiffened and cried out when Morgan plunged his fingers inside him. Cassius clenched and spasmed around him, drawing a curse from Morgan's lips.

Morgan scissored his fingers. He stretched and probed Cassius open, prepping him for his penetration at the same time he teased his prostate. Cassius's cock was soon rising proudly again, his shaft hard and his tip oozing precum.

"Enough!" Cassius reached a hand behind and grasped Morgan's wrist, his gray gaze full of desperation as he met Morgan's eyes over his shoulder. "I want you inside me! *Now!*"

Morgan's heart clenched tightly at Cassius's hungry plea, fire resonating inside his soul core. He slipped his fingers out of Cassius and brought his hungry dick to his hole.

They both groaned as Morgan pushed inside to the hilt, Cassius's body barely putting up any resistance. Cassius shoved his hips back impatiently when Morgan stilled, a whimper tumbling from his lips and his knuckles whitening on the shower wall.

Morgan grasped Cassius's hips, pulled back until the tip of his cock stretched Cassius's entrance, and punched inside with a lustful grunt.

A guttural shout left Cassius, the way his back passage clenched and spasmed around Morgan telling him he'd just come. Morgan set a slow, deep pace as he thrust in and out of Cassius's delectably snug hole, taking his time to drive them both out of their minds, his breaths falling from his lips in heavy pants and groans. Cassius moaned and gasped, his hips meeting Morgan's, matching his movements stroke for blistering stroke. He dropped a hand to his cock and started rubbing himself.

Heat throbbed between their soul cores as they made love, heightening their pleasure. Morgan could almost see the intangible thread running from his belly to Cassius's, fusing their bodies in more than just the physical sense.

It was as if their souls were rejoicing in a long-forgotten connection.

Incoherent sounds left Cassius as he neared his orgasm, his passage pulsing and throbbing painfully on Morgan's cock, his fingers moving briskly on his straining erection.

Morgan sank his teeth in Cassius's shoulder as he finally lost control.

Cassius welcomed it all, his breath hitching over and over again as Morgan's fingers dug painfully into his hips, his body embracing the savage rutting of Morgan's cock where it impaled his insides with sweet frenzy.

They came on loud shouts, Morgan spilling his seed deep inside Cassius while Cassius painted the tiles with his cum.

36

"IT'S BEEN TWO HOURS," ADRIANNE SAID.

"It's still early," Cassius murmured.

"Cassius is right," Julia told the sorceress. "Hunting takes time and patience."

They were back in the sewers under Bayview Park.

Moonlight stabbed through the metal grille high above them, the pale beams dancing down the middle of the confluence chamber piercing the ever-present shadows. Two slabs of steak glistened on the stone altar in the middle of the sunken basin. The meat had been laced with a trace of the Reaper Seed from the Santa Cruz sample Maggie had obtained. All they had to do now was wait for a Lucifugous demon to hopefully take the bait.

Adrianne made a face. "Yeah, well, you guys can keep your hunting to yourselves. I like my meat prepped and marinated, on a platter from a grocery store."

"I thought you two went camping loads when you were going out," Zach murmured to Bailey.

"Hunting was never involved," Bailey said. "Well, not

the kind we're doing right now. We hunted for lots of other stuff in the sack—*ouch!*"

Adrianne had zapped him in the ribs with her magic.

Morgan frowned. "You clowns realize silence is of the essence here, right?"

Bailey winced and rubbed his chest as he indicated the shimmering shadows around them. "Don't worry, boss. This concealment spell is soundproof too."

"That's beside the point."

A faint stirring in the air currents coursing through the sewers brought a familiar scent to Cassius's nostrils some half an hour later.

"Here he comes," he warned.

It took the others longer to detect the sulfurous taint where they crouched behind Bailey's concealment magic. A dark shape appeared in the mouth of the tunnel to the north. It stopped and lurked in the shadows for a moment, its head darting about as it sniffed the chamber.

The Lucifugous demon's stone club scraped across the concrete floor when he finally moved into the light, his gimlet eyes scanning his surroundings warily. His gaze skimmed over the area where Cassius and the others hid as he climbed down into the basin. He made his way to the altar and hesitated before probing a steak with a stubby finger.

Adrianne made a gagging noise as the demon stuck his finger in his mouth and sucked it clean.

The Lucifugous rumbled in approval, dropped his club, and grabbed both steaks. Hungry slurps and gulps echoed around the chamber as he wolfed down the meat.

Cassius could tell from his physique that he hadn't eaten for some time.

"Now!" Morgan barked.

Bailey dropped the concealment spell.

Morgan rose into the air and cast a tempest that wrapped around the surprised demon, lifting him off the ground. Julia sent the stone club flying to the other end of the chamber with a swing of her arm.

Crimson flashed in the demon's eyes, fear and anger twisting his misshapen face. A pulse of darkness exploded above them as he started to manipulate the shadows.

"It's okay." Cassius walked over to the demon, the seraphic energy emanating from his eyes and skin obliterating the mantle of darkness forming around the chamber. "We won't hurt you. We just want to talk."

The demon snarled and grunted as he struggled against the lassoes of wind binding his limbs to his body, too far gone in his terror to be reasoned with.

"Release him," Cassius said.

"Are you insane?!" Adrianne gasped. "He'll go on a rampage!"

Cassius's gaze found Morgan. "Let him go. I'll be okay."

The Aerial hesitated before obeying Cassius's command, his eyes full of unease.

The Lucifugous's feet touched the ground a moment later. The bands of wind holding him prisoner vanished. He roared and charged toward Cassius.

"Stop."

Light bloomed across the confluence chamber.

The Lucifugous demon screamed and stumbled, his vision blinded. A grunt left him as he fell to his knees, the power pulsing from Cassius driving him to the ground.

It took a moment for the radiance surrounding Cassius's Empyreal form to fade. The Lucifugous slowly lowered his hands from his eyes. He gaped at the white wings flaring high above him for a moment before hastily lowering his head to the ground, his body quaking as he prostrated himself in front of Cassius.

Cassius blinked, startled.

"Forgive me, oh Guardian of Light!" the demon quavered.

Cassius glanced at the others, too shocked to speak for a moment.

He hesitated before squatting in front of the Lucifugous. "Lift your head."

The demon stayed put, shivers racking his giant frame.

Cassius reached out and gently tilted the Lucifugous's chin up with his hand. "Lift your head, my friend."

The demon blinked, his dark eyes flaring with surprise.

Cassius retracted his powers, confident the demon would not attack. The Lucifugous gasped as Cassius's wings changed to black and red, gloom descending upon them once more as the brightness faded.

"Angel of Darkness and Blood," the demon mumbled. "Savior of my people!"

Surprise shot through Cassius once more. He sensed Morgan and the others' puzzled stares.

"What do you mean by that?" Cassius said.

"Helped my brethren across the seas," the demon replied, his voice full of awe. "Green place. Eiriu."

Cassius's eyes widened. "You mean Ireland?"

The demon nodded vigorously. He grasped Cassius's hand with both his own. "You kind. You good. You help. Kill." He pressed Cassius's fingers urgently to his chest. "Kill now!"

Cassius swallowed, memories stained with blood filling his mind.

Morgan landed beside him. "What's he talking about, Cassius?"

A muscle twitched in Cassius's jaw as he gazed at the Lucifugous.

"There was an incident on Beenkeragh Ridge, fifty years ago," he said in a hard voice. "A band of wizards and witches went hunting after a herd of Lucifugous demons rumored to be living in the area. The demons were in the middle of their birthing season at the time. Over half of them were butchered with magic spears and arrows, including the female demons and their newborn babies. I helped the rest escape."

Tears glistened in the demon's eyes. His fingers twitched on Cassius's hand. "You kind. You put end to suffering."

"What does he mean?" Adrianne asked, her face pale.

Cassius could sense her and Bailey's shock. The only people who hunted Lucifugous were human magic users and most did so because they considered the demons monsters who did not deserve to live, their hatred born simply of their distaste for their grotesque form.

Angels never participated in those hunts and neither did other demons.

Cassius struggled to keep his anger under control as he continued talking. "The demons the wizards and witches brought down didn't die straight away. They were being tortured when I returned to their den." An echo of power throbbed from his core, making the air shiver. He took a shuddering breath and contained his seraphic energy. "I put down the demons who wouldn't have survived and saved those that I could."

A deathly hush befell them.

"What did you do with the wizards and witches?" Bailey finally asked, anger underscoring his voice.

Cassius knew it wasn't directed at him but at the men and women who had attacked the Lucifugous herd, just as he could tell Adrianne's palpable fury was not intended for him.

"I buried them alive inside the mountain. It took them a week to get out of there." A grim smile curved Cassius's mouth. "I hear several of them were mauled by wolves while they were making their way back to civilization."

"Good," Adrianne said bitterly.

"Kill," the Lucifugous mumbled. He pressed Cassius's hand to his chest. "Kind. Good. Kill. Not want to be here. Not belong."

Cassius's heart clenched at the agony in the demon's voice. In that moment, he wanted to rage at everything and everyone around him. He wanted to scream at the unfairness that had been visited on those who had landed on Earth all those years ago. Those who were deemed not to belong, like the Lucifugous and him.

A hand squeezed his shoulder.

Cassius grasped Morgan's fingers, grateful for his touch and the echo of warm resonance between their soul cores. He knew Morgan could sense his fury and sorrow.

"None of us belong," Cassius told the Lucifugous quietly. "We are all far away from the place where we are meant to be." He curled his fingers around the Lucifugous's hand and gave it a gentle squeeze. "You have every right to be alive. Every right to keep on living. Do not let this cruel world take that truth away from you and your kind. You are all God's creatures. Your home may be in the Nine Hells, but it is also here, for now."

Tears fell thickly down the demon's face. Adrianne

sniffed and wiped her cheeks. Julia cleared her throat, her eyes glistening suspiciously.

"You friend?" the Lucifugous mumbled.

Cassius smiled gently. "Yes. We're friends. What's your name?"

"Akamon," the demon said shyly.

"You can call me Cassius, Akamon."

"I'm Morgan." Morgan pointed at the rest of his team. "That's Julia, Zach, Adrianne, and Bailey."

The demon's eyes glazed over slightly. "Many names."

Cassius chuckled. "You don't have to remember all of them."

"Will remember," Akamon said dutifully.

"We have a favor to ask of you," Cassius said. "Can you take us to see Bostrof Orzkal?"

Akamon startled and fell back on his behind, his eyes rounding. "Bostrof danger!"

"It's okay, we can handle him," Morgan said reassuringly.

Akamon hesitated. "Bostrof strong." He glanced from Cassius to Morgan. "But you...strong too."

"That's right," Adrianne nodded. She smacked her hand with her fist. "We can easily beat that Lucifugous up!"

"*They* strong." Akamon indicated Morgan, Cassius, Julia, and Zach. "Bostrof have you for breakfast."

He blinked at Adrianne and Bailey.

Julia snorted. Zach smiled.

⚡ 37 ⚡

A LOW ROAR ROSE IN THE DISTANCE, THE SOUND different from the drone of traffic coming from above them. Morgan exchanged a guarded glance with Cassius.

"What is that?" Adrianne said.

"It's a crowd," Cassius replied quietly.

They'd been walking underground for a good five miles, Akamon leading them confidently through the maze of tunnels beneath the city. Morgan suspected they were somewhere under Nob Hill, one of San Francisco's most affluent neighborhoods.

Tension stiffened his shoulders when Akamon headed for a watertight service door next to a weir gate. Though Cassius seemed certain the demon would lead them to Bostrof, Morgan still harbored a sliver of doubt about his intentions. The Lucifugous they'd captured and used to guide them to the crime lord in the past had never done so willingly and had always made their distrust of humans all too clear. Akamon could very well be leading them into a trap.

"You can trust him," Cassius told Morgan as they

entered the concrete corridor beyond the service door. "He won't lead us astray."

Morgan recalled the Lucifugous's reaction when he'd seen Cassius's Empyreal form and his red and black wings.

He's probably right. Akamon looked pretty starstruck.

The clamor they'd been hearing for a while became a chant when they turned a corner. A crimson light framed the end of the passage.

"Wait," Bailey muttered. "Are they saying...kill?!"

Morgan frowned.

The noise of the crowd got louder. "*Kill! Kill! Kill!*"

"They not kill," Akamon said reassuringly over his shoulder. "They beat."

Julia's hand dropped to her knife.

"Stay on guard," Morgan warned the others.

They emerged onto a metal walkway above a giant pit some hundred feet deep. Morgan stared, his pulse quickening.

"Is this a fight club?" Cassius asked Akamon warily.

The Lucifugous nodded. "*Ohomgath*. Fight. Beat."

He made a punching movement with a fist.

The space beneath them was a cavernous, concrete auditorium painted black and red. Amber spotlights and fluorescent tubing dotted the periphery and reflected off the glistening walls, turning the air the color of blood. It meant the hundreds of Lucifugous demons standing in the galleries and on the gangways could see without the light hurting their eyes.

The fighting cage in the base of the pit was enclosed in wired fencing and padded at the corners where steel beams formed its frame. A Lucifugous was rising from the floor of the ring, blood streaming from the cuts on his face, his right eye swollen and bruised. He snarled and charged the hulking demon who had brought him to the ground. His attacker moved deftly, hooked an arm around his throat, and sent him crashing into the cage wall.

The demon shook his head, stunned. A grunt left him as his attacker punched him in the gut. Blood spurted from the demon's mouth. He groaned and fell face first to the floor.

The winner placed a foot on the fallen demon's head and drummed his chest with his fists, a loud war cry erupting from his throat. The crowd responded with an even more powerful roar.

"Crusher." Akamon indicated the Lucifugous prancing proudly around the fight ring. "Bostrof champion."

Bailey grimaced. "Nice."

Akamon pointed at an opening on the lower gallery at their two o'clock. "Bostrof."

"Aren't you coming with us?" Adrianne said, surprised.

Akamon shook his head. "Me not belong."

Morgan caught the demon's hungry gaze as he stared at the crowd. It was clear a hierarchy existed even among the Lucifugous and Akamon was at the bottom of the feeding ladder.

Cassius turned to the demon. "Thank you, Akamon. I'll see you around."

Akamon nodded, his gaze gleaming. "Friend."

He turned and disappeared into the shadows of the service corridor.

Morgan narrowed his eyes as they descended the metal stairs leading to the galleries beneath them. He'd spotted several humans among the Lucifugous.

"There are angels and other demons here too," Cassius observed. "Seems Bostrof's fight club is not exclusive to his kind."

A ripple washed through the auditorium when they neared the lower level. The noise died down a fraction before resuming with an added frenzy, the eyes of the crowd focusing on Morgan, Cassius, and their team.

They reached the opening Akamon had indicated and entered a crimson-lit corridor. A black, leather-padded and metal-studded door appeared at the end. Two demons guarded it.

"Vorzof, Goran." Morgan stopped and nodded to the two Lucifugous eyeing him coldly. "I need to speak to Bostrof."

"You have appointment?" Vorzof sneered.

Morgan sighed. "You know I never have an appointment."

"No appointment, no see Bostrof," Goran grumbled.

"Boys, boys, boys." Julia shook her head and cracked her fists. "It seems you two have forgotten our last encounter."

The Lucifugous demons paled slightly.

"No appointment, no see Bostrof," Goran repeated sullenly.

Morgan glared up at the camera to the left of the door.

"Call your guard dogs off before we hurt them, Bostrof," he snapped. "We don't have time for this shit!"

A long silence followed. The door finally swung open on silent hinges.

"My, my, how impatient," Bostrof Orzkal drawled.

Cassius looked up. And up again.

Bostrof was a beast even among the Lucifugous. Standing eight feet tall and almost half as wide, the demon was a mountain of muscle and sinew. The expensive suit he wore did little to mask his strength and overpowering presence.

Morgan frowned. *No wonder he climbed to the top of the food chain so quickly. Bastard probably ate his competition.*

Bostrof's dark gaze found Cassius. A stillness came over the demon. One that made Morgan shift protectively toward the angel.

"The Guardian of Light," the Lucifugous said quietly. "What brings you to *Ohomgath?*"

Cassius frowned faintly. "Akamon called me that too." He studied the Lucifugous without fear. "What does it mean?"

A brooding look came over Bostrof. "Come, we must not speak of such things where the walls have ears."

The Lucifugous turned and beckoned them to follow him with a wave.

The room they entered was opulent and designed to intimidate. Half office, half lounge, it boasted black crystal chandeliers, leather and glass furnishings, and fur rugs. Morgan suspected Bostrof carried out many of his business dealings in the place.

Bailey stared at the gigantic TV taking up a third of the wall to their left. It showed the fighting cage in the club. Two demons were cleaning up the ring and getting it ready for the next match.

Bostrof walked over to a mini bar and poured himself a whiskey.

"Drink?" he asked, holding the bottle up.

"We're on the job," Morgan said.

He looked around the room. He couldn't help but feel someone else had been in there just a moment ago.

Cassius was staring at a beaded-glass curtain at the far end.

Bostrof followed the angel's gaze and smiled faintly.

"Your sense of perception is as formidable as the rumors say."

The Lucifugous tilted his glass at Cassius in a mocking toast before taking a sip.

Cassius frowned. "I have no idea what those rumors you speak of are, but the gossip about me is rarely flattering."

"That's because the people of this world are blind fools," Bostrof said shrewdly, his eyes gleaming. He addressed Morgan. "Now, tell me, why are you here?"

"We need information on a Lucifugous demon who was seen with a warlock who attacked us last night," Morgan said gruffly.

Bostrof's expression turned aloof. "Are you talking about the incident at *Occulta?*"

"Yes."

Bostrof swirled the contents of his glass around before gulping them down. He turned his back to them and poured himself another shot of neat whiskey.

"And what will you give me in exchange for this information?"

Morgan traded a guarded glance with Julia.

"What do you want?" he said reluctantly.

Cassius looked at him, surprised.

Morgan masked a grimace. There was no point beating around the bush with someone like Bostrof. The more straightforward their interaction with the Lucifugous, the better it would be for both parties.

Bostrof twisted on his heels and perused Morgan and Cassius over the rim of his glass. Unease danced through Morgan at the way the Lucifugous looked at Cassius. Just like before, the demon was studying the angel as if he were a prized good that would fetch a fortune on the black market.

"A fight."

The demon's quiet words echoed around the room.

Cassius stiffened. Julia, Adrianne, and the others went deathly still.

Morgan scowled. "Like hell I'm going to let you fight him!"

Bostrof smiled grimly. "You misunderstand me." His dark gaze focused on Morgan. "I meant a fight with you."

"Are you insane?" Julia snapped. "Why the hell would we agree to such an asinine demand?!"

"Because I will tell you who I think that Lucifugous is and more." Bostrof's gaze locked with Cassius's. "I will tell you where you may find the answers you seek, Guardian who does not belong to this world."

38

"Don't do this," Cassius said grimly.

"I have to," Morgan retorted stubbornly. "It's the only way we'll get some answers and prevent another sacrifice."

The clamor of the crowd echoed around the auditorium, the concrete walls amplifying the savage sounds. The excited buzz in the air was unlike the one Cassius had witnessed when they'd first walked into the fight club.

Having Bostrof personally enter the ring was evidently an unprecedented event.

Everyone seemed keen to see the mettle of the demon who ruled the biggest crime syndicate in this part of the world, just as they appeared eager to watch him fight an Argonaut agent.

Morgan handed Cassius his gun and dagger before stripping out of his jacket and T-shirt. Cassius's pulse quickened as he watched the Aerial step inside the ring, his heart full of misgivings. Adrianne, Julia, and the others had fanned out behind him on Morgan's instructions, guarded stares carefully scanning their surroundings for imminent threats.

The noise rose to fever pitch when Bostrof emerged from a corridor across the way. The Lucifugous had stripped out of his suit jacket and shirt. Cassius's eyes widened as he observed the patchwork of scars criss-crossing the demon's body.

Bostrof was no stranger to fights.

The words the Lucifugous had spoken earlier danced through Cassius's mind once more, doubling his unease. *How is it he seems to know more about me than I know myself?*

"What are the rules?" Morgan asked Bostrof when the Lucifugous entered the ring.

Bostrof shrugged. "There are no rules, bar no weapons. The first one who surrenders, or falls and stays down for ten seconds, loses."

"Fine by me," Morgan said nonchalantly. "By the way, we never did agree the full terms of this arrangement. Not that I think I'll lose, but what do you want in exchange if I do?"

"Your lover."

Cassius stiffened. Morgan froze.

A deathly hush descended on the auditorium in the wake of those two simple words.

"I am sure I will find ways for him to entertain me," Bostrof drawled, his dark gaze skimming Cassius from his head to his toes. "He is quite...appealing."

Morgan moved. Bostrof blocked his fist an inch from his head.

"You said no rules, right?" Morgan snarled, his gray wings snapping open.

Bostrof smiled. "Correct."

Morgan grunted as the demon's fist slammed into his gut.

Cassius cursed and took a step toward the cage.

Bostrof was shockingly nimble for a demon his size. He could tell Morgan hadn't seen his hand move. Morgan brought his right fist up in a swift uppercut. The demon barely shifted when it struck his chin.

"Is that all you have, Aerial?" Bostrof muttered.

His next strike smashed into Morgan's solar plexus and sent him flying across the ring and into the cage wall.

"Morgan!" Cassius shouted.

Morgan dropped down from the wired fencing and rubbed his left pec, a scowl darkening his face. Fear surged through Cassius at the sight of the red mark on the Aerial's skin.

Shit! Not even a bullet would have caused that!

"Stop holding back, damnit!" Julia barked. "He said there are no rules, so use your goddamn powers!"

Morgan nodded, his eyes full of determination. Wind swept across the fighting cage as he unleashed his Aerial ability.

Bostrof grinned. "That's more like it. Come at me, angel!"

The next few minutes were a blur of motion as Morgan and the demon engaged in fierce hand-to-hand combat. Only those with preternatural sight could keep up with their movements, while those who couldn't had the sound of fists striking flesh and the grunts of the combatants to track what was going on.

Disquiet gnawed at Cassius's insides as he stared unblinkingly at the unfolding brawl. Bostrof was holding his own against Morgan.

"That bastard is strong," Zach said grimly.

The cage trembled, Morgan and Bostrof striking the fencing hard, fists locked as they fought to push each other back. A crimson light lit the demon's eyes, his expression that of one reveling in his sheer animal side. He slipped past Morgan's defenses and landed a blow on his right flank.

Cassius gasped at the sound of bone snapping, his knuckles blanching where he clung to the fence. Morgan paled before gritting his teeth. A growl left him as he unleashed a tempest. Wind wrapped around the Lucifugous in ever-tightening bands.

Bostrof frowned, his feet lifting off the ground.

Sweat beaded Morgan's face as he carried the demon to the roof of the cage before driving him into the floor of the ring with a violent blast of his Aerial powers. Blood burst from Bostrof's mouth when he crashed into the concrete. The demon stayed still for a moment before climbing to his feet, stone and cement crumbling beneath him. He wiped away the crimson trail dripping from his lips, narrowed his eyes at Morgan, and moved.

Cassius's breath stuttered as the demon jumped onto the wired fence and ascended the cage in a flash. He leapt at the peak of his climb, his enormous body soaring toward the shocked Aerial watching him.

Morgan grunted as Bostrof smashed into him. They crashed into the cage and landed hard on the ground. Bostrof rolled, straddled the Aerial, and started pummeling him with his fists.

"*Morgan!*" Cassius yelled, alarmed.

Julia yanked her dagger from her back. "Shit!"

"No!" Zach grabbed her hand, staying her motion. "We need to see this through if we want the information Bostrof promised us."

A muscle danced in Julia's jawline.

"Zach is right, Julia," Adrianne ordered stiffly. "Stand down."

Cassius's heart clenched as he watched blood bloom from the cuts on Morgan's flesh, the angel's strong skin splitting under the demon's powerful strikes. Morgan was doing his best to block Bostrof's ferocious attacks, his teeth exposed in a snarl as he attempted to shove the demon off him.

How the hell is Bostrof so strong?! He's just a Lucifugous!

Darkness throbbed across the cage as Bostrof unleashed his demonic powers.

"*No!*" Cassius shouted, gripping the fence hard.

He was about to draw on his Empyreal powers and smash his way inside the ring when the air trembled violently.

Cassius gasped, heat flaring through his soul core.

The darkness was fading, the shadows shrinking rapidly to wrap around the angel on the floor. Morgan's eyes flared as he finally appeared amidst the inky clouds sinking into his flesh, his body absorbing Bostrof's powers while his irises darkened to a deep cobalt. Black wind exploded around him.

Faint cracks appeared in the walls of the auditorium as the Aerial climbed to his feet and rose amidst a swirling storm, carrying the surprised Lucifugous he'd effortlessly gripped around the throat into the air.

The ground shook under Cassius's feet, the power pulsing from Morgan so strong it caused him to gasp. Alarmed cries rose from the crowd, scores of figures falling semi-conscious to the ground, unable to withstand the sheer energy of Morgan's midnight-black, wind-wreathed presence.

Darkness exploded around Morgan's left hand. It shimmered and throbbed before lengthening to form a sword of pure black wind. Cassius's eyes widened, stunned by what he could feel echoing through his soul core from Morgan.

Bostrof said something, his face distorted in a grimace of pain. His hands locked around Morgan's wrist where the angel grasped his neck.

"No," Cassius mumbled, Morgan's intent suddenly clear. "Don't!"

Morgan scowled and drew his arm back.

"*STOP!*" Cassius shouted, a pulse of sheer seraphic power bursting from him and lighting up the air.

Morgan froze, the blade of shadows an inch from the Lucifugous's heart. His head moved mechanically as he turned and locked eyes with Cassius, his cobalt gaze reflecting the blazing bond connecting their soul cores in the dark depths of his pupils even as he frowned thunderously.

"Stop," Cassius whispered.

He stared past Morgan, fear twisting his heart. Morgan looked over his shoulder. He froze, shock flaring across his face.

His wings had turned midnight black, the same wind wrapping around his hand and making up the dark sword he held trembling around the inky feathers.

The gale subsided as he retracted his powers. So did the blade of shadows. The black wind finally died down and vanished with a whisper.

Relief swamped Cassius as Morgan's wings slowly brightened to gray once more.

"I surrender," Bostrof wheezed, repeating the words he'd said to Morgan.

Morgan shuddered and closed his eyes, as if struggling to control his bloodlust. When he opened them again, his irises had brightened to their usual, dazzling aquamarine.

Cassius watched breathlessly as the Aerial drifted to the ground amidst the stunned silence. He rushed inside the cage, heedless of the attempts by Bostrof's men to stop him.

Bostrof coughed and wheezed when Morgan let him go. He waved his demons away from Cassius before grimacing and rubbing his throat, Morgan's fingerprints livid, red lines on his dark skin.

"I'm sorry," he said apologetically. "I wanted to see it for myself."

"See what?" Morgan said numbly, his face still reflecting his utter bewilderment as to what had happened.

Trepidation filled Cassius all over again. He couldn't help but share the confusion and dismay he could feel resonating from Morgan's soul core. He bit his lip.

Morgan's wings turning black could very well condemn him to the same cursed life Cassius had lived these past five hundred years, shunned and ostracized by the very society and agencies that once embraced him.

He couldn't bear it if that were to happen to the Aerial.

Bostrof straightened, regret darkening his eyes.

"I wished to see for myself if your powers had indeed returned," the demon said quietly. "I did not think you would manifest them so...spectacularly."

Cassius startled. *Wait. He knows about Morgan's newly awakened abilities?!*

"Do not look so surprised," Bostrof grunted.

Feverish murmurs rose around them as the crowd began to recover from all they had just witnessed. Cassius knew news of the fight would spread through the city before morning came. He clenched his jaw, angry at the

Lucifugous demon for having provoked Morgan into displaying his hidden powers.

Bostrof sighed at Cassius's expression. "Come. There is much we need to talk about."

The Lucifugous turned and exited the ring.

39

MORGAN HESITATED BEFORE FOLLOWING BOSTROF, Cassius at his side and the others on their heels. He was still reeling from what had just taken place inside the fighting cage, the echo of the power he had unleashed shivering through his soul core.

Why the hell did my wings just turn black?!

Bostrof led them to his office, went into a bathroom, and returned with a couple of towels. He threw one at Morgan, poured two whiskeys, and handed the Aerial a glass.

This time, Morgan accepted the drink wordlessly. He sat down in a leather chair, wiped the blood from his face and body, and swallowed the contents of the glass in one gulp, his wounds healing with faint tingles.

"I don't get it," Julia told Bostrof with a heavy frown. "Why the hell did you want to fight him if you weren't serious about winning in the first place?"

"Oh, I was serious all right," Bostrof said wryly. "But I knew I would lose if Morgan revealed his true powers, now that he's managed to unlock them in this realm." He glanced from Morgan to Cassius and back. "I'm sorry for taunting you. Threatening to take Cassius was the only way I knew to rile you enough for you to show me what you are truly capable of."

Morgan stared at his right hand. He clenched his fist, a frown marring his brow. "Even I'm shocked by what I'm capable of." He shared a troubled look with Cassius. "That's the first time I've manifested a sword made from that black wind."

"Your powers will only grow from now on," Bostrof said confidently.

Morgan stared at the demon, his belly twisting with unease.

"How do you know all this?" Cassius asked in a deadly voice.

Morgan glanced at Cassius, sensing his smoldering anger. He knew Cassius was as deeply perturbed as he was by what had just transpired in that ring.

A tired expression came over Bostrof. The demon seemed to shrink slightly where he stood. "Because I did not lose all my memories after the Fall. And neither did many Lucifugous."

Morgan's pulse stuttered.

"Wait," Julia said hoarsely. "You know who you were before the Fall?!"

"Yes," Bostrof said quietly. "My recollections are hazy, but some things I am certain of." He paused. "I was the King of the Lucifugous and the rightful ruler of the Shadow Empire."

Shocked silence reverberated around the room. Morgan's stomach dropped.

Damn. No wonder he's so strong!

"The Shadow Empire?" Adrianne mumbled, the color

265

draining from her face.

"The place where ghouls and dark alchemists are said to dwell?" Bailey murmured, similarly pale.

"And Lucifugous demons." Bostrof sighed. "The Shadow Empire used to be part of the Nine Hells and the rightful home of my kind. Like the other realms where the otherworldly now dwell, it was ripped from its true place when the Nether tore."

Morgan's pulse thumped rapidly as he took this in. "Do you know our true identities?" Hope burned brightly inside him as he stared unblinkingly at the demon. "Do you know who Cassius and I really are?!"

A guarded look darkened Bostrof's eyes. "I have some knowledge of who you were before you fell, yes. Cassius more than you."

Morgan waited breathlessly, aware Cassius was as stupefied as he was.

Bostrof met Cassius's expectant gaze. "The Guardian of Light is but one of your titles. Your true name eludes me still but, like I said before, you do not belong in this world."

Cassius swallowed. "Where do you think my rightful place is?"

"In the Nether," Bostrof said quietly.

"What?!" Morgan gasped.

"The Nether?!" Julia exclaimed, exchanging a startled look with Zach.

"Yes." The Lucifugous turned to Morgan. "As for you, I believe your true self and name lie in your abilities. My wife refers to you often as the Prince of Night. Your black wings are a testament to this."

Cassius clutched the back of Morgan's chair, as if his legs had suddenly gone weak. The title Bostrof had just spoken made Morgan's soul core tremble with an echo of memory. The way Cassius paled when Morgan looked over his shoulder to meet the Empyreal's astonished stare told him he'd felt the same thing.

"Your wife?" Bailey repeated, puzzled.

The beaded-glass curtain at the end of the room clinked and parted. A woman appeared, one unlike any that walked the Earth. The rich, earthy smell of soil and unspoiled woodland suffused the air as the Nymph crossed the floor, grass and flowers blooming briefly beneath her bare feet. The gauzy dress she wore shimmered as she moved, ethereal and full of grace despite revealing her tall, naked form.

Morgan stared. He'd detected her presence briefly across his bond with Cassius when they'd entered the office the first time. Her soul core had appeared as a bright, warm ball of light in his mind's eye. She'd rapidly suppressed it to evade Cassius's senses.

She stopped in front of Bostrof and rose on her tiptoes. The Lucifugous leaned down so she could press her lips to his.

"This is Lilaia, my wife," Bostrof said proudly as he straightened, a hand on the Nymph's back.

"Hello," Lilaia murmured, a soft smile lighting up her beautiful face.

Morgan gazed at the River Spirit, her divine energy dancing across his skin in comforting waves. Nymphs were nature deities, often confused with woodland sprites and fairies. They were Goddesses of the forest who dwelled in Rain Vale, the realm of the Nymphs.

It was exceedingly rare to see one in this world.

"Er, no offense," Adrianne said leadenly. "But how the heck did you two end up as husband and wife?"

Bostrof and Lilaia exchanged a secret smile.

"I have but a vague memory of our first meeting," Lilaia said, her melodious voice ringing in Morgan's ears. She caressed Bostrof's cheek lovingly. "I was the commander of an army who invaded the Shadow Empire after a group of Lucifugous kidnapped some of my kind from Rain Vale. Full of rage and unwilling to negotiate with those I deemed to be savages, I challenged their king to a fight to the death. But Bostrof laid down his sword when he entered the battlefield and knelt at my feet. He apologized for what his demons had done, promised to return my sisters unharmed, and swore that he would punish the fiends who had brought us to the brink of war, even as I brought my blade to his heart." Her eyes brightened. "I saw his soul and who he was in that moment. How could I do anything but fall in love with him?"

Bostrof kissed her palm, his dark eyes gleaming with affection.

"Of course, I would not mind if you wanted to bring another into our bed," Lilaia added in a saccharine voice.

She arched an eyebrow at Cassius.

Bostrof paled slightly at the steel underscoring her words. "I was only jesting, wife. I have no wish to mate with the Guardian of Light."

"Thank God for that," Morgan muttered.

"Good." Lilaia patted Bostrof's face gently. She studied Cassius appraisingly. "Although, truth be told, I wouldn't have minded a taste of him myself."

Morgan stiffened.

"My love!" Bostrof protested, shocked.

"Is it pheromones?" Bailey hissed sideways to Zach. "Is Cassius oozing the stuff or something?"

Morgan cut his eyes to them.

❦ 40 ❦

A HARD EXPRESSION TIGHTENED BOSTROF'S FACE AS HE and Lilaia finished watching the videos Morgan had had Maggie send through of the fight from *Occulta* and the Lucifugous who had been in the alley behind the bar the night Jerry Carneiro died.

"Alas, it is as I surmised," Bostrof said grimly.

"Do you know who that demon is?" Cassius asked.

Bostrof hesitated before nodding. "It confirms what I suspected at the time when I heard what had happened between you and the warlock at *Occulta*. The Lucifugous on that recording is my brother, Oroak."

Cassius exchanged a shocked glance with Morgan and the others.

"Your brother?" Morgan repeated.

"Yes." An unhappy expression darkened Bostrof's face. Lilaia placed a gentle hand on his arm. He closed his fingers over hers, his features softening at her reassuring touch. "Oroak is my younger brother. He was the commander of my armies before the Fall. He was always a demon with deep ambitions, but being on Earth for so long has truly corrupted his mind and soul. I have long suspected him of trading Reaper Seed from the Shadow Empire, but I couldn't find any concrete evidence of his crimes until now." Bostrof's eyes hardened. "That drug is causing a wave of addiction through the communities of Lucifugous on the West Coast. If left unfettered, it will soon affect humans, magic users, and the otherworldly too."

"The Reaper Seed isn't just being used to turn your kind into junkies," Morgan said stiffly. "It's a key ingredient in a series of human sacrifices we've been investigating for the past two months. Our suspects are a group of black-magic sorcerers led by that warlock."

Morgan indicated the frozen image of Eric Crawford on the screen.

Lilaia frowned. "They are killing humans?"

"They are stealing their souls, to be precise," Cassius said. "We think they are attempting to harness the power of fractured souls to breach the Nether."

Lilaia paled. Bostrof scowled.

"They will cause another Fall," the Nymph murmured.

Cassius clenched his jaw, more convinced than ever that Eric and his master's goals had nothing to do with simply tearing the Nether open. "I don't think so. We captured one of their sorcerers and interrogated him. He said the warlock and their master were after the Eternity Key and the Keeper of the Key. I believe that's their true end goal."

Bostrof and Lilaia stared at one another, their eyes rounding.

Cassius's heart thumped against his ribs. "You know what it is, don't you? The Eternity Key?!"

Lilaia swallowed and dipped her head. "Like Bostrof

and his kind, the Nymphs also retain certain memories from before the Fall, although they are often just vague dreams that taunt our consciousness with distant knowledge, such as your identity as a Guardian of Light and Morgan's as a Prince of Night." The Nymph's eyes grew troubled. "All I recall is that it is a weapon of immense power. One that was used to lock Chaos, the first Primordial God, in the Abyss. Its last known whereabouts are said to be in the Seventh Hell. Only the Keeper of the Key knows its precise location in that realm."

Cassius's stomach plummeted.

"Chaos?" Morgan repeated, stunned.

"The Seventh Hell?" Julia mumbled.

Of all the Hells, the Seventh was the most vicious, its dark lands wreathed in smoke and fire and its inhabitants monsters of the worst kind.

"I heard a recent rumor about the Keeper of the Key," Bostrof said in the stunned hush. "He apparently left the Nine Hells a while ago and came to Earth. He is reputed to be wandering this realm disguised as an animal."

Cassius stiffened. "An animal?"

Bostrof nodded. "He is a very clever imp is the Keeper of the Key."

Cassius sucked in air and met Morgan's shocked stare. "Loki!"

"What?" Adrianne said, her confused stare swinging between them.

"Loki is an imp," Cassius said. "Benjamin told us so!"

"You spoke to the Reaper again?" Julia asked curiously.

Cassius's cheeks grew warm. "He, er, kinda turned up last night."

"Shit." Morgan scowled. "That sorcerer must have been after him when he went to Joyce's house!"

"Who's Loki?" Bostrof said, puzzled.

"He's a cat I rescued from the sewers a few nights ago," Cassius explained. "The one that got me into this whole mess in the first place."

Lilaia observed Cassius solemnly. "The Fates work in mysterious ways. It seems the Keeper of the Eternity Key chose you for a reason, Guardian."

"Maybe he knows Cassius is the only one who can protect him," Bostrof murmured, rubbing his chin thoughtfully.

"Do you know where Oroak is?" Morgan asked urgently.

"No." Bostrof frowned. "But I can find out." He paused. "Leave him to me. I will take care of my brother. As for Chester Moran, you should try and use the witch to locate him."

Cassius's breath locked in his throat at the name Bostrof had just uttered.

"What—what did you just say?!" he stammered.

Bostrof pointed at the frozen image of Eric Crawford. "That man is Chester Moran. Judging from what you've just told us, I am pretty certain he is Tania Lancaster's son." He narrowed his eyes at their dazed expressions. "You didn't know Tania had a son?"

"We were aware she had a child. He would have been above five at the time of the battle in London." Cassius raked his hair with a hand, his heart thundering at the enormity of what Bostrof had just revealed. "But Chester is said to have perished shortly after his mother died. The house Tania was hiding him in burned down." He stopped and swallowed. "Rosen and Hexa discovered the remains of a male child that fit his physical description in the ruins of the property. We never found out who was behind the arson attack."

"We know that man as Eric Crawford," Morgan said in a hard voice, his cold gaze on the Lucifugous and the Nymph. "He is Francis Strickland's former apprentice and was a member of Hexa until he disappeared from Seattle a few years ago. Why are you so sure he's Tania Lancaster's son?"

"Because magic never lies," Lilaia said steadily. "He carries his mother's powers in his blood and more. We crossed paths with him briefly, a long time ago, in Europe. The fact that Tania had a son was never made official, so we couldn't be certain until now."

Bostrof's gaze grew distant. "Hmm. Chester may have approached Strickland knowing full well the mage was one of his mother's murderers."

"That's what he meant," Cassius mumbled, the blood draining from his face. He met Morgan's puzzled gaze. "What he told me in the alley that night. About me deserving to die for what I did. He meant killing his mother!"

Tense silence befell them.

"What did you mean about using the witch to find Chester?" Zach said with faint frown.

"She broke his leg with her magic, did she not?" Bostrof said.

Zach's eyes widened. "You mean Suzie?"

Bostrof nodded. "Her magic is powerful. A Level One, from what I can see on the video? It should have left a trace on him if she managed to pierce his flesh. The Guardian may very well be able to sniff it out."

He indicated Cassius.

Cassius blinked. "I may?"

Lilaia smiled. "It seems you are still not aware of all that you can do."

"He's an Empyreal, can summon Reapers, can see and destroy soul cores, and can awaken latent powers," Adrianne mumbled in the silence that followed, counting on her fingers. "And he can also apparently detect magical remains and is some powerful guardian of sorts." She stared at Morgan and cocked a thumb at Cassius. "You should marry him."

Morgan rose from his chair. "He's already mine. Putting a ring on his finger is neither here nor there."

Cassius narrowed his eyes, annoyed. "Since when was I yours?"

Morgan gaped and spluttered. Bostrof patted the Aerial lightly on the back, causing him to stumble forward a couple of steps.

The demon's expression had turned sympathetic. "The road to love is a thorny one, my friend."

Morgan scowled. "Who said we were friends? You've been busting my balls non-stop for the past eight years!"

Bostrof sighed. "That was just business. And you're hurting my feelings."

"Do you know the name Ivmir?" Cassius asked the couple.

Bostrof and Lilaia glanced at one another, puzzled.

"It is not a name we are familiar with," Lilaia said. "Why do you ask?"

"It's what I called Morgan when I was in that armored form in the alley," Cassius said.

Morgan explained how he'd been plagued by visions of Cassius in his dreams since he fell to Earth and how their soul cores had resonated since they met.

Lilaia studied them solemnly. "Your bond is truly special."

"You said you would tell me where I might find answers," Cassius said in the hush that followed, his gaze on Bostrof.

"The Spirit Realm," the Lucifugous murmured. "If there are any who recall what happened before the Fall, they will be there. That's if you can get to the place."

Cassius's pulse quickened. He glanced at Morgan and saw his own surprise reflected in his blue eyes.

The Spirit Realm was the reputed home of the Gods of the Underworld and other lesser spirits. None had traveled there since the Fall and neither had its inhabitants ever set foot on Earth.

"Who sits on your throne?" Cassius asked the demon as they got ready to leave. "Now that you are no longer king?"

"Therreg," Bostrof said with a faint frown. "I believe him to be a former subordinate of mine, one who was not ripped from our realm when the Nether tore. From the rumors that have reached my ears, he is drunk on power and addicted to Reaper Seed himself."

"Can't you just reclaim the Shadow Empire as your own?" Bailey said curiously.

"Few can travel between the realms at will," Bostrof replied sedately. "Otherwise, the Fallen would have left Earth a long time ago, even if it was to return to a watered-down version of their true homes. If I were to reclaim the Shadow Empire, most of my people would not be able to follow." He smiled at Lilaia. "A king is nothing without his subjects."

Lilaia clasped his hand, her expression loving.

They were about to walk out the door when Cassius stopped and turned. "I have a favor to ask of you."

Bostrof and Lilaia shared a surprised glance.

"We will grant your wish if it is within our powers to do so," the demon murmured.

The Nymph dipped her chin regally.

"There's a Lucifugous who lives in the sewers close to Bayview Park. His name is Akamon. Can you take him under your wing?"

Bostrof's expression grew guarded. "Why? What is he to you?"

"He's a friend," Cassius said.

"Your kindness will be your downfall, Guardian," Lilaia murmured after a pause.

Cassius smiled faintly. "But at least I will remain true to myself."

Lilaia's lips curved in an answering smile, her eyes full of sadness.

Bostrof dipped his chin. "He will be taken care of. Now, go."

MORGAN AND CASSIUS SLOWED AS THEY APPROACHED Cassius's apartment, the sound of their footsteps dampened by carpet.

The front door was ajar and hanging off its hinges.

"Argonaut definitely did *not* do that," Adrianne murmured behind them.

The sorceress drew her gun, the others following suit.

They'd driven straight to Mission Bay and Cassius's place after they'd left Bostrof's club, eager to secure Chester Moran and his sect's apparent primary target.

Julia indicated Zach. "We'll take the outside."

Morgan nodded, apprehension coursing through him.

They waited until Julia and the demon had taken up position on the terrace before storming the apartment fast and low. But they didn't find any enemies nor a trace of the demon cat inside.

The place was empty, the stillness inside absolute.

Burn marks scorched the walls and floors of the living area and the bedroom, as if a fierce battle had taken place. The smell of sulfur still stained the air, the currents shifting agitatedly in the breeze blowing in through the terrace doors.

"Whoever they were, they're long gone," Julia said briskly as she and Zach returned from inspecting the exterior. "We can't find any trace of them outside the building."

"Where's the cat?" Zach asked, glancing around.

"They've taken him," Adrianne said grimly.

Morgan looked over at Cassius.

The angel was standing in the middle of his living room, his hands fisted at his sides and his face locked in a furious scowl.

"You think Loki did this?" Morgan asked quietly. "Fought them off?"

A muscle jumped in Cassius's cheek. "I've never seen him engage in battle. But he must have done something to evade them for so long. That cat is a devious little bastard."

He stormed toward the exit.

"Where are you going?" Morgan said, bewildered.

"To find that stupid imp and teach him some manners!" Cassius snapped over his shoulder. "And he's grounded for the rest of his life!"

Bailey made a face. "I get the feeling the Keeper of the Eternity Key is going to regret choosing Cassius as his master."

Morgan sighed and followed the irate angel.

Dawn was breaking across the city by the time they turned up outside *Occulta*. Suzie opened the private door next to the bar with a scowl, Cassius having pressed the buzzer for her apartment a gazillion times.

"What?!" she snapped.

Morgan and the others stared.

Suzie was wearing a pink T-shirt that matched her hair and came to mid-thigh. The words across it proclaimed that witches ruled.

Zach stared at the fuzzy demon-rabbit slip-ons adorning the witch's feet. "I like the socks."

He raked her figure with his blue gaze, making zero effort to hide his interest. Suzie flushed and tugged her T-shirt lower.

"What's going on?" she muttered.

"Can we come in?" Cassius said.

Suzie sighed before opening the door wider. They followed her upstairs to an airy, open-plan apartment with a mezzanine level.

Suzie indicated the L-shaped couch that took up most of her lounge and plopped down on a Chesterfield sofa. "What's up?"

She crossed her legs and hugged a colorful pillow to her chest, her gaze darting self-consciously to Zach.

The Aqueous demon smiled faintly.

Cassius looked questioningly at Morgan, seeking his permission. Though Morgan could still sense his ire, he'd calmed down somewhat on their drive over. He nodded.

Cassius updated Suzie on their most recent findings under the church in Richmond District, their interrogation of the black-magic sorcerer at the Argonaut bureau, their trap to lure a Lucifugous, and their encounter with Bostrof and Lilaia.

Suzie paled as she listened.

"Damn," she mumbled. "You guys don't mess around. And that warlock is Tania's son?!"

"Yeah," Cassius muttered.

"No wonder he was pissed." Suzie frowned, color returning to her face. "What do you need from me?"

"Bostrof said I might be able to trace the magic you left on him when you broke his leg," Cassius said grimly.

Suzie blinked. "My magic? How?"

Cassius rubbed the back of his neck, his expression turning uncomfortable. "I think I need to touch your soul core."

Morgan blinked, surprised.

Zach frowned. "What?"

"I have to grasp a thread of her magic," Cassius explained as he met the demon's stare. "It's the only way I can think of to do what Bostrof suggested."

"Won't that hurt her?" Zach said stiffly.

"I...honestly don't know," Cassius murmured. "I've never done anything like this before."

"I doubt Bostrof would have suggested it if he knew it would harm Suzie," Julia said.

"That's a big if!" Zach snapped.

"It's okay," Suzie said.

The demon scowled at the witch.

"I'll be alright." A smile curved Suzie's mouth. "You seem to be forgetting that I'm a Level One witch." Her gaze shifted from the worried demon to Cassius. "So, how do we do this?"

Cassius hesitated before getting up and crossing the floor to Suzie's chair. He knelt in front of her, moved the pillow aside, and set it on the floor.

"Let me know if it hurts at any point."

Suzie nodded, apprehension darkening her eyes slightly. Lines furrowed Cassius's brow as he concentrated on a point behind Suzie's lower abdomen. Morgan knew he was visualizing the witch's soul core.

Brightness flared on Cassius's hand. Power throbbed across the apartment, rattling the windows and glassware.

Suzie sucked in air when Cassius carefully laid his light-wreathed fingers on her belly. "Oh!"

She blinked and stiffened as his hand slowly sank beneath her T-shirt.

Zach was at her side in an instant.

"It's okay." Suzie glanced at him before staring at Cassius. "It just feels...warm and tingly."

"Here goes," Cassius warned.

He flexed his fingers slightly. Suzie winced.

Zach grasped her shoulder and opened his mouth to protest. The words died in his throat when Cassius's hand emerged from Suzie's body. A thin thread of incandescent light danced between the Empyreal's fingers.

"Is that my soul magic?!" Suzie gasped.

Cassius stared at the phenomenon as it slowly sank into his skin.

"I guess so," he mumbled, meeting the witch's stare with his own shocked gaze.

He flexed his hand a couple of times, rose to his feet, and went to the window overlooking the street. He pressed his palm to the glass and closed his eyes.

"Did it work?" Adrianne murmured to Julia.

It was almost a minute before Cassius opened his eyes. He turned on his heels. Morgan's pulse quickened at the light burning in the gray depths.

"I can sense him," Cassius said in a hard voice. "He's somewhere north of here. I'll get a better idea of his exact location once I'm up in the air."

Morgan turned to Adrianne. "Call Argonaut. Tell them we need authorization to fly and backup at an address we'll relay shortly."

He took out his phone and dialed Strickland's cell. Strickland answered on the second ring.

"Cassius is ready to track down Chester's location," Morgan said briskly. "We'll let you know once we get there. Warn the other agencies."

"I will."

Strickland sounded even more somber than the last time they'd spoken, the recent revelation of his vanished apprentice's true identity a double-edged sword that had driven the director to a dark place.

Morgan could sympathize. Betrayal was never nice, especially when it came from trusted quarters. He was beginning to suspect Strickland had considered Chester Moran to be more than just an apprentice. The director's marriage had been a childless one and his wife had died many years ago from a cancer that even magic and other-worldly drugs could not cure.

"Brianna called," Strickland said, his tone hardening. "The Hexa agents she assigned to your case came up with something interesting concerning the sites of the sacrificial rituals."

Morgan straightened. "They did?"

"Yes. The information was hidden deep in the Hexa archives, so don't feel bad about it," Strickland continued gruffly. "They're all ancient burial grounds for magic users."

Surprise bolted through Morgan. "What?!"

Cassius cast a frown his way.

"They are arcane places of power. Ones that the Hexa leaders of old never went into detail about, but nevertheless chose for a specific reason."

"Thanks. We'll keep that in mind."

Morgan ended the call. The others traded shocked looks when he told them of Brianna's findings.

"That explains a lot," Cassius murmured. "Those kinds

of burial grounds are where the walls between the realms tend to be the thinnest."

"The walls between the realms?" Bailey said, puzzled.

"He means the Nether," Julia said grimly.

Suzie called out to them as they turned and made for the stairs.

"Wait." The witch bit her lip and hesitated, her gaze locked on Zach. "Oh, what the hell!"

She stormed across the floor, grabbed the demon by the lapels of his jacket, and kissed him. Surprise flared across Zach's face. It was replaced by desire. He wrapped his arms around the witch, pulled her close, and took over the kiss.

"Don't die," Suzie mumbled against the demon's mouth when he let her go, her eyes shining bright.

Zach smiled faintly. "I won't. I have a date with a hot witch to look forward to."

Suzie blushed.

"Great," Adrianne said morosely as they headed outside. "Everyone's gonna get some except for me."

Bailey brightened and opened his mouth.

"Don't!" Adrianne snapped.

CASSIUS AND MORGAN ROSE ON THE WARM AIR CURRENTS blowing in from the Pacific and headed north across the city, Julia and Zach in their wake.

Their passage went mostly unnoticed, the people milling below them too focused on their daily commute and the early morning traffic to pay much attention to the sky.

Suzie's magic pulsed faintly in Cassius's palm, a beacon searching for a signal as he trailed his fingers loosely through the air. He marveled at the strange new sensation and the fact that Bostrof had known about a power he was unaware of. He wondered what other secrets the Lucifugous king and his Goddess wife harbored about him and Morgan.

Cassius's hand tingled, an echo of resonance dancing across his skin from Suzie's magic. His gaze found the spire of a Gothic cathedral on a hill to the right.

"There!" He tucked his wings and dove.

Morgan and the others followed.

They landed on the steps of the church a moment

later. Startled shouts sounded from the pedestrians on the sidewalk. Adrianne's SUV screeched into view a moment later. She slammed on the brakes, brought the vehicle to a screeching halt diagonally across the road, and jumped out with Bailey. They flashed their badges and shouted at everyone to clear the way.

A patrol car approached from the east, siren silent and light bar flashing. Bailey jogged over and spoke urgently with the cop behind the wheel. The woman looked anxiously at her partner, reversed, and blocked off the opposite end of the street.

"We've asked them to set up a one-block security perimeter around this place until Argonaut and the other agencies get here," Adrianne said briskly as she and Bailey joined them. "You guys got anything yet?"

Cassius frowned as he examined the towering stone facade above them, power thrumming from him in subtle waves. "He's here alright. I can sense his magic."

There was movement in one of the towers. Something flashed toward Cassius, leaving inky trails in the air.

Morgan cursed and deflected the dark sphere with his sword. It smashed into the steps to their right and exploded. A four-foot-wide crater appeared amidst the debris clouding the air.

"Those are sorcerers up there!" Adrianne yelled.

Zach rose, Julia close behind. "We're on it!"

Bailey cast a protective barrier around their bodies as they flew toward the towers through a barrage of black-magic balls, their gray wings snapping the air with powerful beats.

Cassius clenched his jaw as darkness throbbed across the ground from somewhere beneath the church.

"Shit," Adrianne murmured. "Even I can feel that!"

"They know we're here!" Cassius said grimly. "Let's go!"

Black-magic spell bombs greeted them when they rushed inside the cathedral. Most bounced off the shield Bailey erected around them and exploded against the volley of offensive spheres Adrianne cast in the air. Cassius and Morgan batted away the ones that got through with their swords.

Morgan flexed his left hand, lifted the benches in the nave with his Aerial powers, and sent them crashing into the sorcerers lurking behind the giant stone colonnades rising to a distant, vaulted ceiling.

"Looks like the whole gang is here," Adrianne muttered, eyeing the horde of dark-cloaked sorcerers converging on them from the transepts and chancel.

Cassius's tense gaze found the circular patterns set into the limestone and marble floor beyond the baptism font ahead. He could feel a corrupt energy emanating from beneath it.

"There's a way to the crypts beneath that labyrinth!"

They fought their way over, Bailey dropping his shield so they could engage the sorcerers directly. Cassius's blade sang through the air as he carved fatal wounds into the enemy, anger stirring his blood.

He could sense something else beneath the labyrinth. Something that felt a lot like over a dozen fractured human souls.

"Anyone else seeing what I'm seeing?!" Adrianne shouted, stabbing a sorcerer in the gut.

She indicated the benches around them. Cassius stiffened when he registered what she'd spotted.

Shoes, bags, and phones lay scattered haphazardly on the ground beneath the seats. There had been people there a short while ago. And they'd left in a hurry.

Cassius cursed. "They must have been attending morning mass!"

"I have a very bad feeling about where they could be," Morgan said darkly. "We didn't see anyone running out of the building when we were making our way over here."

Cassius scowled. They doubled their efforts and soon reached the labyrinth.

"We'll keep them at bay!" Morgan shouted.

He rose and took front guard while Adrianne and Bailey brought up the rear.

A group of Argonaut and Hexa agents burst through the doors of the cathedral just as Cassius pressed his hands against the limestone floor. Figures bearing the badges of Rosen and Cabalista followed close behind.

"What's your status?!" Reuben shouted as he made his way rapidly toward them, Jasper and Brianna on his heels.

Cassius gritted his teeth. "There's an immense source of black magic beneath this floor. I'm pretty sure that's where Chester is."

The limestone felt scalding hot to the touch.

"How do we get down there?!" Jasper barked, destroying a black-magic spell bomb with a large chunk of rock.

Another sphere of corrupt magic shot toward the demon's back.

Reuben deflected it with a burst of wind and cast it back at the sorcerer who had launched it. The man's dying scream faded against the background noise of the battle unfolding inside the cathedral.

"Whatever you're intending to do, do it quickly!" Brianna snapped at Cassius.

Adrianne gasped as the witch transformed into a giant,

white tigress with blazing, blue eyes. Bailey stumbled back a step.

Reuben exchanged a glance with Jasper.

"We haven't seen you in this form for a while," the angel drawled.

"Yeah, well, I missed out on the fun in London," Brianna growled. "I'm not missing this for anything!"

"I wouldn't exactly classify this as fun," Bailey muttered, blocking an attack to his left flank.

Cassius shut out the noise around him. Brightness flared around his fingers as he sent a wave of power through the stone floor, mapping out what lay beneath it.

"They're a hundred and fifty feet below us." A muscle jumped in his cheek. He closed his eyes and concentrated. "There's about forty of them. No, wait." Cassius's pulse stuttered at what he finally perceived. "*Fuck!*"

He jumped to his feet. His Empyreal powers throbbed across the cathedral, making the stained-glass windows and lights tremble violently. Brianna and Jasper startled. The bright incandescence faded to reveal his dazzling white angel form and the crackling energy surrounding his body and his sword.

Trepidation burned in Reuben's eyes as he stared at Cassius. "Heaven's Light."

"What did you sense?" Morgan asked Cassius urgently.

"The people who were in the church are down there, along with an army of war demons." Cassius gritted his teeth. "It looks like these bastards are preparing for some kind of mass sacrifice!" He scowled at the sorcerers fighting the agents around them. "And I can feel Loki. He's hurt, but he's still alive."

He raised his lightning-wreathed blade and stabbed it

into the center of the labyrinth with a harsh grunt. A crack appeared in the floor.

Dark wind exploded next to him as Morgan unleashed his new powers, the windows rattling in their frames once more.

Jasper stumbled back, his gaze shifting from the Aerial's midnight-black wings to the sword of dancing shadows in his left hand. "What the—?!"

"That's new," Brianna said leadenly.

Reuben narrowed his eyes.

Morgan drove his blade into the floor, next to Cassius's sword. Ripples coursed across the cathedral. Glass exploded, several of the windows caving under the percussive force of Morgan's powers. Startled shouts echoed across the church as the closest agents and sorcerers went tumbling to the floor.

Cassius's eyes widened where he'd maintained his position next to Morgan. The lines making up the labyrinth were separating, sinking to form steps that spiraled down into gloom. Morgan stared, similarly shocked.

"It's like what happened back at the alley," Cassius mumbled, his heart thundering against his ribs. He stared at the inky currents fluttering around Morgan's body. "The black wind. I think it nullifies dark magic!"

Reuben indicated Morgan's wings and blade with a scowl. "You and I need to have a conversation about *that*— whatever it is—afterward!"

"That's if we survive this," Brianna said grimly.

"What? You scared of a bunch of sorcerers and war demons?" Jasper scoffed.

The demon tucked his wings and dove down the steps.

"Where the hell are you—?! Goddammit, wait for me!" Reuben snarled.

Julia gazed thoughtfully from the vanishing demon to the angel hot on his trail. "Er, is it me, or is there—?"

"Please don't finish that sentence," Brianna begged as she loped down the steps. "Just imagining those two together is enough to make me bring up last night's dinner."

Cassius and Morgan headed after the witch, Adrianne and Bailey bringing up the rear. Gloom engulfed them as they descended past the ancient crypts that formed the basement of the cathedral.

A shaft opened up beneath it, the walls of the dark pit widening and rising swiftly past them. Screams reached their ears when they neared the floor of the vertical drop. They emerged next to a rock shelf and joined a grim-faced Reuben and Jasper on the edge of a shallow cliff.

Dread twisted Cassius's gut at the sight of what lay beyond.

43

UNLIKE BOSTROF'S UNDERGROUND FIGHT CLUB, THIS space was made of bare stone. Ancient scriptures and magic symbols were carved in the walls framing the shallow recesses where human skulls and bones gleamed. The oval floor was pure obsidian, the rock glistening with an ominous sheen.

People lay strapped to it in concentric circles, children, elderly, and adults alike. Their clothes had been ripped asunder and their skin was being marked with Dark Blight runes by a group of sorcerers, the knives the magic users wielded drawing blood from their victims' flesh. Those who had yet to faint writhed and shrieked in agony, the poison burning into their bodies causing more suffering than the cuts the sorcerers were inflicting. The hordes of war demons thrumming the air near the ceiling of the cavern watched on with hungry eyes.

Morgan realized why the victims whose remains they had uncovered in the past two months had been so viciously mutilated.

"The war demons!" he hissed, baring his teeth. "These

assholes use them to kill the people after stealing their souls!"

Chester Moran stood at an altar in the center of the cave, one hand around Loki's throat where he held the imp down on the dais, a bloodied knife in the other. Crimson oozed under the demon cat's matted fur and coursed down a channel that ran to a shallow basin surrounding the altar, the drops casting ripples in the scarlet pool already filling it.

Loki's eyes blazed red as he glared at the warlock. The imp struggled violently despite the stab wounds he bore, his claws vainly attempting to pierce the shadows throbbing around Chester's hand. A golden object covered in blood throbbed with light on the altar next to him. It was a dagger pulsing with divine power.

Morgan's eyes widened. *The Eternity Key!*

Floating in the air above the demon cat were thirteen pale globes of light.

Morgan knew without looking at Cassius that they were the fractured souls of the humans who had been killed by Chester and his sorcerers. He could feel the truth in the shudder that echoed through him from the white angel beside him.

"Twenty," Adrianne mumbled, ashen faced.

Bailey glanced at her. "What?"

"There are exactly twenty humans down there," Brianna growled. "Which will make the total number of fractured souls thirty-three if they succeed in ripping them from their bodies." The witch met the sorceress's alarmed stare. "That's a powerful magical number."

Adrianne nodded grimly.

"That's more than Tania had in London." Cassius scowled. "We can't wait for back up." His pupils flared with power. "We have to stop Chester, now! Before he kills Loki and those people!"

Morgan cursed as Cassius leapt from the edge of the cliff and shot down into the cave, his blazing wings flaring wide before he tucked them close to his body.

The war demons' heads snapped around as one, their skeletal figures growing still when they detected the enemy in their midst. Clicks echoed from their jaws as they tasted the air with their tongues. They shrieked and plunged toward Cassius.

Morgan jumped, Reuben and Jasper hot on his wings, the demon cursing the Empyreal who had given away their presence. Sulfur wreathed the air as the sorcerers on the ground starting casting offensive spells at them. The black-magic bombs missed Morgan and the others by inches as they flicked their bodies right and left, the war demons screaming above them when they became accidental targets of their summoners' spells.

None reached Cassius as he arrowed down to the altar.

Brianna landed on the floor of the cave with a thud that fairly shook the ground, Adrianne and Bailey clinging grimly onto her back.

"Protect the humans!" Brianna barked at Bailey.

The wizard nodded, magic flaring in his palms and in his eyes.

Adrianne cast a volley of attacks at the closest sorcerers while Brianna maimed two with her massive jaws, the enemy's black spells exploding uselessly against the intangible layer of white magic protecting the sorceress and the witch's bodies. Morgan, Reuben, and Jasper slowed to a hover above them before turning to face the legion of war demons descending toward them.

Morgan cast an anxious glance at Cassius over his shoulder.

Then the monsters of the Nine Hells were upon them and the Empyreal disappeared behind a wall of leathery wings, sharp fangs, and wicked claws.

❧

CHESTER GLARED AT CASSIUS OVER HIS SHOULDER WHEN he sensed his approach. He slammed his knife through Loki's left hindleg, bunched his fist, and cast a spear of darkness at Cassius.

Cassius scowled and flicked his wings, the demon cat's shriek of pain bringing forth another wave of fury. The weapon hissed past him as he rolled, the corrupt energy dancing harmlessly inches from his skin.

He smashed into the warlock and took him to the ground.

Blood splashed onto their bodies as they landed in the crimson pool next to the altar. Chester roared and slammed a shadow-wreathed fist into Cassius's jaw.

Cassius grunted, head snapping violently to the side from the force of the blow even as the corruption burned his skin. He called forth the seraphic light blazing in his soul core and fixed Chester with a hot glare, his flesh healing in a single breath.

The warlock cursed and rolled as Cassius brought his lightning-wreathed sword down upon him. The blade struck the floor in a shower of blood and sparks.

"Why are you doing this?" Cassius barked, swinging the weapon once more. "Who is your master?!"

Chester ducked, an incantation falling from his lips.

The darkness fluttering across his body thickened until it resembled armor.

He bared his teeth. "Die!"

A black sphere exploded from his hands, the ball expanding as it shot toward Cassius. Cassius's eyes widened. He knew this strike was the deadliest one yet that the warlock had cast at him.

Time slowed.

He moved, his legs shifting as if the very air had turned to treacle. Morgan screamed his name from across the way. Cassius turned his head and saw the black-winged Aerial's horrified face amidst a swarm of war demons.

Something exploded deep inside him as their gazes met.

Heat bloomed from his soul core, filling him with power.

Black magic detonated over his body.

44

MORGAN FELLED WAR DEMON AFTER WAR DEMON, HIS arms aching as he carved their bodies into pieces with his Stark Steel sword and his blade of shadows. Still the monsters came, their numbers never ending. He panted and wiped the sweat from his brow. Relief flooded him when he caught a glimpse of Cassius's pale hair and armored body where the Empyreal fought Chester by the altar.

Thank God! Chester can't kill him easily when he's in that form!

Jasper cursed as a war demon slashed his back with his claws. Reuben was there in the next second, his blade ripping through the enemy, a terrifying scowl darkening his face even as his skin throbbed with seraphic light.

Blood and sweat trickled down Adrianne's left temple as she and Brianna strengthened Bailey's defensive magic. The pale shield shuddered violently under the war demons' attacks where it rose some ten feet above them. The humans Chester had wanted to sacrifice trembled and whimpered beneath it, their glazed eyes locked on the unholy battle unfolding around them.

Two winged shapes shot down from the cliff at the far end of the cave and smashed into a group of monsters trying to rip through the magical barrier.

"Where the hell have you guys been?!" Adrianne yelled at Zach and Julia.

"Having a picnic!" Zach cleaved a war demon's head from its chest with his water-sheathed blade and glared at Adrianne. "What else did you think we were doing?!"

"There were sandwiches and lemonade!" Julia grunted as she squeezed a war demon's throat with her bare hand. "And, oh yeah, a fuck load of sorcerers to take care of!" She looked grimly around the cavern. "Drinks are on me if we survive this."

"Are you guys always this thrilled to see one another?" Brianna asked leadenly.

Bailey grimaced. "Sometimes, there are tears."

"Yeah, tears of pain," Adrianne muttered darkly.

"Will you assholes focus?!" Jasper roared, chest heaving and blood dripping off his sword. "There's a sorcerer hiding somewhere in here. He's the one summoning all these war demons. We need to find the bastard and kill him!"

Resonance throbbed across Morgan's skin. The black wind trembled, the currents rising from his flesh to sniff the air for prey. Morgan's gaze found a shadowy recess next to an outcrop some fifty feet to his left.

"Cover me!" he shouted at Julia.

Cassius smashed aside the corrupt sphere Chester cast at him with a flick of his blazing sword, the blood in the pool sizzling and steaming under his armored boots as he advanced toward the warlock backpedaling across the ground.

This time, he was aware of who he was, just as he was faintly conscious that the raw energy coursing through him was not that of an angel. But here and now were not the right place and moment to ponder such things.

"*Who is your master?*" Cassius said.

His voice rang across the cave, raising faint cracks on the walls and bringing a shower of dirt down from the ceiling.

Terror widened the warlock's eyes. It was replaced by rage.

"I will never reveal his name!" Chester snarled.

Sweat beaded his ashen face as he called on his dwindling soul-core magic. Another black spear left his hand.

Cassius shifted to the side, the lance flashing harmlessly past him. "*This will not be like the alley, Chester. You will not win this fight. Now, tell me what I want to know!*"

Lightning crackled as he raised his sword and brought it down. Chester yelped and darted behind the cover of the altar, the blade missing him by an inch.

"*Your master has abandoned you.*" Cassius frowned and walked around the dais. "*You are on your—*"

He stopped, his fist tightening on his blade. A triumphant sneer lit Chester's face as he climbed shakily to his feet, Loki dangling limply from his hand.

"Stay back!" he snapped, holding the cat up defensively before him. "Stay back or I'll kill the Keeper of the Key!"

Movement above the altar captured Cassius's gaze. Something was happening to the fractured souls. The thirteen globes were throbbing and quivering. His eyes widened as they started to merge.

"Yes! *Finally!*" Chester hissed. "Come to me, Master!"

The warlock tilted his head back and closed his eyes, his expression turning rapturous. The shadows around him intensified.

Cassius tensed. He discerned the presence of another rising from within the warlock. One whose essence was made of pure darkness.

A faint whimper escaped Loki. Cassius met the imp's slit-like gaze, his pulse thundering in his veins. The moment to act was now.

"Do you trust me?"

Loki blinked once.

Cassius frowned, drew his arm back, and drove his sword straight through Loki's body and into Chester's heart. Blood gushed from the cat's mouth. He closed his eyes and sagged, motionless.

Chester stood frozen at the end of Cassius's blade, his body rigid.

Cassius stiffened as the warlock released the body of the cat, gripped the lightning-wreathed sword with both hands, and slowly lowered his head. Awareness exploded inside Cassius's consciousness as he met the warlock's eyes.

The man staring at him was not Chester Moran.

"You should have destroyed his soul core," the stranger said with a vicious smile through Chester's mouth.

Pain stabbed Cassius's temples at the sound of his voice, sharp and sudden. He sucked in air, his vision scattering with dark spots and his fingers growing weak on the handle of his sword.

What the—?!

"That's the memory spell taking effect," the man said conversationally. "It's trying to stop you from remembering who I am." He chuckled as he took the Eternity Key from the altar. "Oh, what sweet delight this is! I get to make you suffer once more!"

His last words came out a wicked hiss.

Cassius blinked sweat from his vision. The pounding in his head was getting worse. Bile flooded the back of his throat.

Darkness throbbed across the cave. Dread filled Cassius. He turned his head, his body moving sluggishly.

The fractured souls had merged and were sinking into the altar. The dais split, cleaved neatly in two by the power contained within the throbbing sphere. A thin, black spot exploded where the souls met the obsidian floor.

The blood on the altar and in the pool flowed toward the inky dot as it absorbed the bright globe. Cassius gagged as the phenomenon slurped up the crimson liquid, its hunger all too evident. The spot expanded and lengthened, forming a thin line that started to spread across the floor.

Fear twisted Cassius's stomach.

The Nether! It's opening!

45

MORGAN DREW HIS STARK STEEL SWORD FROM THE DEAD sorcerer's body and kicked aside the summoning staff from his limp hand.

The war demons pouring out of the portal screamed, their bodies rent in two as the doorway to the Nine Hells started to close. One of them snagged the sorcerer's foot and dragged him into the black miasma, the man's leg disappearing down the monster's throat with wet snaps and crunches.

The cave shook with a violent explosion of shadows.

"Sweet hellfire!" Julia gasped.

Morgan whirled around. He froze, his eyes rounding and his swords sagging limply at his sides.

Something was happening to the floor. Something unreal.

"Is that the Nether?!" Julia mumbled.

Morgan's heart thumped rapidly in his chest as he stared at the expanding dark fissure in the center of the cave, the answer rising from his very soul core. "Yes!"

His gaze found the white-winged, armored angel by the

altar and the man standing opposite him. Morgan grew deadly still, recognition sparking across his mind even as sharp pain drilled into his skull.

That's not Chester Moran!

❧❦❧

DEATH!

Cassius blinked. The word danced through his consciousness, faint yet full of power. It was as if something inside him was urging him to remember.

Not something. Cassius's eyes widened. *Someone!*

His soul trembled with sweet violence. His true self was trying to make him recall who the enemy was.

Strength filled him anew, draining the weakness that had overcome his flesh and bones. Cassius straightened, his knuckles whitening on his sword and his dulled mind clearing.

He knew what he needed to do.

And so does he!

A mocking sneer twisted the mouth of the man who oozed darkness and terror. "I have always loathed you. You who were bathed in Heaven's Light by virtue of your birth. You were always so righteous. So kind. So...easy to manipulate."

Sorrow brought tears to Cassius's eyes. He blinked, shocked.

The gut-wrenching misery he was experiencing was not coming from his present self but who he had once been. The being who lived deep inside him. The one whose agony was like a blade threatening to rip his soul asunder.

Cassius wiped the wetness from his cheeks, gripped his

sword in both hands, and tore it out of Chester's heart. Loki slid off the blade, his body striking the ground wetly.

The man grunted. A sick grin split his mouth. "Chester is long dead. You can't kill me—"

A gasp choked his breath.

Cassius scowled and twisted his blade where he'd stabbed the writhing globe of darkness hidden behind Chester Moran's fading, gray soul core.

The man's shocked gaze dropped to the sword of shadows that had pierced his back and exited the front of his body at the exact same moment.

"You've sure stopped being chatty for an asshole who claims he can't die!" Morgan growled in the stranger's ear.

He yanked his blade out and sliced the man's right hand at the wrist.

The stranger cursed as the Eternity Key fell to the ground. Blackness filled Chester's eyes. It bloomed across his face and head and raced down his body.

"Get back!" Cassius yelled at Morgan.

He yanked his sword out of Chester's body and jumped backward, Morgan mimicking his movement opposite.

Chester exploded into thick globules of shadows that dripped into the opening Nether.

Cassius stared. The dark presence he had felt was gone. He frowned. He doubted he'd actually killed Chester's master.

Tremors rocked the cave as the Nether started to expand.

"We need to get out of here!" Adrianne yelled from across the way.

"It's too late," Jasper said grimly where he stood beside her. "This thing is going to swallow the city."

Cassius startled as Morgan closed the distance to him

and hugged him fiercely, lifting him off the ground for a moment.

"Are you okay?" Morgan mumbled.

"Yes."

Morgan drew back in surprise. "You remember who you are?!"

Cassius nodded. *"I do. And I know what I have to do."*

The knowledge had just come to him from his true self. He knew not to question it, however insane the notion sounded in his head.

"Take cover," Cassius ordered Adrianne and the others.

"Take cover?!" Brianna snapped. The witch had returned to her human form. "Where?!"

She indicated the cave with a wild wave of her hands.

"A shield. The strongest you can muster." Cassius's gaze skimmed the terrified humans huddling behind the witch. *"There's no time to get these people out of here."* He looked at Morgan. *"You too."*

Morgan scowled. "I'm staying right here with you!"

Cassius narrowed his eyes. *"We don't have time for this."*

"I'm not going anywhere," Morgan stated between gritted teeth.

Cassius blew out an irritated sigh. *"Alright. But if a giant piece of rock lands on your head and squashes you, don't say I didn't warn you."*

He walked over to the middle of the rift tearing across the floor of the cave, took a deep breath, and concentrated. Heat bloomed inside him, filling his body with a power that did not belong in this realm.

Blinding light exploded on the tip of his sword. It pulsed and throbbed as it condensed down to a fine layer that coated the metal, the heat coursing off it warming Cassius's skin even through his armor.

He stabbed the holy blade into the Nether and twisted it.

Thunder clapped across the cave ahead of a violent detonation of energy. Cassius leaned into the percussive storm even as it sent fracture lines racing across the obsidian floor and up the walls of the cavern. The air throbbed, molecules of darkness expanding briefly before being sucked into the shrinking black fissure that was the Nether.

It took but seconds for the veil to close.

Deafening silence fell in the aftermath.

Cassius released the breath he'd been holding and closed his eyes, his limbs weak with relief. He gasped when Morgan embraced him and took him to the ground.

"What was that?!" Morgan mumbled, rising on an elbow to stare down at him.

"What was what?" Cassius said awkwardly.

His armor had vanished and his Empyreal form was fading fast.

An echo of gratitude danced through him from his true self.

Thank you...

"Did he just close the Nether?" Reuben said dazedly, the shield Adrianne, Bailey, and Brianna had erected fading around their group where they'd been crouching low on the ground.

Jasper scowled and straightened. "I think he did."

Adrianne opened and closed her mouth. "How?!"

"That's what I'd like to know," Brianna said grimly.

They came over just as Morgan rose and pulled Cassius to his feet.

"That was a neat party trick," Julia told Cassius guardedly.

"Yeah," Zach grunted. "Let's not do that again."

"Okay," Cassius murmured.

Adrianne looked over sadly to where Loki lay on the floor. "The cat."

Cassius tucked his dagger back in its sheath and sighed. "I know you're faking, you damn imp."

The others stared at him, startled.

Jasper grimaced. "I really think he's dead. His chest isn't moving."

Loki opened a yellow eye and looked at them guiltily.

"He's not dead?!" Bailey gasped.

"No. I deliberately avoided his soul core when I stabbed him."

The cat sat up and shook himself out, a ripple racing across his hackles before his fur settled back down. His wounds were already closing.

Cassius narrowed his eyes. *I wonder if it's because of the power of the awakened Eternity Key.*

Loki studied them for a moment, twisted around, and promptly ate the artifact where it lay on the floor.

Cassius sucked in air. "Why, you little—! *That's it!* No more gourmet salmon for you!"

"Wait," Adrianne said dully. "You were buying him gourmet salmon?"

Loki licked his paw and meowed innocently.

✥ 46 ✥

BOSTROF LAUGHED OUT LOUD, THE SOUND BOOMING across the bar.

Lilaia smiled. "You grounded the imp?"

"Yes." Cassius sniffed. "That cat is not getting out until at least Thanksgiving."

"You're still buying him gourmet food, though," Morgan murmured.

"His wounds are still healing," Cassius protested. "He needs the protein."

"Just admit you like the damn cat already, Black!" Jasper snapped.

"Yeah, I'm pretty sure the imp's wounds healed the night we rescued him," Reuben drawled.

A tray of beer mugs slammed down on the table, startling them. The golden liquid sloshed over the sides of the glasses.

Morgan followed the knuckles clenched around the tray to Suzie's irate face. "You okay?"

"No, I am *not* okay!" Suzie said between gritted teeth.

"It's opening night and you guys are scaring my clientele away!"

It had been a week since the Nether had opened under the cathedral. Tonight was the first time *Occulta* had reopened its doors for business. Julia had kept her promise and invited everyone out for drinks.

Morgan swallowed a sigh as he perused the mismatched group occupying the extra-large booth and the table that had been pushed up against it.

It's a miracle no one's dead yet. We'd normally be at each other's throats by now.

Julia looked around the thinly crowded bar.

"It's not that bad," she told Suzie.

"Yeah, it's still early," Bailey said.

"I just saw another party of Hexa agents walk in and walk straight out again," Adrianne observed. She glanced at Brianna. "I think they spotted their director."

"I have no idea what you're talking about," the witch said coolly. "I'm a nice boss."

Zach scoffed at that. Brianna narrowed her eyes at the demon.

Morgan studied the pale-faced group that had just done a U-turn in the vestibule. "And there goes a party of Rosen agents."

"What?" Reuben shrugged at Suzie's scowl. "I'm a nice boss too."

"You're the worst one of all of us," Jasper muttered into his beer.

Reuben smiled and draped an arm across the back of the demon's seat.

"There's definitely something going on between those two, right?!" Adrianne hissed at Julia sotto voce, her avid gaze swinging between the grinning angel and the frowning demon.

A party of three men and two women walked inside the bar. They rocked to a halt when they saw Jasper and promptly whirled around.

"Cabalista agents," Bailey concluded with a confident dip of his head.

Charlie bit back a smile next to the wizard. The enchanter had fully recovered from his fever and was back on duty.

Suzie cursed and vanished in the direction of the bar.

"It's not usual to see you out and about like this, Bostrof," Brianna told the Lucifugous. "And I didn't know you were married to a Nymph."

She tipped her glass respectfully at Lilaia.

"It doesn't do his Underworld *Godfather* image well to have me draped over his arm," Lilaia drawled.

The Nymph was wearing an elegant, white Chanel pantsuit that had practically every man in the bar ogling her, and quite a few women too.

Bostrof didn't seem to mind the stares, his expression indicating he had nothing to fear from his competition.

"How's Strickland holding up?" Reuben asked Morgan.

A pang of remorse shot through Morgan at the question. "He's still pretty shocked."

"I'm not surprised," Brianna murmured.

"Yup." Jasper sipped his beer. "It's not every day you find out the kid you took under your wing was double-timing you for decades and planning to wipe your city from the surface of the planet."

Morgan frowned. Even though all four supernatural agencies had been involved in the battle at the cathedral, it was Argonaut who'd taken the brunt of the criticism from the mayor and the media. It didn't matter that they'd saved the lives of the people Chester and his sorcerers had intended to kill that day and prevented the Nether from opening fully. The Anglican Church wanted a scapegoat for the damage and destruction to their property and Argonaut had filled that role perfectly.

The fact that the Nether had almost destroyed the city was a fact known only to Morgan's team, the local bureau directors, and the heads of the four agencies. No one wanted that kind of information out there.

"So, are we finally going to talk about it?" Brianna said quietly.

Adrianne stared. "Talk about what?"

Reuben sighed. "About how *he* closed the Nether." He indicated Cassius with his glass. "And about *his* black wings and that sword of shadows."

The angel pointed at Morgan.

Morgan and Cassius exchanged a guarded glance. They'd already spoken about what had happened that night at length and decided to keep their suspicions a secret for now.

"Guardian of Light and Prince of Night."

Everyone gazed at Lilaia.

"They are the names my kind and Bostrof's race remember Cassius and Morgan by," the Nymph explained to the three agency directors. "It appears their meeting has finally unlocked the powers that were imprisoned inside them."

Morgan wasn't even surprised by Lilaia's words anymore.

He and Cassius had come to the same conclusion. That it was the Fates that had brought them together, here, in this city. And that their predestined union and soul-core resonance had allowed them to tap into their hitherto suppressed abilities. Morgan frowned faintly.

What the Fates intended by it we're still not sure. Nor do we know who confined our powers.

Cassius suspected it was the same force that had erased their memories at the time of the Fall. Morgan wasn't so sure of this himself.

Reuben's eyes flared with surprise as he stared at Bostrof and Lilaia. "Wait. Are you saying you've retained some of your memories from before the Fall?!"

The Lucifugous nodded. "They came in bits and pieces at first. It took me several decades to make sense of what it was I was remembering."

Morgan wondered what the bureau directors would make of Bostrof's status as the previous king of the Shadow Empire.

Brianna sighed. "Well, that little bombshell aside, you realize the agencies aren't happy about those new powers of yours, right?"

She studied Morgan and Cassius with a frown.

Morgan shrugged. "Whether they are happy about them or not isn't really our concern."

The witch rolled her eyes. "Just so that we're clear, I'm not including myself in that group. And neither are Reuben and Jasper. There would be a lot of dead people in this city were it not for what you two did down there."

Surprise flashed on Cassius's face as he gazed at Jasper.

"What?" Jasper said irritably.

"I thought you hated my guts," Cassius blurted out.

Reuben smiled into his drink.

"Yeah, well, I'm over it now," the demon grumbled. "It doesn't mean I like you, though!" he added defensively.

"Have you guys discovered the origin of the

summoning staff Chester Moran and his sorcerers had in their possession?" Morgan asked Jasper.

"No. It definitely wasn't one from the vault in London."

"Which means whoever acquired it had access to the Nine Hells," Brianna said with a frown.

"By the way, what did you do with Oroak?" Cassius asked Bostrof curiously.

The Lucifugous's eyes hardened. "He has been banished to the Shadow Empire for now. He is not allowed to set foot on Earth until I say so."

"And the Reaper Seed trade?" Cassius asked.

"I ordered Oroak to burn the fields with his own hands."

"Did he really do that?" Morgan said skeptically.

"His guard assures me he did," Bostrof said. "You know the guy." The Lucifugous arched an eyebrow at Cassius. "A certain Akamon?"

Cassius brightened. "You gave him a job?"

"Yes." Lilaia smiled. "He is quite sweet. And handsome too."

Bostrof frowned at his wife.

"But not as handsome as you, my love." The Nymph patted her husband's knee.

Bostrof's face relaxed. Jasper grimaced.

Glass smashed behind the bar. Suzie scowled at the floor and blew a lock of pink-white hair out of her face.

Zach sighed, downed his drink, and rose to his feet.

"Where are you going?" Julia said curiously.

"To pacify a witch," the demon drawled.

He headed over to the counter.

Lilaia studied Cassius pensively. "So, the Keeper of the

Eternity Key decided to stay with you rather than return to the Hells."

Cassius's hand clenched around his drink. "Chester Moran's master is still out there. He may have failed to achieve what he wanted to do in London and here, but I doubt that's going to stop him. The imp knows I'm the only one who can protect him."

"You suspect Chester's master wants to free Chaos?" Bostrof said quietly.

Cassius hesitated before dipping his chin.

Reuben frowned. "It would mean the end of all the realms, including this one, if he did. Even the Heavens and the Nine Hells might not survive the destruction that Chaos would wreak upon us all."

Tense silence followed.

"We just need to make sure that never happens," Cassius murmured.

A commotion at the bar drew their gazes.

Brianna made a face. "Is that what he meant by pacifying the witch?"

Zach had Suzie in his arms and was kissing her with dedicated focus. The way the witch clung to him and wrapped a leg around his thigh indicated she was relishing the attention.

"It's like a sex show," Adrianne said morosely.

Julia took a sip of her beer. "It's not as bad as when we walked in on Cassius and Morgan."

"Your team walked in on you two making out?" Jasper said in a disgusted voice, his gaze swinging from Morgan to Cassius.

Color stained Cassius's cheeks.

"In my defense, it was partly his fault," Morgan said, unabashed.

Cassius sucked in air. "In what way was it my fault?!"

"Yeah, in what way was it poor Cassius's fault?" Adrianne said, aghast. "You practically attacked him!"

"You attacked him?" Reuben drawled.

Morgan grinned. "What can I say? He's one delectable piece of—"

Cassius punched him in the ribs.

❦

IT WAS LATE BY THE TIME THEY RETURNED TO THEIR apartment building. A mellow feeling danced through Morgan as they exited the elevator and headed down the corridor to their apartments. It faded when Cassius stopped in front of his door and unlocked it.

Morgan paused next to him.

"Goodnight," he murmured reluctantly.

"Goodnight," Cassius said, not quite meeting his eyes as he headed inside the dark apartment.

He closed the door. Morgan stood there a moment before sighing and walking over to his place.

Though they'd spent most of their days together since the battle at the cathedral, Cassius had told him he needed space to himself to take in all that had happened. Morgan had protested at first, before finally caving in the face of Cassius's steadfast resolve.

He sighed as he headed inside his apartment.

"I really hope he changes his mind soon," Morgan muttered under his breath. "At this rate, my dick is gonna rot and fall off."

It was still too early for bed. Besides, Morgan knew the only way he would sleep soundly was if he were holding

Cassius in his arms. He sighed, poured himself a drink, and headed out onto the terrace.

A cool breeze danced across his skin as he walked over to the railing overlooking San Francisco Bay. He scowled into the darkness and took a gulp of his whiskey.

Damn, I could really do with a smoke right now.

He'd given up on cigarettes a few days ago, after Cassius had made it clear he didn't like smokers.

A sound came from his left.

Morgan turned his head and saw Cassius walk out onto his terrace. The angel shivered slightly before taking a seat on a deckchair. Loki appeared and jumped on his lap.

"Can't sleep?" Morgan called out.

Cassius startled and looked over.

"No," he mumbled.

Morgan downed his drink, put his glass down on the table next to the deckchairs, and hopped over the balustrade separating their terraces.

"What are you doing?" Cassius asked suspiciously.

"If we're both gonna sit out here pondering the mysteries of the night sky, we might as well do it together," Morgan drawled.

Cassius frowned. He shifted over to make space for Morgan nevertheless.

They sat in companionable silence for a while, Loki curling into a ball and closing his eyes.

"So, you're still thinking about Strickland's offer?" Morgan said.

Cassius stiffened slightly. "Yes."

"We make a good team. And the others like you." Morgan glanced at Cassius. "Joining Argonaut makes perfect sense."

Cassius hesitated. "You think we make a good team?"

Morgan nudged Cassius's arm with his elbow. "Of course we do. We can practically read each other's mind on the battlefield. And we fit perfectly outside it too."

Cassius made a face. "Are you talking about sex?"

Morgan grinned. "Maybe."

Cassius blew out a sigh. "You're incorrigible, you know that?"

"And you love it," Morgan said confidently.

"Yes, I do," Cassius mumbled almost to himself.

Morgan stilled at the inherent confession in those three simple words, his belly clenching with emotion. He turned to Cassius and leaned in to kiss him.

Cassius pressed a hand to his mouth and narrowed his eyes. "What are you doing?"

Morgan blinked. "Kissing you. You just admitted you love me."

"I did nothing of the sort!" Cassius protested.

Morgan licked his palm. Cassius cursed and drew his hand away, as if he'd been scalded. Morgan made the most of it and stole a quick kiss from Cassius's lips.

"Oh." Cassius stared. "Is that it?"

Morgan kept a straight face by a sheer act of will and arched an eyebrow. "You sound disappointed."

"I am not!"

"Take the job, Cassius. We belong together."

Cassius's gaze shifted to the dark bay beyond the railing. He was quiet for some time.

"There's something I haven't told you. About what happened that night."

Morgan waited.

"This power." Cassius stared at his hand and flexed his fingers, his expression troubled. "It's more than I should be capable of, as an angel. Even an Empyreal." He looked at Morgan. "Julia was right. I am...other. I sensed it when I was fighting Chester and his master."

"I know," Morgan said. "You're probably a Demi. Like me."

Cassius drew a sharp breath. "You—you knew?!"

"Is that what you've been worried about this past week?" Morgan asked.

Cassius hesitated before swallowing and nodding.

Morgan sighed, wrapped an arm around Cassius's shoulders, and tucked him against his side. "Then don't. We're in the same boat, you and I. And something tells me our Demigod powers have awakened because we need to be able to use them in the future."

Cassius relaxed against him, as if a weight had been lifted off his shoulders.

Morgan's heart clenched. "Do you trust me?"

Cassius blinked and looked at him. "Of course."

"Then don't take everything on by yourself." Morgan stared into the beautiful, gray eyes opposite him. "I want to share your burden, Cassius. And I hate seeing you all anxious like this, as if the troubles of the world are eating at your insides."

"I'm sorry," Cassius murmured.

Morgan sighed. "You don't have to be sorry." He pressed a kiss to Cassius's brow. "Just promise me you won't bottle things up and you'll talk to me."

"Okay."

"Good."

"I'll take the job."

Morgan's pulse quickened. He turned and clasped Cassius by the shoulders. "You will?!"

Cassius smiled and dipped his head. "Yeah. Like you said, it makes sense."

Morgan swallowed. "I'm sorry, but I really need to kiss you right now!"

Cassius gasped as Morgan leaned in and took his mouth in a fierce kiss.

Loki woke up and leapt lightly onto the ground.

Cassius's lips parted and his hands rose to spear through Morgan's hair. A small sound of protest escaped him when Morgan lifted his mouth off his a moment later. It turned into another gasp as Morgan nudged his chin up and rained hot kisses down his throat.

"Mmm, Morgan," Cassius mumbled. "I thought you said you were just gonna—"

Morgan lifted his head and narrowed his eyes at Cassius. "I'm pretty sure we've solved the problem of what's been bugging you this past week, so time's up, buttercup. I am here to collect on seven nights' worth of sex."

Cassius sucked in air as Morgan kissed and nibbled the pulse beating frantically at the base of his throat. "Seven nights' worth?! What are you, a sex mani—! *Oh!* Right *there!* Fuck, that feels good!"

Morgan grinned at the way Cassius hummed and his breath hitched with pleasure, his fingers busy on Cassius's nipples. He pulled Cassius to his feet and walked him backward inside his apartment, hands on Cassius's ass and mouth dancing across his face and neck.

"Don't you have a meeting in the morning?" Cassius shivered as Morgan ran his tongue inside the whirls of his right ear. "Like, at six a.m.?"

"You mean *we* have a meeting."

"We should get an early night," Cassius murmured. "We don't want to be—*ah*—late!"

Morgan smiled lazily as he stroked the hard bulge

denting the front of Cassius's jeans with his palm. "You were saying?"

Cassius's eyes burned brightly as he glowered at Morgan. "Shit!"

His hands moved to Morgan's belt, his lips crushed against Morgan's mouth, and he dragged Morgan urgently inside the bedroom.

THE END

Cassius and Morgan's adventures continue in Spellbound.

WANT A FREE PREQUEL STORY?

Sign up to Ava's newsletter to get Unbound now, as well as new release alerts, sneak peeks, giveaways, and more.

AFTERWORD

I hope you enjoyed Fractured Souls, the first book in
Fallen Messengers. This is my first MM urban fantasy
romance series and I'm having a blast mixing my favorite
genres! Please consider leaving a review of Fractured Souls
on Amazon or Goodreads. Reviews help readers like you
find my books and I truly appreciate your honest opinions
about my stories.

Make sure to stay signed up to my newsletter to get more
free stories in the Fallen Messengers universe!

BOOKS BY AVA MARIE SALINGER

FALLEN MESSENGERS

Fractured Souls -1
Spellbound - 2 (coming soon)
Edge Lines - 3 (coming soon)

ABOUT THE AUTHOR

Ava Marie Salinger is the pen name of an Amazon bestselling author who has always wanted to write MM urban fantasy. FALLEN MESSENGERS is her first MM urban fantasy romance series. When she's not dreaming up hotties to write about, you'll find Ava creating kickass music playlists to write to, spying on the wildlife in her garden, drooling over gadgets, and eating Chinese. She also writes contemporary MM romance as A.M. Salinger.

Here are some places where you can connect with her:

www.amsalinger.com
Ava's Angels